Human Traffic

P N Thompson

GW00459082

Acknowledgements

Cover Creation

Jake J Thompson

Edits

Sherri Weber

Eve Vangeline

The Createspace Minefield

Leon Gray

Special thanks

Thank you to my son Jake for creating the cover for Human Traffic after six weeks of continuous nagging.

Thank you to Eve for your edits.

Thank you to Leon who showed me that Createspace isn't so much of a minefield after all and made this paperback version possible.

Thank you to all of my friends that have and continue to support me as I chase my dream.

My special thanks and deepest gratitude goes to Sherri Weber, who without a doubt kept me reasonably sane from the start until the finish and I truly believe that without her it would never have been possible.

Sherri....Thank you for everything.

Human Traffic

One
Saturday July 7th 2001

Today just like yesterday would prove to be the hottest day of the year for more than two decades on the Indonesian island of Sulawesi.

At 3:10pm the temperature reached its scorching peak as a battered old green former Serbian military truck slowly trundled into the seemingly deserted village of Tapalang on the island's north-west coast.

Forty three year old Spaniard Miguel Sanchez peered through his bug smeared windscreen and appeared to search for signs of life.

However none of the local villagers were naive enough to even attempt to work outside in this ridiculously hot and incredibly humid climate.

Miguel was a thin man and stood at five feet seven inches and he had a mop of black curly hair and sported a thick black bushy moustache that just started to creep over his upper lip.

He had very narrow dark brown eyes that always gave the impression that he squinted.

He wore a filthy white cotton shirt that showed darkened soaked patches of sweat beneath his armpits and across his chest and he also wore dark brown corduroy slacks with filthy old white training shoes on his feet.

It was difficult to comprehend that over the years Miguel had become an incredibly wealthy man.

His beloved old truck slowly rolled to about halfway through the deserted village.

Miguel continued to search the area in front of him with both windows of the rusty pale green cab lowered in an attempt to get some much needed cooler air inside.

He shook his head with disbelief when he heard children playing somewhere in the distance.

They were probably down on the beach to his left.

A wry grin suddenly appeared because he realised that at their age he would have ignored warnings from his parents and would have been outside with his friends too.

As he neared the northern end of the dirt track road he slowed the truck down to an almost dead stop and stared out to the left from his driver side window.

He knew that it was around this area somewhere.

His eyes scanned for a narrow discrete fork in the dirt track road.

There was a concealed turning here somewhere and he knew it because he had made this trip many times in the past but for some reason he always missed the hidden turning.

The concealed turn passed beneath trees and would lead him toward the perilous cliffs edge.

The dirt track would then bank right and lead him to a more perilous journey over a mountainous region heading north.

This dangerous road was only ever used by the Indonesian military because it led to just one place.

However Miguel Sanchez was no soldier and had never been one.

He bought his beloved truck from a man that knew a man that knew another man and there were no questions asked.

His foot suddenly slammed down hard onto the brake as he stared at the darkened narrow dirt track beneath the trees on his left where he could just see very faint old tyre tracks embedded into the earth.

A wry grin suddenly appeared.

"Ahí está" He quietly uttered in his native Spanish tongue.

'There you are.'

Beneath the faded green canvas awning at the back of the truck, Miguel's thirty eight year old wife sat on the wooden bench that ran the entire length along the right side.

Theresa Sanchez was these days a very large woman thanks to a near fatal illness that was followed by a lengthy medicated recovery with a heavy and consistent use of steroids.

She was five feet six inches tall and had long straight jet black hair that was pulled back into a ponytail.

Her very dark brown eyes were the only remaining evidence that she was once an incredibly beautiful woman.

Theresa was dressed in a khaki military style short sleeved shirt that was far too tight as were her almost matching lighter khaki knee length shorts.

On her feet she wore beige desert boots and her outfit showed that what were once long and slender tanned legs now displayed large clusters of black and blue varicose veins.

The couple were childhood sweethearts until twenty years ago when Theresa grabbed her opportunity and moved to the bustling Spanish city of Madrid to become a clothing catalogue model.

She was struck down by her illness three years later.

Back then Miguel walked his own path too and with his cousin Louis he created what would become a thriving export business.

He didn't see Theresa again until ten years ago when he returned to his sleepy home town to attend the funeral of his mother.

It was only then that he discovered that his beloved Theresa was back at her family home and stricken with illness.

The romance was immediately re-ignited and as Theresa slowly recovered she involved herself in Miguel's business with Louis.

These days she was responsible for monitoring the cargo prior to its delivery just as she was doing today.

In their native Spanish tongue their cargo was known as *el Ganaderia*.

Translated into English it means *the Livestock*.

Lying on the scorching hot steel floor of the truck were three women.

The woman furthest from Theresa lay slumped against the back of Miguel's rusty green cab.

She was around five feet six inches tall and had long matted blonde hair.

She was dressed in a filthy black sleeveless cotton vest and a just as filthy short faded blue denim skirt.

There were no shoes on her feet and her ankles were very tightly tied together with stiff blue nylon rope that caused bloody red sores despite the fact that she hadn't moved for the entire journey.

Her wrists were chained behind her back with solid steel handcuffs and strapped over her face was a filthy white paper industrial mask that was lightly doused with chloroform to keep her completely subdued for the journey.

Lying in front of her was a woman with shoulder length reddish brown hair dressed in a ripped filthy white cotton blouse and a pair of what used to be tight fitting light grey pinstriped slacks.

Her ankles were just as tightly tied with the same stiff blue nylon rope and her hands were chained together behind her back too.

She also wore a white paper mask that kept her completely unconscious.

Just like her blonde travelling companion this woman was rendered and kept unconscious for what was now the better part of three months.

These women just like all of the others were only ever partially woken to be given just enough liquid food and water to survive before they were returned to unconsciousness.

It was the simplest way to manage them on such a grand scale.

These two women could in some way consider themselves fortunate that they knew nothing of this trip or where they were headed.

The same however could not be said for the third woman.

On the burning hot steel floor in front of Theresa's beige desert boots was another blonde woman in her early to mid-thirties.

Her shoulder length blonde hair was matted because she had spent so long in captivity and most of it unconscious.

Theresa stared down into her pale blue eyes and saw that they were full of anger and frustration as they glared straight back up at her.

She was dressed in a filthy black sleeveless vest and a pair of beige denim shorts with no shoes on her feet.

Theresa had taken a liking to her beige leather sandals and concluded that this woman most certainly no longer needed them just like her two unconscious travelling companions no longer needed theirs.

Before this woman was revived to a semi-conscious state a large filthy brown rag was pushed into her mouth and shiny black duct tape was then firmly pressed over it.

More extra strong tape was then very firmly pressed over and wrapped around her entire head three times to ensure that she couldn't speak.

Theresa Sanchez liked to talk and taunt during these longer journeys but she saw no reason to debate or to listen.

This blonde woman's hands like the unconscious women behind her were tightly chained behind her back and the same stiff blue nylon rope caused more profound bloody red sores around her ankles.

Her sores were more painful and defined because she had the ability and would occasionally attempt to kick out at Theresa's sadistic taunts.

Her bare thighs showed redden marks that were provided by the scorching hot steel floor because she had intentionally been given the ability to move albeit just a little.

Like Miguel she heard the sounds of those children playing somewhere in the distance.

They were too far for her to hear single defined words so that she could try to work out where in the world she had been brought to.

She was absolutely certain of only one thing.

This was without a doubt far, far too hot to be London.

Two
Saturday July 7th 2001

Anchored eight miles south of the same Indonesian island in the Flores Sea was one of the largest ocean faring vessels in the world.

She was a giant Spanish cargo ship named the Indigo.

Her overall length was a little more than 1,200 feet and her width spanned 161 feet with a depth or draft of more than 50 feet.

She was anchored so far south of the southern ports to prevent her from running aground which she undoubtedly would especially during low tide.

The alternative was an associated feeder ship named the Madagascar.

The smaller vessel was a giant of the sea in her own right but still at roughly half the size of the Indigo.

Five hours ago the South African Madagascar sailed out to meet the Spanish colossus where she hoisted two of the forty feet long steel containers using her upper deck crane.

The smaller vessel then returned to the disused southern port of Bontosunggu where she unloaded the cargo from the Indigo.

Inside one of those steel containers was Miguel Sanchez in his beloved battered old green truck, his wife Theresa and their cargo *el Ganaderia*.

The exchange as always went like clockwork.

Unofficially associated to the Indigo were sixteen more feeder ships.

They operated in and around northern Scandinavia, southern France, Spain, Portugal, Italy, Greece, Turkey, North Africa and all of the countries within reach of the Mediterranean.

More of the smaller yet giant vessels operated out of South Africa, India, Western Australia and the Indonesian and Malaysian islands.

The latest feeder ship to be added to the list of unofficial associates operated in the English Channel the river Thames and into the heart of the city of London itself.

She was a British vessel named the Candlelit Queen.

On the vast bridge of the Indigo dressed in his smart crisp white Spanish merchant Navy uniform was her skipper.

He was a rotund man with a shiny balding head and he stood and stared north toward the island of Sulawesi although from eight miles out he could barely see it.

Fifty seven year old Captain Louis Frederick Fernandez very nervously waited for a call from his cousin Miguel who would inform him that the delivery was complete and payment was made.

Captain Fernandez would not, could not rest until that call from Miguel was made.

Three
Saturday July 7th 2001

The battered old green truck struggled up the southern face of a high mount.

Miguel Sanchez pushed his foot hard down onto the accelerator and prayed that she would make it to the top.

They were now eleven miles past the sleepy fishing village of Tapalang and his final destination was just a little over a mile in front of him so long as his truck made it to the peak of this last hill.

At the top he would witness the optical illusion that always made him smile.

It always meant the end of a perilous journey because the drive back to Bontosunggu where he and Theresa would eventually re-join The Indigo would be at a much less hurried pace.

The truck screamed as it reached the top of the hill and as it began to level off Miguel released his foot from the accelerator.

He stared at the white rooftops that seemed to magically rise from the ground at the military base in the distance.

It was his favourite illusion and he smiled as he stared.

He then he lovingly patted the steering wheel because together they had made it once again.

Miguel now allowed his four tonne truck to roll down the bumpy northern face of the hill.

At the bottom he slammed his foot back down hard onto the accelerator and raced along the one mile strait toward the closed large white iron gates where he saw a familiar soldier dressed in a khaki uniform.

A little more than two minutes later in the back of the truck on the hot steel floor the bound and gagged blonde in front of Theresa's feet listened as the driver in the cab spoke with another man outside.

They spoke in a language that she didn't understand at all.

Soon the talking stopped.

She looked up to see that the large Spanish woman seated on the bench above her was completely focussed on the lowered dusty green canvas flap at the rear of the truck.

Suddenly the flap was violently pulled back from outside and a bright burst of broad daylight filled the back of the truck and temporarily blinded her.

Just like the two unconscious women behind her she had not seen natural daylight in three months.

As she squinted at him, all she could see was a large silhouetted figure of a man that stood at around six feet tall and he stared back at her in silence.

She noticed that when he glanced up at Theresa and spoke to her in his native tongue the large Spanish woman could only nod with acknowledgement.

It probably meant that she didn't understand a word that he said.

'Where the hell, am I?'

Her heart pounded as her fear and anxiety increased but she still managed to conclude that contrary to her earlier belief she hadn't been transported to Spain.

The soldier suddenly dropped the canvas flap and returned the truck into a state of relative shade although still stiflingly hot.

Her heart continued to race because she knew that this was it.

Whatever was going to happen to her was going to happen here and very soon.

Theresa Sanchez returned her attention to the floor.

"I think this one, he likes you." She said with a wry grin.

The blonde once again attempted to kick out but of course her tightly tied legs prevented any kind of impact and only served to amuse the large Spanish woman.

"Many, many lovers await you here I think." She added with a chuckle.

She attempted to control her emotions as the engine restarted and the truck slowly rolled forward from the rough dirt track road onto what felt like smooth tarmac or concrete.

Then she heard a large heavy gate slam shut behind them.

Her heart rate continued to climb as beads of sweat trickled down her face and her breath became very short.

For the entire journey of taunts and assurances from the *'fat Spanish bitch'* she made a point of showing Theresa no fear.

She offered only contempt but now, whatever was about to happen was imminent and she knew it.

The truck slowly took a left turn and travelled for around thirty seconds before it took a right and she felt sheer panic start to flood over any other thoughts.

Suddenly the wheels slowly squealed to a dead stop.

Her entire body suddenly jumped when the steel door of the cab was slammed shut.

Now she heard another foreign conversation that seemed to slowly pass behind her outside from the front to the back of the truck.

She was aware that there were many other conversations taking place all around outside.

She breathed heavier and heavier through her nose with panic and when she glanced up at Theresa, she saw that her attention was again focussed toward the back and at whoever was outside talking with her husband.

Suddenly the dusty green flap was violently pulled back and the unbearably bright Indonesian sunlight again burst inside and completely destroyed her vision.

She could make out five silhouetted figures that all stared back at her and for a few moments they all stood in complete silence.

The man on her right was a huge figure and when he eventually spoke the others laughed as they continued to stare inside.

Of course she was the only conscious woman and it meant that all attention was focussed on her.

She couldn't make out faces only silhouettes due to the bright sunlight behind the five men as they all continued to stare in at her.

Suddenly the huge man lunged forward and his enormous hand grabbed the tightly tied blue nylon rope around her ankles.

She squealed with pain as it bit into her already deep red bloody sores.

He started to drag her across the hot steel floor and although she tried to squeal through the gag and kick out with her feet he effortlessly pulled her helpless frame toward him.

She knew that she was fighting a very one sided losing battle.

Again he spoke to his friends as he held the stiff blue rope around her tightly bound ankles.

Again they all laughed as she helplessly lay there and listened to a conversation of which she didn't understand a single word.

Her heart pounded faster and heavier than it had at any time before.

Suddenly he hoisted her up and effortlessly threw her over his left shoulder.

She squealed again as he continued to mock her arrival to his friends who all seemed to laugh at every available opportunity.

Suddenly his huge flat hand came crashing down onto her left bottom cheek and she squealed through the tight gag with shock more than from the stinging pain.

He turned and started to walk toward a long single storey red brick building that had a rusty green steel door and no windows.

She lifted her head in a state of panic and saw that her unconscious travelling companion with reddish brown hair had been lifted in the same way by another of the men.

Suddenly her attention was drawn toward a young female soldier that was dressed in the same uniform as the others but hers was clean and neatly pressed.

For a very brief moment they made eye contact and for the first time she silently pleaded with her eyes from one woman to another.

'Help me!'

The young female soldier with long straight black hair that was pulled back into a ponytail seemed to half-smile at her with acknowledgement.

She then returned her gaze to the direction that she was walking and paid the bound and gagged blonde no more attention.

Her heart suddenly sank because that woman was her last desperate hope.

The huge man suddenly kicked the green steel door and entered the brick building and as it closed behind him she found herself in a stale smelling darkened corridor.

As he carried her toward the far end she saw several closed wooden doors on both sides before he eventually stopped in front of a brown steel door on the right side at the very end.

He fumbled inside his filthy khaki trousers for keys.

The green door at the other end of the building was again violently kicked and she saw the unconscious woman with reddish brown hair being carried inside over the other man's shoulder.

When the huge man finally unlocked the door she watched the far end of the corridor.

The green steel door that led into the building slowly closed behind the unconscious redhead.

In her terrified state she now wondered if she would ever taste freedom again as the sight of daylight disappeared as the green door slowly closed.

As soon as he carried her inside her nostrils filled with the combined stenches of stale body odour and urine.

She already felt the intense humidity because this room was even more stiflingly hot than the back of the truck.

Sweat poured down her face and when she inhaled through her nose the hot dusty air was almost unbearable but impossible to avoid.

She turned her head to her right and saw on the floor a filthy white single mattress and crouched on it was a completely naked young woman with short blonde hair.

She now turned her head to her left and saw more filthy mattresses and more naked young women that knelt on top of them.

They all crouched and avoiding eye contact and she guessed that it could only be because he was here and that he was some kind of violent monster.

Her heart continued to heavily pound and her fear and anxiety were completely overwhelming as he unceremoniously dumped her down onto a filthy stained mattress in front of him.

He then climbed to his feet and headed to a small grey rack of rusty shelving that was obscured by the opened door when she was carried inside.

This room was absolutely stifling and with her hands tightly chained behind her back she couldn't even wipe the beads of sweat that continued to pour down her face.

When he returned he held in his hand a large rusty padlock.

He then pulled a length of rusty chain that was somehow attached to the wall above her head.

Her eyes suddenly widened as she realised why none of these women had ever escaped from this place or even attempted to.

She saw why she wouldn't either.

She rigorously shook her head and muffled squealed pleas through the gag as he pulled the length of rusty chain around her neck.

He then tightly fastened it into place using the old padlock.

Throughout all of it she shook her head and pleaded to him not to do this to her.

If she could just communicate with him she could make him understand that she was wealthy.

She knew that she could make him an offer that would be impossible for him to refuse but she needed him to listen to her.

She needed to be able to speak to him and make him understand.

But he stared down into her eyes and when he grinned he displayed yellow tobacco stained teeth.

He shared with her his rotten breath as he leaned closer to whisper something in his native tongue.

Her nostrils were now filled with the stench of his rotten decayed teeth as he slowly climbed to his feet and headed back toward the door.

Her terrified eyes followed his huge frame until they suddenly saw Theresa Sanchez standing in the doorway.

Theresa displayed that same wry grin that she showed before.

"He said that he will return for you in one hour." She chuckled.

In truth she had no idea what he said.

"He always tries his new purchases before he allows others to pay him to use them."

Around Twelve Months Earlier

Four
Wednesday June 28th 2000

Estate agent Susie Long sat inside her small red company car outside the only vacant property at Oakland's avenue near Ponders End north London.

She was five feet six inches tall with straight shoulder length blonde hair and for the house viewing today she wore a plain black business suit and a white open necked blouse with black low heeled shoes on her feet.

Susie parked directly in front of the three bedroomed semi-detached property and her eyes scanned the immediate vicinity to make sure that he hadn't arrived before her.

After a short while she leaned across and picked up a pale blue file from the passenger seat and after she checked her appearance in her rear view mirror she slightly lowered the driver side window.

Today was a warm sunny day and the opened window allowed a cool breeze into the car that gently brushed against her face.

She then stared toward the other end of Oakland's avenue and could see an elderly man pushing a lawn mower in his front garden.

The smell of that freshly cut grass soon filled her nostrils and brought a smile to her lips.

"I just love that smell." She quietly told herself.

For Susie this was the calm before the storm prior to the arrival of a somewhat executive client that was keen to view this particular house but she didn't understand why.

She continued to read the file for around fifteen minutes before a black London taxi cab pulled up behind her car and she discretely watched via her rear view mirror.

"This must be him." She uttered.

Susie knew that she needed to make a good impression today because the man that currently sat inside the taxi was in fact a Russian Diplomat.

He was looking to rent a property in a quiet suburban area of London with his wife and two small children.

Susie continued to watch as he climbed out from the back.

Her eyes suddenly widened as she studied this mountain of a man dressed in a black suit jacket with a white shirt beneath it and he wore blue denim jeans with dark brown leather shoes.

"Wow you're a big guy!" She uttered.

She continued to observe him for a few more moments.

Forty seven year old Vladimir Kolov was six feet five inches tall and he had a very large frame and a mop of thick black slightly greying curly hair and he also sported a thick black bushy beard.

Susie again checked her appearance in her rear view mirror before she grabbed the file from the passenger seat and then climbed out of her car.

She immediately made eye contact with the huge Russian and he smiled in her direction as he paid the taxi driver.

As the black cab reversed and began to turn Susie walked toward him and looked up into his green eyes as he smiled down at her.

"Mr Kolov?" She asked.

She held out her hand to shake.

His huge paw immediately enveloped her tiny hand in comparison but he then very gently shook it.

"Good morning." He replied in perfect English.

His Russian accent was only slightly evident.

Together they walked along the short narrow garden path toward the white front door of the house and Susie made polite conversation in an attempt to put him at ease.

"Your English is remarkably good Mr Kolov." She told him with a smile.

She fumbled inside her black leather bag for the keys to the property and Vladimir smiled as he watched her.

"And yours is also." He eventually replied.

Susie glanced up at him and saw a grin and she realised that he was toying with her.

She immediately broke into a giggle and he chuckled too.

She unlocked the front door and pushed it to allow the musty smell from the house that had been vacant for some seven months to waft out as the huge Russian politely ushered her inside ahead of him.

Her hard low heels echoed on the hardwood floor in the hall as he followed her inside and then she closed the door behind him.

Vladimir Kolov immediately started to view his surroundings.

"My office manager told me that you're a Russian Diplomat Mr Kolov, is that correct?" Susie asked.

Vladimir turned and smiled down at her again.

"Not as such." He replied in his usual very calm and quiet tone.

"Think of me as a glorified secretary to one of the minor Diplomats." He added.

He completely played down his minor role within the Embassy at Kensington Palace Gardens.

Susie glanced back up at him with surprise at his modesty.

"My main job is to read and validate visa applications for Britons that wish to visit Russia." He explained.

"This is why I wish to live in a quiet area such as this one." He continued.

Susie continued to stare up at him with confusion.

Vladimir now broke into a grin.

"I can work from here and not in one of the provided apartments that are too close to the Embassy building." He told her in a mock whispered tone.

Susie started to giggle again.

"I wondered why you wanted to rent somewhere so far from Kensington." She confessed.

Again he chuckled.

"Scotland would have been better but they tell me only London." He replied.

When Susie eventually started to show him around the house they discussed his family.

"So as you can see this is quite a spacious property and I understand that you have children Mr Kolov?" She asked.

She turned at the top of the stairs to face the huge Russian and again he smiled.

"My daughters are twins." He replied.

Then now stood on the landing too.

"Three years old." He added.

When Susie finished showing him around the upper floor of the house he followed her back down the staircase and eventually they stood in a spacious kitchen.

"Do you think Mrs Kolov will like this room?" She asked.

Vladimir slowly turned full circle and viewed the kitchen but then he turned and looked directly down into Susie's eyes.

"I hope not." He eventually replied.

"She is terrible cook!" He added with another chuckle.

Susie started to giggle again.

"I cook or my children and I would never eat."

There was more laughter between them.

Susie concluded that Vladimir Kolov was an extremely nice guy and she took a genuine liking to him, particularly to his very warm and caring family orientated personality.

She headed toward a small very out of place brown mitre shaped wooden door on the right side of the kitchen.

Before she opened it she stopped and turned to Vladimir because she believed that this would be the deal clincher.

"Do you drink wine, Mr Kolov?" She asked.

It was his turn to display a look of confusion.

"Do I drink wine?" He asked.

Susie nodded before she beamed another grin.

"During World War Two the owner of this house, a builder, built what was then a bomb shelter to protect his family during the Blitz." She began to explain.

Vladimir raised his eyebrows.

"It was converted during nineteen fifty something into a wine cellar and as far as I'm aware there are no other properties in the area with one of these." She added.

Susie opened the small wooden door and that same stale musty smell that they had become accustomed to returned, now stronger as it wafted up from the damp basement.

Vladimir still looked confused.

"Wait, he built a hole beneath his house?" He asked with a chuckle.

Susie nodded with that same beaming grin.

"But this hole meets with the required building regulations." She assured him.

She disappeared behind the door and started to climb down a flight of twelve narrow stone steps.

Vladimir then crouched to partially enter.

He stared down into the dimly lit basement and saw that Susie had already flicked a switch to turn on the single low watt bulb and there was a pause as they stared at each other.

"I...I cannot come down there." He told her.

Susie stared up at him.

"I suffer with claustrophobia."

Susie suddenly felt a wave of embarrassment.

"Mr Kolov I'm so sorry." She replied.

He still smiled back down at her.

"It is fine." He assured her.

"Is there no natural sunlight down there at all?" He asked.

Susie immediately started to climb back up the stone steps.

"No like I said, it used to be an air raid shelter." She replied.

Susie felt terrible that she hadn't even considered that he might be claustrophobic or at the very least comfortable in confined spaces.

More importantly she had just risked failing to rent this property to him all because of her lack of consideration.

When she stepped back out she closed the door behind her and still displayed a reddened face of regret as she looked up at the huge Russian.

He beamed a reassuring smile back down at her.

"Now there will be somewhere for my wife to store my children's too many toys and games." He joked.

Susie suddenly felt relief that he wasn't angered or put off.

She desperately needed to win this twelve month contract to meet her personal monthly target figures.

Together they walked through the spacious living room and back out into the hall where she turned and smiled up at him again.

"There's one more room that I'd like to show you Mr Kolov." She informed him.

Her low heels again echoed across the hall where she opened a white painted door and stepped inside.

"You requested a house with a study." She reminded him.

Vladimir followed her inside where his green eyes scanned the room.

"This is perfect." He quietly uttered.

With her back to him Susie beamed a grin before she turned to face him without it.

'Now clinch it!' She told herself.

"My office already has all of your details so I can make you a formal offer right now." She told him.

The gentle giant smiled back down at her again.

"Good, I like this one." He replied.

Five

Monday July 3rd 2000

Thirty six year old former web designer Jane Chapman lived alone at her luxurious five bedroomed detached house at Glade road Watford.

She was five feet six inches tall and had straightened blonde shoulder length hair.

She was dressed in a white long sleeved cotton blouse and a pair of faded blue denim jeans with beige leather sandals on her feet.

Her house was recently redecorated throughout after Jane made huge profits following some quite radical changes three years ago.

She decided on a completely different career path and now owned one third of an import / export business with two of her friends.

Her large house was now fully paid for and she drove a red top of the range convertible Audi car.

The imported and exported goods were however living and breathing people and it made no difference to her that her human cargo had absolutely no choice in the matter.

In her opinion she was providing the city of London with a service.

Chapman, although assisted by two friends was largely responsible for the sale and transportation of forced labour to thirty seven underground mines scattered across eleven different European and Asian countries.

Her contact list was still growing.

Everything changed for Chapman and her friend thirty year old Lisa Moore who at the time worked as a freelance digital photographer.

Moore worked for the same web design company and it was how and where she first met and became friends with Chapman.

The two women sat outside a small coffee shop at Drury lane just five minutes walking distance from Covent Garden underground railway station.

On this particular occasion they were joined by Lisa's former sister in law thirty two year old Debbie Davies.

Both Chapman and Moore knew that Debbie Davies was involved in the trafficking of young girls from Poland Bulgaria and Romania into London.

They were encouraged in under the belief that there were jobs and accommodation awaiting them beneath the bright lights of the city.

Davies worked with a small team of Turkish traffickers.

Her personal role was to collect the young illegal immigrants from their point of entry into the UK and house them in one of three properties that were owned by the leader of the Turkish gang.

At a later date Davies would arrive at the same house to collect the unwitting young women and drive them to London under the pretence that housing and employment awaited and of course by now she was a friendly and familiar face to them.

Upon arrival at the house or flat in London the girls were systematically severely beaten by their new Turkish handlers just to show and enforce their control over them.

The vulnerable young women, usually no older than twenty one and often as young as sixteen would be brutally beaten while Debbie Davies watched on.

When the beating eventually ceased each girl in turn would be dragged into a different room where she would be tied or chained down onto a bed so that the second stage of her new involuntary working life would begin.

It was another role of Debbie Davies to administer just the right amount of Heroin into the bloodstream.

The captive young women would be kept in dimly lit rooms and administered Heroin for weeks until they became completely dependent addicts and dependent on their Turkish handlers to supply it.

At that point each girl would be taken to a brand new location where she knew nobody but her handler and he or she would supply her fix as long she did exactly as she was told.

It would be now that some would be put out onto the streets to earn that fix and to work for their addiction.

Both Jane Chapman and Lisa Moore knew how Davies made her living.

They also knew that she was driving around in a brand new top of the range convertible Mercedes and that she lived in an almost palatial home at Amersham not far from Jane Chapman's house at Watford.

Of course how Davies made her living was never a topic that came up in general conversation between them.

That day at Drury lane would however be different and it would prove to be a major turning point in how each woman viewed the other two.

Outside the coffee shop fate would bring them to a mutual understanding just twenty three minutes after they all sat down together.

A young man in his mid-twenties that was obviously homeless approached them and begged for some small change.

Jane Chapman was a people-watcher and she closely observed the unfortunate young man as Lisa Moore vividly explained to him where and how to leave them alone, much to the amusement of Debbie Davies.

When he left, Jane turned her attention to Davies.

"Maybe we should get involved in kicking his bone idle kind out of the country." She suggested in a mocking tone.

Chapman was also testing the water to see what kind of response she would receive.

Lisa Moore stared across at her not quite believing what she had just heard.

"Well if they don't want to get off their backsides to work here it'd be their own fault!" Davies explained.

Lisa Moore now nodded in full agreement with her former sister in law.

That afternoon provided a theoretical discussion about how it could be done and for the productive and more importantly financial end with the help of Debbie Davies's group of Turkish friends.

During that conversation Debbie Davies reliably informed Jane and Lisa that there were an abundance of recently discovered underground mines that were located across Europe that required a vast ongoing and rotating labour force.

Debbie Davies of course had the contacts and the ability to ship the homeless men out of London in much the same way that she was already moving young girls in.

That initial conversation outside a small coffee shop at Drury Lane would later reshape and affect the future lives of so many.

That was almost three years ago.

Today Chapman sat in her beautifully redecorated lounge and admired the finished product as she sipped coffee and waited for the arrival of three guests on this warm and sunny morning.

It wasn't long before she heard the new doorbell chime.

She stood up from her brand new cream coloured leather sofa and spied through the curtains to see Lisa Moore's new blue Jaguar parked on the drive behind her own red Audi.

She casually walked out to the hall still holding her coffee cup where she opened the door and saw both Lisa Moore and Debbie Davies standing on her doorstep.

Lisa Moore was five feet six inches tall and had straight shoulder length reddish brown bobbed hair.

She wore a pale green sleeveless vest and a short blue denim skirt with brand new white designer training shoes on her feet.

She lowered her large dark designer sunglasses and grinned.

Debbie Davies was also five feet six but with blonde shoulder length hair and she also beamed a grin at Jane.

"Is our mystery man here yet?" She asked.

Jane shook her head as the two women entered and the door was closed behind them.

The three seemingly average women were already responsible with the help of Davies's Turkish group, for the abduction sale and transportation of over eight hundred of the homeless population of London over the past two and a half years.

They knew that their highly illegal enterprise was completely undetected because their victims were the homeless and nobody would even notice that they were missing.

But Chapman would soon take that security to a whole new level.

All three continued to believe that they were doing London a favour.

It was how they justified their actions to each other and it was how they slept at night.

The reality was that they were forcibly taking and shipping living and breathing and already unfortunate young men and occasional women.

They were then worked beaten and starved to death hence the need for continuous supply.

It was a reality that none of them chose to acknowledge because in almost three years they had each amassed a small fortune but of course it wasn't enough.

It would never be enough.

Eight months ago Jane Chapman was contacted via email by the man that dealt with the transportation of her shipments on land after they were removed from the giant cargo ship.

It was he, Miguel Sanchez that informed her of the existence of a man that operated a very similar operation to her own but on a much, much larger scale.

His in fact covered most of Europe.

In his email Sanchez suggested that she should meet with this third party to discuss business and that he could arrange it on her behalf.

Jane travelled to Rome for her annual holiday where she met with this man and during that meeting a brand new plan was discussed and formulated.

It was a plan that Chapman relentlessly worked on since.

As soon as she closed the front door Lisa Moore approached the subject of why they were getting involved with this new player and bringing him in.

"We're doing really well on our own Jane." She reminded Chapman.

"We made over eight thousand pounds each last month."

Debbie Davies nodded with agreement but Chapman casually walked passed them both.

"Do you two want coffee?" She asked.

All three women walked through into the kitchen where Jane turned to face her two friends.

"Why don't you both just wait until after he's been before we do this discussion?" She asked.

"Because until you see what I've done you have no idea what you're talking about." She assured them both.

The conversation was interrupted by the second chime of the doorbell.

"That's him now."

"Remember just wait until after this meeting before you make any judgements."

She then walked past Moore and Davies and headed back out to the hall where she opened the front door to see a black London taxi cab heading away from her house after it dropped its fare.

The giant Russian Vladimir Kolov stood on her doorstep and smiled down at her.

"Jane it is lovely to see you again." He told her.

He lowered his huge frame and gently kissed her cheek.

After Kolov was invited inside and the formal introductions were made the four of them moved into Chapman's small study that was a simple walk across the hall from the lounge.

Jane started to explain her prepared show and tell for her two best friends in particular.

Vladimir Kolov already knew of its existence.

Lisa Moore stared at the bland green and brown home page of a website that had taken Jane Chapman some six months to create.

"You built a dating website?" She asked.

She continued to stare at the computer screen as Jane grinned.

"It's a little more than that." She replied with a chuckle.

Vladimir Kolov watched in silence as Chapman revealed more of her creation.

"When you log into the administration area you'll find that a twelve digit password is required." She explained.

She clicked the white cursor arrow onto the tab at the top of the screen that read *'Administration'*

Both Moore and Davies watched her type in the twelve digit password and while she waited Chapman turned to them both again.

"This website isn't registered on any search engine." She explained.

Both ignorantly shook their heads.

"It won't just show up if somebody searches for an online dating site." She explained.

"And if by chance somebody does stumble across it they'll find it far too expensive and ugly to want to register for membership."

Lisa and Debbie looked at each other in silence before they both returned their attention to Chapman's computer monitor that suddenly began to upload miniature jpeg images.

Jane nodded in the direction of Vladimir Kolov.

"The twelve digit password has already been given out by Vladimir to many of his trusted clients in the Middle East." She informed them.

She clicked on the first minimised jpeg image that enlarged to show a beautiful woman with long wavy dark brown hair that casually walked along a beach somewhere dressed in just a shiny gold two-piece bikini.

Debbie Davies still hadn't grasped what she was looking at and she glanced back at Jane.

"Who's she?" She asked.

Chapman shook her head.

"That's not important." She replied.

"But the figure below her picture is very important though."

Davies glanced back at the image to see a numerical attachment beneath it.

00065000

Again she stared at Chapman.

"So what do the numbers mean?"

Jane's smile broadened.

"That my dear Deborah is how much the bidding is up to in order to buy and own that beautiful little Spanish madam." She replied.

"And just out of interest the bidding started at forty thousand."

Suddenly Debbie Davies spun her head back toward the screen and her eyes widened.

"It's up to sixty five thousand?" She asked.

Again she turned to Chapman who nodded to confirm that she was correct.

Both Davies and Moore stared at the screen and could see that there were at least three hundred different minimised images of more women of exceptional beauty.

Now Lisa Moore found the words that she was looking for.

"Holy shit!" She quietly uttered.

But now it was her that turned to stare at Chapman.

"So let me understand this." She began.

She then nodded in the direction of Vladimir Kolov.

"His rich friends are given this twelve digit code to log on and view these women who are for sale?" She asked.

Vladimir Kolov chuckled at her question.

Chapman nodded in response.

"These women on the screen are in Italy, Spain and Portugal." She explained.

"Our role will be to supply the same type of cargo from London."

Lisa glanced at the screen again and then back at Chapman.

"But Jane these aren't going to be homeless pot heads, addicts and drunks." She reminded her.

"And we can't trust those idiot weed smoking Turks to take women from their homes." She correctly pointed out.

"So how are we going to take them and where the hell do we keep them?"

Jane glanced across at Vladimir Kolov as the giant Russian now slowly walked toward Lisa and Debbie.

"In Europe I have been using former soldiers from Spain Romania and Albania that all specialised in such tasks during their military service." He explained.

Lisa Moore nodded still reluctantly as he approached her.

"That's all well and good but where do we find soldiers from here in Britain?" She asked.

Kolov looked down at her with his usual warm smile.

"There is no need." He informed her.

"I brought mine with me."

"They are all taking their security license training as we speak." He added.

He saw the look of confusion on Lisa Moore's face.

"You'll understand the reasons for that later." He assured her with another smile.

Jane Chapman now turned her attention to Debbie Davies.

"We're still going to need your Turks to do the running around and we'll still be supplying the mines with the homeless."

Davies nodded but she still displayed a look of stunned surprise at what she had just been shown.

"I'll speak to Mark Downing about renting a larger warehouse than the one that he's been using to keep the homeless in." Jane told them all.

Jane Chapman and Vladimir Kolov continued to reveal their new joint business venture.

Between them they explained that Debbie Davies would need to rent three more houses in quiet residential streets in the London suburbs.

These houses would become needles in a stack of needles so to speak.

The new cargo could be held inside them until it was eventually transported to a warehouse that wasn't yet chosen or operational.

They needed these new houses now because this new venture would begin almost immediately.

Six
Saturday July 8th 2000

The giant Spanish cargo vessel the Indigo anchored in deep water twenty six miles north-west from the coast of Spain.

From the bridge her fifty seven year old Captain Louis Fernandez stared at a feeder ship far on the horizon to the north east as he calmly sipped coffee.

He knew that the smaller vessel was the British Candlelit Queen and that she was heading towards his own ship to rendezvous.

Fernandez looked down onto the vast deck of his colossal ship and saw that his crew prepared for the arrival of the smaller but still vast British vessel.

She would in around thirty minutes anchor alongside the Indigo at a distance of no greater than thirty feet.

What was about to happen was a very dangerous manoeuvre.

Five long reinforced lockable telescopic steel poles would be carefully navigated over to the British vessel from the Indigo.

These specially designed extendable poles would be carefully navigated from the Indigo and latched into position aboard both ships to maintain a safe distance between them.

The poles would prevent them from drifting into each other at a combined weight of 253,000 tonnes.

Twenty three minutes later from the bridge of the British vessel, her own skipper forty six year old Captain Karl Flannigan continued to watch as the colossal Indigo grew larger and larger in his forward window.

His own crew prepared on the deck below for the clandestine transfer of cargo.

Flannigan was five feet nine inches tall with short grey hair and he was of average build and dressed in his white Merchant Navy uniform.

"Steady as she goes." He instructed the pilot.

They began their approach in what was thankfully today a very calm blue sea.

As the Candlelit Queen very slowly drifted alongside the vast Indigo Flannigan looked across to his pilot.

"All stop." He instructed.

His pilot nodded.

"Aye sir all stop."

Flannigan turned and glanced at the positioning of the Candlelit Queen with the Indigo.

"Lower all anchors."

Again he heard his command repeated.

When the main anchors dropped into the calm blue ocean and eventually rested onto the sea bed Flannigan watched his crew receive the locked long steel poles from the starboard side of the Indigo.

They were then latched to the port side of the deck of his own vessel.

The two colossal ships would now maintain a safe distance of thirty feet and it was impossible for either to drift toward or away from the other.

In whatever direction the Indigo drifted so would the Candlelit Queen.

When all five of the forty feet long poles were tightly latched into position he looked up high to the cab of his forward crane and nodded to the operator.

The red steel crane slowly hoisted a forty feet long rusty orange steel container to around thirty feet from the deck and then slowly turned anti-clockwise and toward the Indigo.

Flannigan watched as the large container soon gently swayed between the two huge vessels.

He glanced across from his portside window toward the bridge of the Indigo and nodded his head to the Spanish Captain.

Louis Fernandez nodded back in acknowledgement as the large crane slowly continued to extend across.

After ten minutes the crane gently lowered the orange container onto the deck of the Indigo where the Spanish crew immediately started to unfasten the couplings.

The crane of the Candlelit Queen immediately began its return.

Time was of the utmost importance.

The empty crane returned to the Candlelit Queen a lot faster and after a few minutes it had retracted and returned to its original position.

The crew of the British vessel already started to unfasten the forty feet poles from her deck that were then slowly retrieved by the Spanish crew.

Flannigan again looked toward the bridge of the Indigo and nodded to confirm that the transfer was complete before he turned again to his pilot.

"Let's get out of here." He uttered with a sigh of relief.

This well-practiced illegal transfer of cargo from the moment that the Candlelit Queen anchored beside the Indigo took just twenty seven minutes before she continued her voyage to Turkey.

It wasn't long enough for the Spanish Port Authorities to raise concerns and react as they viewed the close proximity of the two giant vessels via Radar.

Inside the heavily locked orange steel container were thirty seven unconscious men that were taken from outside a soup kitchen at Finsbury Park, another near Charing Cross railway station and a third near Clapham Junction London.

Most of them, those that would survive this trip were destined for a recently discovered mine on the island of Madagascar.

None would ever return to the United Kingdom.

Seven
Thursday July 13th 2000

It was 2:31am on a cold and wet morning and inside a mobile soup kitchen stood sixty two year old retiree Joyce Markham and twenty two year old college student Sasha Willows.

Together they waited for the last three regular homeless visitors to the soup kitchen where they volunteered at Lant Street Southwark central London.

A black Audi pulled up in front of them and in the driver seat was the familiar sight of Joyce's thirty year old son Carl.

Carl arrived to pick up his mother to take her home just like he did every night that she worked inside the mobile kitchen.

Sasha Willows pulled back the sleeve of her black duffle coat and checked the time before she glanced across at Joyce.

"Why don't you go home with Carl now?" The pretty young blonde asked.

"I can lock up when the last three finally get here." She added.

The older woman frowned as she glanced back at Sasha and shook her head.

"You know I don't like leaving you here by yourself." She replied.

Sasha giggled.

"I live right there!" She laughed.

She pointed toward her rented flat on the corner of Lant Street itself.

Eventually she persuaded Joyce to go home with Carl and as Joyce finally climbed into the passenger seat she stopped.

"Are you working here tomorrow night?" She asked.

Sasha nodded with a grin.

"You've got to put up with me for three nights in a row!" She replied with another giggle.

Sasha stood behind the counter of what was once a fish and chip van but converted into this mobile soup kitchen that was owned by the charity that the two women volunteered for on a part time basis.

Sasha wore a bright red woollen hat with her shoulder length blonde hair just visible, a long black fully fastened duffle coat and black denim jeans with bright pink fingerless gloves that covered most of her hands.

While she waited for the last three of the regular homeless visitors to hand them a steaming hot cup of soup on this dark cold and wet morning, Sasha stared down at the bright pink gloves that her brother had given her as a birthday present.

She grinned.

"Richard, what the hell is the point in gloves with no fingers?" She quietly asked herself with a giggle.

She stared at her blue fingers that were a result of the cold damp very early morning air.

A quiet sound made her look up and when she stared toward the far end of Lant Street she saw the three late arrivals slowly heading toward her and she smiled.

"Thank god for that!" She quietly uttered to herself.

She started to pour the soup into polystyrene cups and as the three homeless men approached Sasha turned to face them.

"This chicken soup was getting ready to lay eggs!" She told them.

She handed one his cup.

"Here you go Jerry." She said.

He gratefully accepted it.

"Thanks Sash and sorry we're so late, we were waiting for it to stop raining."

"There's nothing worse than being soaked through all night." He assured her from experience.

She saw that all three men in their late thirties to early forties carried many flattened sheets of cardboard.

Sasha knew that she was in fact looking at their bedding for the night.

"So where are you lot sleeping tonight?" She asked.

She poured three more cups with soup and pressed plastic sealable lids on top and handed the extra cups out to the three men as Jerry pointed to half way down Lant Street.

"You know the alley down there?" He asked.

Sasha nodded.

"There's lots of shelter in there." He informed her.

Sasha smiled because she knew that there were other members of the homeless community in the alley between two closed down shops.

She also knew that there was safety in numbers.

"Go and get yourselves settled in then and I'll see you tomorrow." She said.

Again the three men thanked her for waiting before they slowly made their way toward the alley.

Sasha started to clean out the boiler of the remaining dregs of chicken soup.

Around four minutes later she saw a long sliver security van as it slowly passed right in front of her.

She waved with a smile as she continued to clear up and the man in the passenger seat half smiled and waved back at her.

"If you were here earlier I'd have given you some soup." She quietly uttered.

It was around ten minutes later that she stepped out from the soup kitchen and closed the door and when she pushed the key into the lock she glanced to her right.

She saw that the nose of the same security van that passed her just a short while ago was backed into the alley where Jerry and his two homeless companions earlier headed to bed down for the night.

She knew that the two large shops on either side of the alley were empty and had been closed down for some time and she also knew that neither of them employed the services of a security company to protect them.

"I hope you bastards aren't selling them drugs!" She quietly uttered.

She finished locking up but continued to stare at the nose of the silver van.

Despite the fact that it was now after three in the morning, Sasha headed toward the van instead of walking in the opposite direction toward her flat at the end of Lant Street.

As soon as she neared it her heart began to pound.

"What the hell are you going to do if they're up to no good?" She quietly asked herself.

She felt a tremble in her tone as she whispered.

She placed one hand onto the nose of the van and stared toward the opened back door and past it into the pitch black alley.

She suddenly sensed a very eerie silence as her heart thumped heavily against her chest.

"What are you doing you silly bitch?" She very quietly asked herself.

She took in a long deep breath before she exhaled it.

She could see nothing at all in the pitch dark alley in front of her.

Somehow she slowly and very nervously forced one foot in front of the other and stepped toward the back of the van but the back doors were wide open and obscured her view.

"J...Jerry?" She nervously called out.

She received no response.

When she reached the opened back door of the van she eased herself sideways passed it and again stared down into the pitch black alley.

"Hello!" She called out.

Still she received no reply.

"Is anybody down there?"

There were no sounds and no movement anywhere in the alley.

Sasha's heart now hammered against her chest.

"Jerry, are you ok?" She called out again.

Sasha only heard the eerie echo of her own voice.

The hairs on the back of her neck stood up as she squinted down into the far too silent pitch dark alley.

She suddenly felt something gently brush against the right side of her neck.

She raised her right hand to instinctively brush away whatever touched her but before her fingers could reach her neck there was a sound that seemed to echo loudly in the dark still of night.

CLACK!

It came with what sounded like an electrical snap at almost the exact same moment.

Suddenly an incredibly intense pain violently jolted through Sasha's entire body and she completely stiffened and everything immediately turned brilliant bright blinding white.

Her eyes flickered and her entire body violently trembled before she slumped down onto the floor where she continued to convulse.

Eight
Saturday July 15th 2000

It was a warm and sunny evening when twenty three year old Hannah Anderson sat in front of her dressing table mirror where she carefully applied mascara to her long lashes before she painted her lips deep glossy red.

Her long wavy auburn hair was down past her shoulders and she was dressed in a black sleeveless shimmering top and an incredibly short tight fitting white mini skirt with glossy black patent leather platform shoes on her feet.

Hannah was a beautician at her home town of Lewisham south London.

Eventually she climbed to her feet and walked across her bedroom to the full length mirror where she stared at her own reflection where she pointlessly tugged down her mini skirt.

She grinned.

"Lock up your sons, Soho."

Downstairs in the living room at Morley road was her best friend and she desperately hoped that Hannah would hurry.

Twenty two year old Amanda Golding very quietly sat in an armchair while Hannah's parents watched their favourite TV soap opera.

Amanda was five feet five inches tall and she had long wavy blonde hair that tumbled down over her slender bare shoulders.

This evening she had the most beautiful dark brown eyes that were accentuated courtesy of a full makeover by the beautician upstairs.

Hannah's mother glanced across the living room at Amanda.

"Where are you two going tonight Amanda?" She asked.

Amanda uncomfortably forced a smile.

"We're going up west to Soho Mrs A."

Hannah's father sat in an identical armchair across the living room and remained disapprovingly silent.

Amanda was dressed in a figure hugging black sleeveless mini dress with the same black patent leather platform shoes that were essentially worn to make them both appear just a little taller.

"I hope you two don't get cold out there tonight." Hannah's mother sarcastically said.

Amanda forced another smile but this time without reply.

"How's the new job going?" Mrs Anderson then asked.

"I'm really enjoying it." Amanda replied.

'Will you stop with the conversation?' She thought to herself.

She glanced up at the ceiling in the general direction of Hannah.

Amanda recently started a new job as a secretary at a local highly respected law firm and her wages were now incredibly high considering her young age.

The door suddenly opened and broke the uncomfortable silence as Hannah stepped into the living room.

Her father who had been silent until now slowly looked Hannah up and down.

"That's a nice belt." He sarcastically uttered.

He referred to her ridiculously short tight white skirt.

The girls were suddenly saved by a loud thump on the front door and Hannah glanced down at her best friend.

"That's our cab."

Amanda smiled up at her as she climbed to her feet.

'Thank god for that!' She thought.

Hannah strode across the living room where she kissed her mother on her cheek.

"I'll see you in the morning mum." She said.

She then walked to where her father sat and she kissed him on his cheek too.

"See you tomorrow grumpy." She giggled.

The two beautiful young women left the house and climbed into the awaiting black London taxi cab.

"If you ever leave me alone with your parents again I promise I'll disown you as a friend." Amanda uttered.

Hannah chuckled at her best friend's remark before she turned her attention to the driver at the front of the taxi.

"Soho square please."

For the next three hours the girls travelled from pub to wine bar to pub around the Soho area until they entered Soho square itself at a few minutes before midnight.

They stifled giggles as they walked arm in arm toward the large glass frontage of one of their favourite nightclubs when Hannah leaned into Amanda.

"Try to act sober!" She whispered with another giggle.

When they stopped outside the building they were approached by a very large man dressed in a black suit with a black shirt beneath it and even a black tie and he had a completely bald shiny head.

"Good evening ladies." The bouncer greeted with a complimentary smile.

Hannah and Amanda immediately reached into their shoulder bags to produce fake driving licences that would show him that they were twenty five years old, the minimum age limit that was reserved by the management of the club.

The bouncer smiled at them.

"Just go straight in girls." He told them.

"I've seen you here plenty of times before."

Hannah and Amanda approached an oval shaped desk inside the foyer where they paid twenty five pounds entrance fee each before they were issued small brown tickets.

The young woman behind the oval shaped desk pointed toward her right without looking up.

"Go through that door and up the stairs." She told them.

She still didn't look up from the magazine that she was reading.

Hannah and Amanda walked through the door that slowly swung closed behind them as they climbed a steep narrow grey tiled staircase on their right side.

Amanda slowly shook her head.

"She's one happy bitch isn't she?"

The girls walked along another silent narrow corridor toward the back of the building and at the far end they could see another large bouncer dressed entirely in black.

"Good evening ladies." He said with a grin.

He watched Hannah and Amanda as they both tugged down their short skirts.

He eventually relieved them of the two small brown tickets before he opened the white soundproofed door and filled the corridor with extremely loud thumping dance music.

"Have a good night girls!" He yelled over the thumping beat.

They both entered the vast darkened two tiered hall that was filled with bright multi-coloured flashing lights when Amanda reached behind her and took a hold of Hannah's hand.

"Let's get a drink and hit the dance floor!" She yelled over the music.

Hannah was already dancing as she followed and she nodded.

Within twenty minutes they were both dancing on the white multi-coloured flashing dance floor with two very handsome well-dressed young men.

After around half an hour Amanda turned to Hannah.

"After this dance let's go upstairs and get another drink!" She yelled over the loud music.

Hannah nodded as she danced with her handsome young man.

A short while later the girls climbed a wide staircase that led up to an area known as the VIP lounge.

It was in fact just a slightly quieter surrounding balcony with seating and tables that was in fact available to all and when they reached the top of the sticky red carpeted stairs Hannah smiled at Amanda.

"It's your turn to buy the drinks before you try that one again!" She giggled.

Amanda opened her mouth and appeared shocked.

"Good try!" She eventually chuckled.

When Hannah went to the bar to order two more drinks Amanda sat down on a dark red leather bench seat that almost completely encircled a small silver table.

She glanced over the balcony and down onto the multi-coloured flashing dance floor.

She saw the same two handsome young men that they were earlier dancing with now talking and they both occasionally glanced back up at her.

Eventually Hannah returned with two drinks and sat down opposite Amanda and she wondered the exact same thing.

"Do you think they'll come up here?" She asked.

Amanda glanced over the balcony and then back at her best friend.

"They're coming up the stairs now!" She replied with a grin.

"Free drinks!"

Both girls burst into laughter.

It transpired during the following conversations that Jamal was twenty five.

He stood at six feet one with short cropped black hair and he had olive toned skin being of Turkish descent although he was born and raised in London.

He wore a smart black suit with a white open necked shirt and because he was previously dancing with Amanda he naturally sat beside her.

"Do you want another drink?" He asked.

Amanda glanced across at Hannah with a telling grin and Hannah grinned back at her.

The other young man was Ali and he was a little shorter at five feet eleven with the same short cropped hairstyle as his cousin Jamal.

Ali also wore a smart plain black suit with a white open necked shirt and he had of course been dancing with Hannah.

"Can I get you ladies another drink?" He asked.

Both girls although already quite drunk nodded.

"We'll both have Brandy and coke." Hannah replied to his offer.

When Ali was away at the bar Hannah slid herself across the seat and looked over the balcony to watch people dancing on the flashing floor below.

It was preferable to sitting and playing gooseberry to Amanda and Jamal who were now kissing.

Jamal suddenly broke off.

"We're going to a party in a little while do you want to come with us?" He asked.

Amanda glanced across at Hannah before she returned her attention to him.

"Where's this party at?" She asked.

"In Sidcup, do you know it?" He asked and she nodded.

"Sidcup isn't that far from where we live." She replied.

Ali reappeared with two half pints of weak lager for himself and Jamal and two glasses of Brandy and coke for the girls.

He sat down beside Hannah but stared directly across at Jamal.

"That came to thirty five quid!" He begrudgingly announced.

"Firat is going to pick us up in ten minutes." He then informed his cousin.

Hannah turned to Ali.

"Who's picking you up?" She asked.

Ali glanced at her as he sipped his beer.

"My uncle Firat owns a black cab so he's going to pick us up in ten minutes to take us to a party." He eventually replied.

Hannah beamed a grin.

"I know about the party because we're coming with you." She informed him.

Ali suddenly beamed a bigger grin than Hannah's.

"Brilliant!"

Amanda suddenly stood up and again tugged down at the hem of her short and ultra-tight black mini dress.

"If we're leaving soon I need to go to the little girl's room." She announced.

She then glanced down at Hannah.

"Are you coming with me?" She asked.

Hannah nodded before she again turned to Ali.

"Don't go without us!" She playfully warned him.

Ali chuckled.

"Just don't spend four hours in there chatting." He sarcastically replied.

As soon as the girls were out of sight Jamal and Ali stared at each other for a few moments.

"Ready?" Ali asked.

His cousin nodded.

Jamal then reached inside his left black sock and removed a small piece of folded brown paper.

He held it in his hand while Ali stood up leaned across the table and appeared to be talking to him.

"I'm right in front of the camera so all it can see is my back." He quietly informed his cousin.

"It looks like we're just talking."

Jamal carefully opened the small slip of paper and tipped roughly half of the powdered contents into Hannah's dark Brandy and coke.

Then he tipped the remaining into Amanda's before he tucked the slip of brown paper back into his sock.

"It's done!"

Ali then returned to his seat and tapped a number into his phone and talked in his parent Turkish tongue.

'Uncle Firat come pick us up, we have two.'

It was around twelve minutes later when Hannah and Amanda returned to find Ali and Jamal standing.

"My uncle's outside waiting for us." Ali informed Hannah.

He handed her the dark Brandy and coke before she sighed and gulped it down in one go while Amanda picked up her glass from the table and did the same.

Ali and Hannah with Jamal and Amanda left the club and climbed into the back of an awaiting black taxi cab that immediately headed south east toward Sidcup.

Hannah and Amanda sat on the long red leather bench seat at the back of the cab while Ali and Jamal sat on the two single pull down seats facing them with their backs to the driver.

Already something wasn't right.

Rohypnol is an incredibly powerful sedative and after around twenty five minutes the effects became apparent as both Hannah and Amanda felt very drowsy and disorientated.

Hannah stared across at Ali with a blank expression and she could vaguely comprehend that Jamal spoke to the taxi driver in a foreign language.

In her confused and disorientated surreal state nothing registered as the sedative started to take its full effect.

Hannah attempted to speak to Ali.

'What have you done to me?'

Her words were completely slurred not that he was in any way interested in anything that she had to say.

Amanda slumped forward in her seat held back only by the safety belt that she was wearing.

Ali laughed before he pushed her forehead so that she slumped back into her seat.

"Sit back you silly little bitch." He laughed again.

Within thirty five minutes, the inside of the taxi cab was violently spinning and Hannah's eyes became very heavy although to an extent she remained conscious.

She was vaguely aware of what was happening and that something had been done to her despite the fact that her levels of comprehension and understanding were now severely diminished.

She sat barely conscious slumped in the back seat of the cab beside her best friend Amanda.

It was just after three in the morning when the black cab slowly turned left into a long dark and very quiet tree lined residential street with well to do semi-detached houses on both sides.

The cab then slowly turned into one of the driveways and straight into the opened attached garage.

Before the engine was even switched off the large brown metal garage door started to electronically close.

As soon as it was fully lowered, the bright light inside suddenly flickered into life.

Hannah's head slowly swayed as both back doors of the cab were opened.

She knew very little of her experience of being dragged from the garage into the house by Jamal and Ali where she was unceremoniously dropped into the middle of a cannabis-smoke filled living room.

She now lay motionless on her front.

Three middle aged men sat on an old dark brown leather sofa.

Forty seven year old Barak Yazici, thirty nine year old Atif Rahman and forty year old Doruk Gezmen all stared down at her in silence.

The group of now five Turkish men with Ali and Jamal were soon joined by the cab driver forty two year old Firat Alican who had for some reason taken some time to join the group.

Alican looked to Barak Yazici who sat between his two other friends on the tatty old dark brown sofa and he discretely shook his head.

Suddenly from the kitchen thirty two year old Debbie Davies appeared.

She stared down at the barely conscious Hannah lying face down on the floor.

Davies turned her attention to Jamal as he stood over Hannah.

"Where did you find them?" She enquired.

"We picked them up from a club in Soho." He replied.

Davies nodded before she walked back out to the kitchen but soon returned carrying a small grey rag and a wide roll of shiny black sticky duct tape.

"What did you give her?" She asked.

She knelt beside Hannah where she unfastened the black platform shoes from her feet.

Jamal glanced beside him at Ali and then back down to Davies.

"They've had about a gram of Rohypnol each." He replied.

"There's another one in the back of the cab." He added.

Again Davies nodded as she unfastened Hannah's tiny tight white mini skirt and tugged it down her bare legs.

"So I owe you two hundred and fifty pounds for this one, right?" She asked.

She then tore off Hannah's black satin sleeveless top.

Hannah was now dressed in nothing but a black bra with pale pink cotton briefs.

Jamal nodded.

"Her mate is in the back of the cab too." He pointed out again.

Davies again nodded without looking up at him.

"I know but I'm not paying for that one." She replied.

She folded Hannah's arms behind her back and very tightly wrapped several layers of sticky black duct tape around her crossed wrists.

Hannah was still conscious although completely disorientated and thankfully couldn't comprehend the conversation between Davies and Jamal.

She was however aware that she was being tightly bound with duct tape whilst lying face down on a filthy brown carpet in front of watching men.

She could also comprehend a woman's voice very nearby.

Jamal glanced toward Barak Yazici on the sofa for some kind of support and saw that it obviously wasn't coming.

He then returned his attention to Davies.

"You're not paying for both Debbie?" He asked.

Davies shook her head as she began to tightly wrap tape around Hannah's ankles.

"Nope I'm not." She eventually replied.

Jamal now looked to his cousin Ali and then returned his attention to Debbie Davies.

Davies rolled Hannah over and pushed the small grey rag into her mouth before she firmly pressed and covered her lips with two layers of the extra-strength black tape.

"Can I ask why not? Jamal asked as he watched.

Davies now turned her attention to Barak Yazici.

"Can you take her up to the empty room at the back?" She asked.

Yazici nodded before he tapped on Doruk Gezmen's thigh for help to carry Hannah.

Davies climbed to her feet and then walked back into the kitchen and she was gone for around a minute.

She eventually returned with a wad of cash and in front of Jamal she counted out two hundred pounds and handed it to him.

Jamal was becoming increasingly frustrated with this woman.

"What about the other girl in the back of the cab?" He asked.

"And that's only two hundred not two fifty like we just agreed." He reminded her with a snap in his tone.

Debbie Davies nodded and then stared up into his brown eyes.

"First of all, the girl in the back of the cab is dead." She informed him.

"And I kept back fifty pounds to pay Firat to get rid of her." She added.

They stared at each other for a few moments before Davies offered him the cash again.

"Do you want this or not?" She asked.

Eventually Jamal took it.

Twenty four minutes ago the pretty twenty two year old recently hired legal secretary Amanda Golding's blood pressure became so low that her heart simply stopped beating.

The vast quantities of alcohol that she consumed combined with a dose of Rohypnol became a lethal combination and she suffered heart failure.

Later that same morning under the cover of darkness, Amanda's body was weighted and unceremoniously dumped into the river Thames near north Woolwich pier east London.

Nine
Monday July 17th 2000

At just before nine the morning a black London taxi cab slowed to a stop outside a Home Office building at John Islip street Westminster.

Fifty four year old Martin Roberts climbed out from the back of the cab and stared up at the grey cloud filled sky and his pale face grimaced.

He was a thin man and stood at five feet eleven inches and he had slick dark brown swept back hair.

He was dressed in a fully fastened long black raincoat and neatly pressed black trousers with highly polished black leather shoes on his feet.

"Only in England does it rain in bloody July." He quietly uttered as he paid the taxi driver.

Mr Roberts then climbed the five stone steps toward a glossy dark green Georgian door where he pressed his thin bony forefinger onto the doorbell and waited.

He glanced back up at the grey cloud filled sky with another grimace because he could see that the rain was going to soon fall heavily again.

The green door suddenly opened and Mr Roberts spun around to see a woman that he judged was in her mid to late fifties.

He also guessed that she was around five feet five inches tall and he could see that she had a mop of grey shoulder length tightly permed hair and she wore half rimmed glasses on the tip of her nose.

She suddenly broke into a welcoming smile.

"Good morning." She began.

"I assume that you're Mr Roberts."

Roberts immediately stepped inside where he unfastened and removed his raincoat to reveal a smart black police uniform tunic with shiny silver buttons and three silver pips on his narrow shoulders.

"As a matter of fact it's Chief Inspector Roberts, madam." He informed her.

He then attempted to hand her his now neatly folded raincoat.

Fifty eight year old Sheila Marriot glanced down at his awaiting coat and then back up into his pale blue eyes.

"I have a nine o'clock appointment with Sir Christopher Dwyer." He informed her.

He then glanced up at the clock on the wall behind her to make his point but Sheila Marriot continued to stare up into his eyes.

"I'm more than aware of your meeting with Sir Christopher, Mr Roberts." She replied.

"I made it for you." She continued.

"My name is Sheila Marriot and I'm the senior secretary to Sir Christopher." She added.

She glanced back down at the long black raincoat that was draped over his still extended forearm.

Again she stared back up at him.

"I'm not the bag lady of Westminster Mr Roberts so take your raincoat up to the waiting area with you." She told him in no uncertain terms.

"You're not the only person here to meet with Sir Christopher."

There was a short pause of uncomfortable silence as Roberts glanced around his quite lavish new surroundings.

The high walls were painted deep burgundy and displayed gold ornate framed paintings and portraits of Ministers past and present and the floor was covered with a burgundy wall to wall fitted carpet.

"Please follow me Mr Roberts." Mrs Marriot eventually said.

She then stepped behind him and walked toward a wide staircase on the right.

Roberts followed her up the staircase and along a narrow corridor on the first floor where he saw more ornate framed portraits on either side as they made their way toward the rear of the building.

He could see directly ahead of him a tall narrow window that provided a view of the rooftops of the buildings behind this one and beyond them just a glimpse of the far side of the murky brown river Thames.

He followed Sheila to a wide open waiting area where on his right he saw a closed white panelled door with a brass plaque with the name 'Sir Christopher Dwyer' inscribed upon it.

On his left were two matching burgundy Chesterfield sofas that were separated by a rectangular smoked glass coffee table that was covered with glossy magazines.

Seated on the further of the two sofas and facing Roberts was a woman with long straight blonde hair that was pulled back into a ponytail from high at the back of her head.

Roberts guessed that she was around five feet eight inches tall maybe five feet nine and he knew exactly who she was.

'What's she doing here?' He wondered.

She sat reading one of the magazines from the table dressed in a black suit jacket with a white open necked blouse and matching smart black slacks.

At no point did she glance up to make eye contact or acknowledge the Chief Inspector.

Seated directly opposite the woman on the nearer sofa and with his back to Roberts was a broad shouldered man with thinning greying light brown hair.

He wore a navy blue pinstriped suit with a white cotton shirt and he was just as engrossed in one of the provided glossy women's magazines from the smoked glass table.

Sir Christopher Dwyer sat behind his solid oak four feet by four feet partner desk with his back facing a window that provided the exact same view of the buildings and the murky river behind him.

He read a very recently released file.

He was a portly man of fifty one and stood at five feet nine inches tall and he had short dark brown hair that was swept back and greying at the sides.

He was dressed in a dark brown three piece pinstriped suit and a smartly pressed white shirt with a light brown club tie.

His spacious office was painted in pale blue with an ornate white painted non-usable fireplace on his left that was filled with fake colourful plants with the exception of the Lavender that provided the scented aroma inside the room.

On his right beside the closed white panelled door was a large portrait of her Majesty Queen Elizabeth II.

He heard a light tap on the door that broke the silence and his concentration.

When Sir Christopher eventually glanced up he saw the smiling face of Sheila Marriot.

"Chief Inspector Roberts has arrived Sir Christopher." She informed him.

Her smile broadened into one of a wry grin as she watched and heard him quietly sigh before he broke into a smile of his own.

"Please show him in Mrs Marriot." He eventually replied.

He placed the paperwork back down onto his desk.

Sheila ushered Chief Inspector Roberts into the room before she quietly closed the door behind him.

She then walked toward the burgundy leather Chesterfield sofas where twenty nine year old Detective Inspector Nicola Garwood was seated on her left and forty seven year old Detective Inspector Samuel Henning on her right.

Sheila smiled.

"Would either of you like a nice cup of tea or coffee while you wait?" She asked.

Eventually after a short conversation Mrs Marriot disappeared and Detective Inspector Nicola Garwood smiled across at the man opposite her.

"You must be Sam Henning." She said.

The broad shouldered man glanced up from his magazine again.

"Before I answer that, is this an official enquiry?" He asked.

A playful grin then appeared.

Nicola Garwood chuckled as she extended her right hand for him to shake.

"I'm DI Garwood from Dulwich." She announced.

Henning took her hand in his and shook it.

"Sam Henning Acton CID." He replied with a smile of his own.

Behind the closed door Sir Christopher watched Chief Inspector Martin Roberts deliberately very slowly take his seat.

As he watched, Sir Christopher considered that the high ranking police officer in front of him had used his influence to persuade certain members of the parliamentary select committee to push his own name to the top of a shortlist.

The shortlist of names was to head a task force that was being assembled and he could only conclude that the Chief Inspector's motives were selfishly plain and simple.

Sir Christopher understood that the obnoxious Chief Inspector in his personal opinion, was due to retire from the force in less than two years and it was common knowledge that he had ambitions to throw his own hat into the political arena.

This, again in the well versed and highly respected politician's personal opinion provided Roberts with a perfect grand stage from which to launch his political career.

The appointed chief of the task force would be responsible for all matters relating to the press and public affairs and this of course included televised press conferences.

It meant again in Sir Christopher's opinion, Roberts had positioned himself perfectly.

He was about to launch himself into the public spotlight prior to the start of his own political career.

If his assigned senior officers cracked the case in good time he as the face on everybody's televisions would obviously assume much of the credit without ever leaving his new office chair.

It was something of a political masterstroke in Sir Christopher's opinion.

The meeting eventually started and it was initially quite informal until Sir Christopher announced that there had been *certain recent developments* regarding the situation.

"As you're aware Mr Roberts, so far we seem to have mislaid more than six Hundred of London's homeless community over the past eighteen months." Sir Christopher began.

The realistic figure was in fact now fast approaching nine hundred but Sir Christopher had no way of knowing this from the research and data provided to him.

"This task force was initially thought up to combat this growing situation." He continued.

He watched the Chief Inspector as he continuously attempted to interject.

"It has become blatantly obvious that these people as unfortunate as they already are..." Sir Christopher continued.

He raised a single forefinger to indicate to the police officer that he wanted him to wait.

"It has become blatantly obvious that they're being forcibly taken from our streets." He added.

The Chief Inspector finally nodded in agreement.

"I've been trying to tell you people this all along." He finally interjected.

Sir Christopher gently tapped his pen onto the desk as he considered the situation.

"But as I said there have been recent and quite significant developments." He eventually continued.

Chief Inspector Roberts raised his eyebrows.

"What developments?"

Again Sir Christopher pondered on how to word this correctly considering the man that sat front of him.

"It appears that there has been a separate seven percent increase in reports of other missing people." He started to explain.

Roberts continued to stare back at him.

"Mr Roberts I'm talking about everyday working, housed and *voting* Londoners." He eventually continued.

There was a lengthy silent pause as Roberts digested what the politician had just revealed.

"A seven percent increase?" He eventually asked.

Sir Christopher slowly nodded his head.

"And just like the missing homeless none of these people have shown up anywhere else." He replied.

"And I want you to take into account that we're discussing the reported cases Mr Roberts." Sir Christopher continued.

"I suspect that there are realistically many, many more."

Sir Christopher paused and allowed Roberts to digest this new information before he moved on to what he considered an even more delicate matter to approach.

Again he took into account the Chief Inspector's somewhat volatile personality.

"As you're aware this task force is being assembled as we speak and two Detective Inspectors have already been assigned to combat these two separate issues." Sir Christopher started.

He went on to emphasise that *two separate issues* meant that the situation with the missing homeless would run alongside the also growing number of the non-homeless missing people.

Right now nobody knew if the two were in fact connected.

Regardless Chief Inspector Roberts promptly interjected.

"Wait, wait, did you just say that two senior Detectives have already been assigned?" He asked.

As Sir Christopher nodded and pointed toward his office door Roberts rigorously shook his head.

"Now hold on a moment!" He suddenly snapped.

"I was led to believe that I would personally select and assign the senior officers to this task force!" He strongly protested.

Sir Christopher sighed as he stared down at his desk and regathered his thoughts.

"Mr Roberts." He began again.

"The Prime Minister himself thought it prudent to form a select committee for such tasks as the assembly of the task force." He continued.

"They have in their wisdom, like it or not assigned Detective Inspector Nicola Garwood from Dulwich and Detective Inspector Samuel Henning from Acton." He added.

"They are waiting right outside that door as the two newly appointed senior officers at task force headquarters."

Sir Christopher ignored the fact that Roberts now rigorously shook his head.

"The reality of this situation is that your role will be to manage press conferences along with the day to day administration of the task force." He continued.

"It might be prudent to remain focussed on your own role Chief Inspector, and leave detection to the senior Detectives of this case."

Roberts mocked a chuckle that Sir Christopher saw as contempt for the select committee's decision.

"I'd like to point out that Detective Inspector Garwood is nothing more than a product of a fast track promotion scheme based on the fact that she has blonde hair and long bloody legs." The Chief Inspector retorted.

Sir Christopher raised his eyebrows with genuine shock at the statement.

"Because some idiot in an office at Westminster with no comprehension of how things really work decided that we didn't have enough of them in upper management!" Roberts snapped again.

"This is precisely why the assignment of officers should be left to those of us that know what we're doing!"

The usually unshakable Sir Christopher was for once taken aback by the Chief Inspector's outrageous statement.

He took another few moments to compose his thoughts before he continued after a long deep sigh.

"Mr Roberts, I have it on good authority that at some point in the not too distant future you intend to enter the world of politics is that correct?" He asked.

He received no response from Roberts whatsoever.

Sir Christopher then somehow managed a half smile.

"Feel free to take a little advice from somebody that's been around the block once or twice."

"Try to keep your personal views and opinions to yourself." He advised the Chief Inspector.

"Oh and by the way, I'm the idiot at Westminster that assigned DI Garwood to the task force." He now revealed.

After another lengthy pause of uncomfortable silence Sir Christopher slid one of the files in front of him across the desk toward Roberts.

"Seven hundred miniature cameras are soon to be installed onto the streets of London." He started to explain.

"Inside the building that's about to be allocated to the task force a sizeable team of CCTV operators will have the ability to watch every single major road within the city of London." He added.

"And we're currently in negotiations with several borough councils with regard to the loan of safe houses to begin temporarily housing as many of the homeless community as possible."

Roberts concentrated on the file and purposely appeared to hear nothing of what Sir Christopher was telling him.

'You really are an obnoxious little prat!' Sir Christopher thought to himself.

However he stared across at Roberts but took his own advice and kept this personal opinion to himself.

It was around half an hour later that the somewhat disgruntled Chief Inspector departed from the meeting and the office before Detective Inspectors Nicola Garwood and Sam Henning were ushered inside.

Sir Christopher explained the same situation to them although in a much less stressful environment and with far fewer eggshells for him to step onto.

Chief Inspector Roberts was initially intended to be included in this secondary meeting with the two senior Detectives who would together run the day to day investigations of the two cases.

But in his wisdom after the chief's outburst regarding the woman that now sat in front of him with blonde hair blue eyes and long legs Sir Christopher concluded that it would be more than counter-productive.

Both Detective Inspectors Garwood and Henning listened as the politician explained the intended details along with the internal workings of the task force that they would manage together.

This meeting would last considerably longer due to the fact that Sir Christopher wasn't in so much of a hurry to get them out of the door unlike a short while ago.

When the secondary meeting was finally over and after many questions were asked by both Henning and Garwood they were finally and more cordially dismissed.

As they were leaving the office Sir Christopher called back Sam Henning.

After Sheila Marriot closed the door behind Nicola Garwood Sir Christopher turned and stared out of the window behind his desk.

"I'm going to need your help to protect her to an extent Henning." He sighed.

He then nodded toward his closed door and the general direction of Detective Inspector Nicola Garwood on the other side of it.

He then very loosely explained the views of their soon to be new boss regarding the fast track promotion schemes and Detective Inspector Nicola Garwood.

He slowly turned back in his chair and smiled up at Sam Henning.

"This is strictly off the record of course." He reminded Henning.

Sam nodded with a smile of his own.

"I understand Sir Christopher." He replied.

"I'll do whatever I can."

Ten

Tuesday July 18th 2000

At just after eight in the morning two teenage girls casually strolled along Larchwood Drive on their way to college.

As they passed a house with a dirty white front door, behind it Debbie Davies climbed the narrow brown threadbare carpeted staircase.

She was followed by the Turkish leader Barak Yazici and his thirty nine year old countryman Atif Rahman.

They reached the top of the stairs and turned left and walked along the landing toward the back of the house where Davies used a key to unlock a white door.

The small box room behind the door was badly painted in pale blue with no carpets covering the wooden floorboards and closed thin light brown curtains kept the room in a semi darkened state.

Twenty three year old Hannah Anderson who was taken from the night club at Soho Square with her friend Amanda Golding three nights ago was now fully awake.

She lay writhing on the hard wooden floor as she desperately tried to free her hands from behind her back.

Her long auburn wavy hair was now matted and sweat ran down her face as she tried to breath much more heavily than usual thanks to the grey rag that had been stuffed into her mouth with the same sticky black duct tape that rendered her hands and feet helpless.

Her muffled squeals and whimpered pleas were to absolutely no avail because nobody other than those that kept her there could hear them.

Within an hour from now she would struggle no more and the tightly wrapped duct tape around her wrists and ankles would be removed.

Black mascara ran down her face from several earlier flows of terrified and confused tears but now her eyes suddenly widened when she heard the key turn inside the lock of the door.

When Debbie Davies pushed open the door her nostrils filled with the stench of stale urine.

Hannah had been kept locked inside this room bound and gagged for what was now the third day and of course she had unavoidably urinated in her underwear several times.

Davies stared down at Hannah with the two very ominous figures of Yazici and Rahman standing on either side of her.

There was a short pause as the two women silently stared into each other's eyes.

"Ok get on with it." Davies uttered.

She then turned to leave the room but she stopped at the opened doorway and then turned and glanced down at Hannah again.

"I want you to understand something." She began in a calm and quiet tone.

"What these two are about to do to you is nothing compared to what'll happen if you ever decide to do anything other than what you're told."

Davies then turned her attention to Barak Yazici.

"When you're done take her to the front bedroom." She told him.

Yazici nodded his head in silence.

Hannah's already widened eyes grew even wider with terror as she watched Yazici and Rahman slowly remove the belts from their waistbands.

Debbie Davies left the room and closed the door behind her.

She still had no idea that her best friend Amanda Golding had in fact died in the back of the black cab three nights ago.

Hannah believed that she was being kept somewhere else in this house but right now her best friend's whereabouts and welfare were distant thoughts from her mind.

She lay mostly naked and helplessly bound as she watched the two men remove their belts and she knew that she could do absolutely nothing to protect herself.

Debbie Davies started to climb back down the narrow staircase and immediately heard the muffled screams from Hannah as she lay helplessly bound and gagged on the hard wooden floor.

Both wide leather belts started to land with ferocity onto and all over her bare unprotected flesh.

It was actually worse than that, much worse than that.

As Davies climbed down that staircase the sounds of Hannah Anderson's brutal beating at the hands of the two Turkish men slowly became nothing more than a quietened background din.

When she reached the bottom Davies glanced out from the glass window of the front door and saw the two teenage girls, one blonde and the other brunette walking arm in arm and laughing hysterically.

"You're a silly pair of cows." She quietly uttered with a chuckle.

It was twenty minutes or so later when Davies finished preparing the plastic medical syringe that was now half filled with murky Heroin.

She walked through the living room and into the hall beside the front door where she again stared out at Larchwood drive and listened to the ongoing brutality upstairs in the small box room at the back of the house.

"Great, kill the second one why don't you?" She quietly uttered with a sigh.

She stared up the narrow staircase.

"I said give her a good hiding not kill her you pair of dickheads!" She finally yelled up the stairs.

The muffled sounds suddenly ceased.

"Take her into the front bedroom now!" She yelled up.

She walked back into the living room and watched the news channel on the TV as she waited and eventually she heard the whimpering bound and gagged Hannah being dragged across the landing.

"It's about time!" Davies quietly uttered.

After another ten minutes she heard the heavy footsteps of both Turkish men as they climbed down the staircase and when she turned to face them Davies saw that both Yazici and Rahman were out of breath.

"They can't make you money if they're dead!" She angrily pointed out.

She then climbed back up the narrow staircase but this time at the top she turned right and headed toward the front of the house.

She opened the door on her left and the same strong stench of stale urine immediately filled her nostrils.

The master bedroom was twelve feet by twelve feet with walls that were badly painted in beige and on the floor was a lighter brown just as badly fitted threadbare carpet.

In each corner of the room was a small single bed and all were now occupied due to the addition of Hannah Anderson.

The other three women, a redhead and two blondes were like Hannah dressed in nothing but urine stained underwear and they were all chained down on their respective beds.

All of these women and three more in an adjacent bedroom were sold to Davies and her Turkish gang at a price of two hundred and fifty pounds courtesy of Jamal and Ali.

They were all coaxed from various London night spots over the past five to six weeks.

It was only Hannah that could be heard quietly sobbing through her duct tape gag after receiving the most brutal beating at the hands of Yazici and Rahman.

Her now battered bruised and lacerated body provided the evidence that she wasn't just beaten with the belts.

It was worse, much worse than that.

The two men had in fact beaten her with the metal belt buckles.

Now tightly padlocked around her right wrist was one end of a rusty chain that travelled down the right side of the bed and beneath it to reappear on her left side where the opposite end was just as tightly padlocked around her left wrist.

Debbie Davies smiled down at Hannah as she approached the bed.

"Did you enjoy that?" She asked.

She sat down on the mattress beside the sobbing Hannah who just wanted to go home and be with her parents.

Hannah eventually slowly shook her head as she attempted muffled pleas through her gag but Davies placed her forefinger onto the duct tape that was firmly pressed over her mouth.

"If you keep quiet for me I'll take the pain away for you." She said in an almost warm and caring tone.

She then studied some of the black and blue bleeding bruises that now covered Hannah's entire body.

She then stared back into Hannah's tear-filled eyes.

"I don't want you to take another beating like that." She said.

"So from now on you only ever do as you're told or the next one will be ten times worse, I promise." She assured Hannah.

"Do you understand?"

There was a momentary pause before Hannah eventually nodded as she wept uncontrollably.

She then let out a whimper as she felt a sharp prick as Davies pushed the tip of the needle of the loaded medical syringe into her upper left thigh.

"You won't feel a thing in a few moments." Davies assured her.

She then slowly pressed down onto the small plunger and watched the murky liquid travel down the clear plastic tube and into Hannah's leg.

Davies was absolutely right because very soon the twenty three year old beautician Hannah Anderson would feel nothing.

Her journey had begun.

Eleven
Friday July 28th 2000

Tranton road Bermondsey south east London was a quiet through road between Keeton's and Drummond road with Bermondsey Underground railway station just five minutes walking distance around the corner.

There was some kind of friendly neighbourhood competition occurring in Tranton road regarding garden showings of colourful plants and neatly trimmed lawns.

Passers-by would see ornate wooden wishing wells and one garden was almost completely full with brightly painted garden gnomes.

But another in the centre on the left from Keeton's road was completely covered with drab grey concrete and enclosed by a low and dirty white painted brick wall.

This particular property was faceless in comparison.

It was designed to be faceless.

After viewing the gardens before it from both directions, passers-by would usually hurry to the next colourful or extravagant showing and pay it absolutely no attention.

It stuck out like the proverbial sore thumb but nobody wanted to give it a second glance.

Behind this house in the small back garden was a large corrugated steel shed that seemed to have a sliding roof that could actually extend open.

Inside it was a large grey fully operational satellite receiver.

Directly opposite this strange construction was a permanently closed and locked white kitchen door.

Inside the long and narrow galley style kitchen was a spotless oven on the left and it was spotless because it had never been used.

The work surfaces on both sides showed many stacked red empty pizza boxes and the white fridge was almost completely filled with various coloured bottles of fizzy pop.

Opposite the fridge was an empty void where a washing machine should be but the occupant of this house was without a doubt a creature of habit.

A washing routine inside the house as opposed to the local launderette would only serve to break the habit and that was completely unacceptable.

Through the kitchen and into the badly wallpapered light brown hallway leading toward the front door were a narrow flight of stairs on the left and a closed door leading into the living room on the right.

Inside the living room two large glossy posters of the latest girl band were taped onto the beige painted walls and a tatty old dark brown sofa and one matching just as tatty armchair sat on the dark blue threadbare carpet.

But opposite the old sofa was a brand new state of the art dark blue leather reclining chair and directly in front of it was a large brand new TV with three of the latest games consoles connected into it.

The room itself was darkened due to the fact that the blue lined curtains were hardly ever opened.

On the wall up the threadbare burgundy carpeted staircase, were two crooked pictures and there was a loose bannister rail too.

At the top of the stairs were four white painted wooden doors that were all fully opened.

The door on the far left side of the landing led into the sparse master bedroom that had a dark brown carpet and white painted walls with no pictures whatsoever.

The dark brown curtains were partially pulled shut just like almost every other room inside the house.

There was an unmade double bed with a white Formica wardrobe on the left and one small white painted chest of drawers on the right.

The top drawer was fully opened and showed one black and one navy blue sock inside it.

Inside the opened wardrobe was one pair of hanging blue denim jeans and a brand new black suit that was still covered in its clear plastic wrapping because it had never been worn.

The same could be said for the brand new shiny black shoes that were inside a yellow box on the wardrobe floor.

Every other item of clothing was stuffed inside the completely full washing basket and awaited another trip to the launderette.

At the far end of the hall directly opposite the master bedroom was an opened bathroom door that had a bath on the left that was still wet from recent use and a purple toothbrush remained in the porcelain sink on the right.

On the grey tiled floor was a discarded crumpled dark blue bath towel.

The first of the two spare bedrooms on the left of the bathroom was darkened and spanned ten feet by ten feet with white painted walls and it had a new dark blue fitted carpet on the floor and matching closed dark blue curtains.

In the centre of the room was a fully operational white satellite dish that spanned eight feet in diameter and it was positioned on top of a tall thin black tower that displayed various tiny multi-coloured continuously flashing lights.

Placed on the floor around three of the walls were more identical functioning black towers that displayed identical tiny multi-coloured flashing lights.

Cables ran from each tower into a small hole at the bottom left corner of the room and disappeared into a second larger spare bedroom next to this one.

The next spare bedroom spanned twelve feet by twelve feet with beige painted walls and a dark brown carpet on the floor.

The curtains were actually opened and the bedroom window was ajar allowing natural sunlight and real fresh air into the room.

A home-made wooden work surface ran around three of the walls.

On the left side were five switched off computer monitors and there were three identical black leather chairs tucked beneath.

A further four working monitors were beneath the window directly in front of the door.

There were four more computers that were all switched on that ran along the right side of the room.

Seated and scrutinising the information on three of them at the same time was a thirty three year old autistic genius.

His name was David Stringer.

David was five feet eight inches tall and came with a chubby build courtesy of the stacked empty pizza boxes and the fridge full of fizzy pop down in the kitchen.

He had short straight mousy brown hair that was combed into a centre parting directly above his incredibly thick prescription glasses.

In fact his glasses were so heavily magnified that they made his eyes look three times too large for his head and when he blinked they somehow often gave the impression that it happened in slow motion.

He wore a dark blue t-shirt and blue denim jeans with one black sock and one navy blue on his feet thanks to his incredibly poor eyesight whenever he wasn't wearing his glasses.

Just like when he climbed out of bed this morning and quite literally fell into the bath.

The story behind David Stringer was that he used his somewhat unique and completely self-taught skills to hack into the computer files at New Scotland Yard mostly because it wasn't actually in Scotland.

He also hacked the computer system at Buckingham Palace and in his ignorant innocence and his own words he immediately confessed.

"I was just having a nose around."

His multiple unauthorised visits subsequently led to his arrest but because of his quite obvious unique talents, David Stringer immediately vanished from the grid.

Today he didn't officially exist.

Nobody even back then could know that he could so easily do this.

This was initially a precaution because they had no intention of ever releasing him because he posed such a threat to national security.

David Stringer hacked the computers of computer hackers for fun and during several interrogations it was clear that his nature displayed a somewhat naive innocence.

Autism in the year 2000 was still only just being recognised but it soon became very clear to all concerned that he knew more about the inner workings and capabilities of a computer than any government expert.

He was of course completely self-taught so there really was no working manual that came with him and this led to the next problem.

What to do with David Stringer?

He was eventually employed by an involved organisation that also didn't officially exist however this non-existent organisation often performed tasks on behalf of high ranking government officials.

'It's better to have him working on our side than somebody else use him against us if he's ever released.'

It would never be allowed for him to be recruited by any similar organisation.

The management of this one already knew that he could gain access to their files whenever he chose to regardless of any type of safeguards or security in place.

He had already proven that on nine separate occasions but of course this meant that he could also gain access to the systems of their competitors and enemies.

Stringer actually regarded the entire eleven week ordeal in incarceration beneath Whitechapel as something of an adventure.

He simply didn't comprehend the trouble that he was in at the time.

With a little help he soon learned to gain access to any overhead passing satellite to *'borrow'* it for viewing on the ground while remaining completely undetected by its owners.

He masked his IP (Internet Protocol) address so that his presence automatically pointed the owners in the direction of several rotated Nigerian internet chat rooms.

David Stringer became an invaluable asset.

Today one of his roles was to watch from above and guide military styled operations feeding intelligence along the way.

He had over the past two years become an absolutely invaluable asset although most that he directed on the ground had never met him in person.

One operative however that had met him was a former Captain of the elite British Army SAS Regiment.

He was now a civilian called Richard Willows.

Thirty four year old Captain Richard Willows was the older brother of Sasha who mysteriously disappeared from the mobile soup kitchen at Lant Street in Southwark just over two weeks ago on July 13th

When Sasha disappeared on that cold and wet early morning as her next of kin Richard was notified around thirty six hours later.

He knew at the time that there was some kind of case being constructed by the metropolitan police regarding many of London's missing homeless and he was certain that his sister as a volunteer had somehow been caught up in it.

Sasha would never have simply disappeared without telling him.

Richard eventually contacted his friend David Stringer to ask for help and of course David immediately agreed.

As Richard's friend he had met and knew Sasha personally.

Richard on the other hand was in fact David's one and only friend.

Right now displayed on the first monitor on his left David stared at the very bland green and brown home page of an online dating website.

For some reason the website wasn't listed on any search engines whatsoever.

Online dating was a subject that he knew quite well but this was completely unappealing even to him and besides the membership fees were staggering.

He could, had he chosen to hack into the dating site and issue himself with solid gold membership free of charge.

However the reason that he now viewed this particular site was not to search for love and romance or for once pictures of half-naked young women to view.

On the second monitor to the right of the first was the image of a blonde woman.

Her name was Jane Chapman and he viewed her courtesy of the DVLA (Driver Vehicle Licensing Agency) website.

"So you built this heap of crap?" He asked her image.

He nodded in the direction of her dating site.

Of course he received no reply because it was just an image and she had no idea that he was even viewing her.

Neither did the DVLA.

David believed that he was now onto something.

It was the first plausible break but he didn't yet know exactly what that was.

Something just wasn't quite right.

Earlier that morning he tracked vast cash payments from a single source that eventually led him to this ugly and unappealing green and brown dating website and at that time he also viewed her dimensions.

"Well you're a very big boat!" He uttered.

He viewed an overhead image of the Indigo from a passing Russian satellite while she was anchored off the coast of Syria.

There had been many payments from various eastern European banks averaging between sixty and seventy thousand pounds but when he back-tracked those payments they all pointed to the exact same source no matter where she sailed or anchored.

It was always the Indigo.

After tracing most of the payments onto this ugly dating website he discovered Jane Chapman from her own IP address.

He now knew what type of vehicles she was entitled to drive and what she looked like and inside an attached file he discovered her home and mobile telephone numbers too.

He also discovered from cross reference and more research that Jane Chapman was a former web designer and that she had worked for a web design company until a couple of years ago when she suddenly resigned for no given reason.

On monitor three he viewed the internal banking details of her dating site and his over-magnified eyes widened.

"That's from a dating website?" He asked out loud.

"Are you sure?" He uttered as he continued to stare.

"No wonder you quit your job!"

He glanced back at her DVLA photograph as if he were talking to her in person.

It was something that David often did regardless of the fact that he was talking to nothing but a photograph.

For reasons that he didn't yet know David's attention continued to return to the ugly green and brown dating site home page displayed on what he referred to as monitor one.

There was something right in front of him that greatly bothered him but he didn't know what it was and this was how it always happened for David Stringer.

It was there right in front of him but he couldn't yet see it.

He continued to scrutinise the banking details on monitor three but again he glanced back at the bland green and brown home page and now in particular at the available tabs that ran across the top of the screen.

"What's Administration?" He asked himself.

Stringer knew that something was wrong with this particular tab because he had already viewed behind the scenes of the site.

He wondered what could be behind this 'Administration' tab because it wasn't the route that he had used *'to take a nose around'* inside earlier.

It was somehow completely separated and isolated from the rest of the dating site.

"It's not actually connected to this site." He uttered.

"It's actually a crafty link to something else." He added.

His over-magnified eyes widened again when he discovered that a twelve digit password was required to enter this so called administration area.

"Are you bloody kidding?" He asked her photographic image.

"What have you got inside there, dancing girls?" He asked as he nodded toward the monitor.

He inserted a disk and ran some home-made software that immediately started to work on cracking the huge code.

He left it running while he continued to scrutinise the internal banking information that was created by Chapman herself as an account summary.

In particular he viewed the details displayed shortly after the date that Sasha Willows was reported missing.

After around twenty five minutes the fourth monitor flickered into life and as he stared he saw hundreds of tiny minimised jpeg images that automatically uploaded onto his screen.

"At last we have your dancing girls!" He said with a beaming grin.

He sat back in his black leather chair and watched as the tiny images continued to upload.

Eventually he leaned forward and clicked his mouse icon onto the very first and it immediately enlarged.

"Ok we have lots and lots of dancing girls!" He added as he watched images continue to upload.

David now stared at a photograph of a very beautiful woman with long dark brown hair who at first glance appeared to be posing as asleep.

David frowned.

"Why do they do that?" He asked Chapman's photograph.

Again he nodded in the direction of monitor four.

"I like them to pretend to be awake when I work the old Stringer magic!" He told her.

He clicked on the second image and found another supposedly sleeping beauty and the third appeared to be sleeping too.

David leaned forward to take a closer look because he understood that it often took a few minutes to fully grasp certain things.

Now he clicked on a fourth image to see a woman that appeared to be shopping for groceries in a supermarket and to David it appeared that she had no idea that her picture was being taken.

"These can't be members of a dating website." He uttered.

He clicked on more images of supposedly sleeping women.

All of these women were quite beautiful as were more images of women that were awake and again who didn't appear to know that their picture was taken.

"I don't get it." He quietly told himself.

He returned to the very first image and studied the dark haired sleeping woman again before he clicked on more images of women that seemed to be posing in the same way but once again he returned to the very first.

They all had one thing in common with her.

He knew it.

He just didn't know what that common factor was.

Suddenly everything slotted into place.

He realised why he continuously clicked on her image.

"Holy crap it's the floor!" He yelled.

For the first time David was rattled and that didn't often occur.

He reached for his telephone and dialled a number while his eyes remained fixed on the photograph and   continued to stare at monitor four until the recipient of his call picked up.

"Richard I found them!" He blurted into the mouthpiece.

There was a pause as Richard Willows on the other end of the line replied.

"When do you come back?" David asked.

"Ok, come here the day after tomorrow then." He said.

He continued to stare at the jpeg image and there was another pause as Richard nervously asked the most important question of all.

"No, I'm going to go through them all now but I haven't seen her yet." David replied.

Twelve
Friday August 4th 2000

Eighty seven year old Stanley Morton suddenly died from a massive stroke in the bathroom at his home at Love lane Micham just four miles from Croydon on the outskirts of south London and he had no known living relatives.

A reporter from the local Gazette took an interest in the story and he wrote an article regarding Stanley.

He discovered that in 1944 shortly after the D-Day landings on June 6th Stanley Morton from Micham Surrey was awarded a posthumous medal for bravery.

It transpired that while completely alone Stanley incapacitated a German Panzer tank after he became lost and found himself in the French town of Carantan under heavy enemy fire.

The compelling story generated much public interest particularly at quiet Love lane where Stanley lived with his wife and childhood sweetheart Hilda since 1946 until she passed away a little more than five years ago.

The posthumous medal came as a surprise particularly to the residents of Love lane who only knew Stanley as a quiet old man that kept himself to himself and he never once spoke of it.

Forty eight year old Ian Carter was the journalist from the local Gazette that discovered the heroic past of Stanley also discovered during his research that Stanley and Hilda had no children.

Hilda only had an older brother Robert who was himself killed during the Normandy landings which meant that there were no known living relatives to inherit the three bedroom house and a small estate and of course Stanley's posthumous medal that was in fact awarded to him by the King himself.

The search began to find a distant relative and innocently on the part of the local journalist Ian Carter.

He wrote and published in the Gazette many articles regarding the exploits of Stanley Morton during the then war torn Europe hoping to jog the memory of somebody still living or maybe a family story told that somebody might recall.

Seven weeks after the first article and twelve weeks after Stanley's sudden death there was still nobody.

The story picked up momentum and public interest but it possibly divulged a little too much information because during week fourteen of the articles written by Mr Carter something did occur as a direct result.

Six squatters gained access to the empty property of Stanley and Hilda Morton and took up residence.

This brought anger particularly from the residents of Love lane where a few incidents of violence were recorded and police were called to the address on several occasions.

After a few weeks the local council became involved and a private Bailiff company that were contracted by the council arrived to enforce evictions.

The squatters however knew more about their legal rights than the Bailiffs and the rushed eviction attempt ended in disastrous failure and more police presence followed on a daily basis.

Eventually the local council got it right and the following week notice was served at the former home of the late Stanley Morton.

The six squatters were given twenty eight days to move from the property or they would this time be removed by force and possibly arrested.

The story for the journalist Ian Carter rolled on for another four weeks.

By now the squatters had received many threats of violence and there was a permanent police presence outside the house and one night the story reached the heights of the regional six o'clock TV news.

The TV news report led to the discovery of Mr Robert Wise, a fifty one year old plumber from Bethnal Green London.

Although Mr Wise was not directly related to Stanley Morton he was a second cousin of Hilda and this of course made him Stanley's cousin too and their only known albeit distant living relative.

When it was validated that Mr Wise was related to Hilda the property and belongings of Stanley essentially became his and it was in fact he that calmed the public outrage with a plea via the local radio station.

He pleaded with the local residents of Love lane to allow the legal process to run its course and he also pointed out that valuable police resources were being used that could and should be used elsewhere.

His calming radio interview seemed to make sense and eventually the angry protestors bowed to his wishes and the permanent presence outside the property dwindled away as eventually did the constant police presence.

It was 3:08am on August 4th and just three days before local officials were due to remove the six squatters by force in the now much quieter Love lane.

It rained earlier that morning for an hour or so which meant that the roads were wet and the only announcement of the security van's arrival was the splashing sound from the tyres as it rolled to a stop directly outside the house without the engine running.

The luminous markings revealed that the van was from a London based security firm called *Indigo Security Services* and beneath the company logo was boasted *'London's Finest!'*

A small black Fiat parked at the far end on the junction of Love lane and the A236 Western road and waited with three occupants inside it.

The role of the 'spotters' inside the car was initially to alert the occupants inside the security van by way of two-way radio of any activity heading their way.

Their secondary role was to enter the house later to perform the clinical clean up that was required to remove any evidence that their colleagues had ever been there.

The other end of Love lane was a dead end so there was no need for a second car on this occasion but under normal circumstances there would be two.

There was a large tree in the front garden that partially obscured the view of the house.

Thirty five year old former Romanian army Captain Abel Barbu stared over it at the completely darkened upper floor of the house from the passenger seat of the security van.

He was a well-built man and stood at around six feet tall with dark brown eyes and olive skin and with a thin neatly trimmed moustache above his lip.

The Captain turned to his driver thirty year old Lucian Banica who was once a sergeant in his old unit.

They made brief eye contact before the Sergeant checked in his driver side wing mirror and turned to his boss and nodded.

The Captain turned his attention to the back of the van where twenty nine year old former sniper Emil Hagi and twenty nine year old explosives expert Dorin Christescu awaited his orders.

Captain Barbu pulled down his black balaclava and his three Romanian associates did the same before he pointed to Emil Hagi and showed him a single forefinger.

'You are number One.'

He then showed Christescu two fingers.

'You are number Two.'

Dorin Christescu like Emil Hagi nodded.

They had just silently been given specific roles.

Barbu returned his attention to the driver Lucian Banica who checked again in his wing mirrors before he looked back at the Captain and nodded again.

No words would be spoken.

Barbu for the final time turned to the two soldiers at the back and showed them a thumb that prompted both to exit via the sliding side door that Hagi then very quietly closed behind him.

The Captain and his driver watched Hagi and Christescu disappear behind the large tree that obscured their view of the front door.

At first they couldn't see that Hagi had taken seventeen seconds to unlock the door using what looked like two thin slithers of silver metal.

It was Hagi's job to unlock the door and then gently push it to the full extent of the security chain from the door to the frame so that Christescu could then silently cut it.

They were surprised under the circumstances to discover that the chain had not been used at all by the occupying squatters.

Christescu stepped to the side of the tree and indicated to his Captain that they had gained entry into the property.

There was an eerie silence inside the darkened house when the Captain and his driver quietly entered.

As usual Captain Barbu's heart began to pound against his chest as his adrenalin rush began with all of his senses now fully heightened.

Dorin Christescu carefully closed the front door behind him with a resounding and almost earth shattering 'CLICK!' that caused the Captain to cringe.

The hallway was dark and there was a closed white door on the left that was once Stanley Morton's living room.

They already knew that it was currently being used as a bedroom.

The Captain stood in front of it and silently indicated to Emil Hagi and Lucian Banica to wait on either side of him while Dorin Christescu waited at the front door as back up should anything go wrong.

Sleeping inside the room was twenty seven year old Mark Pritchard and his girlfriend twenty three year old Nikki Fright with their small white Jack Russell dog Ben.

Christescu actually stroked the dog in a nearby park just yesterday when Nikki Fright walked him.

Captain Barbu's heart pounded faster against his chest as he fought to compose himself as his three soldiers patiently waited.

He took in a long deep breath before he pressed down onto the handle and carefully pushed the door away from him.

He also very slowly removed his tranquiliser pistol from the holster.

Hagi and Banica silently entered the darkened cluttered room where Mark Pritchard and Nikki Fright slept on a double mattress on the floor on the left beneath a large bay window.

Suddenly the small white head of Ben the Jack Russell dog looked up from the bed.

It was the Captain that encouraged it to come to him while Hagi and Banica completely ignored it and silently drew their own tranquiliser guns.

The dog slowly stood up and stretched before it made its way toward Barbu and as it stepped completely off the mattress wagging his tail the Captain fired his tranquiliser gun and the dog silently slumped unconscious to the floor.

Hagi and Banica carefully stepped through the strewn objects on the floor before they both knelt on either side of the still soundly sleeping Mark Pritchard and Nikki Fright.

They both slowly reached down and took a hold of the dark blue covers before they stared back up at each other.

Hagi nodded his head.

Together they slowly pulled back the covers.

Hagi reached down and firmly covered the mouth of Nikki Fright with his black gloved left hand while Banica reached down with his gun in his left hand and used his right to cover the mouth of Mark Pritchard.

The well-drilled sequence was almost immediate as Hagi fired directly into the chest of Nikki Fright as Banica also fired into Mark Pritchard.

Both had just enough time to open their eyes and briefly see their attackers.

The Captain now pointed to Lucian Banica and made a T shape with his hands and the driver nodded.

Banica removed several black plastic cable ties from his left breast pocket as Emil Hagi followed the Captain back out of the room.

Before he left, Hagi broke Ben the dog's neck with a quiet but effective snap!

Four minutes later the Captain stood directly outside what used to be Stanley Morton's bedroom with Hagi again on his left and Dorin Christescu on his right.

Again he took time to compose as his two soldiers waited patiently.

Inside the room and sleeping in Stanley's old bed were twenty four year old Michael Stott and his twenty two year old girlfriend Jackie Miles who was unmistakable with her long bright red hair.

Captain Barbu tapped the barrel of his reloaded pistol onto the shoulder of Emil Hagi and the former Sniper nodded.

He then turned and did the same to Dorin Christescu and he also nodded.

The Captain then very slowly pushed down on the handle and then quietly opened the door.

As Hagi and Christescu entered the bedroom Captain Barbu was suddenly gripped with panic as he heard very quiet padding footsteps behind him.

He slowly turned with widened eyes to see Lucian Banica grinning from behind his balaclava.

Banica knew that he had caught out his nervous Commanding Officer.

Captain Barbu sighed with relief.

Their eye contact was broken by the muffled sounds from inside the bedroom as both Jackie Miles and Michael Stott were rendered unconscious in exactly the same way as Nikki Fright and Mark Pritchard.

Both Hagi and Christescu looked back at the Captain and again he formed a T shape with his still trembling hands.

He then quietly turned to the Sergeant Lucian and pointed to the room at the end of the landing where twenty eight year old Robert Croft slept.

Eleven minutes later and after the Captain tranquilised nineteen year old Jim Creasley he was binding the young musician's wrists behind his back with black cable ties.

Nikki Fright, Dan Pritchard, Michael Stott, Jackie Miles, Robert Croft and Jim Creasley were carried outside where they were unceremoniously dumped unconscious onto the steel floor inside the van.

Ben the Jack Russell dog was left for the clean-up team, the spotters inside the small black Fiat that would spend most of that day inside the house.

Passers-by were completely unaware that they were inside and they would wait to leave in the dead of night.

At precisely nine o'clock in the morning three days later the local authorities arrived in force to remove the six squatters from the home of Stanley Morton.

They discovered that the squatters already fled under the cover of darkness probably as late as just last night or so it was believed.

The journalist Ian Carter closed the now long running story with a feel good factor because everything eventually turned out well.

He publicly thanked Mr Wise the new found relation of Stanley Morton for his intervention in his closing article and a few weeks later the Gazette published the responses and comments to Ian Carter's articles.

Most were negative toward the squatters and also toward the local authorities for both allowing this to happen in the first place and because of the farcical failed eviction attempt.

In general the responses were those of *'Good riddance'* toward the squatters.

They would undoubtedly reappear, living at somebody else's property.

But they were all wrong.

The six squatters wouldn't reappear anywhere.

Thirteen
Sunday July 30th 2000

It was just after nine on a dry but cloudy morning when a black Saab convertible pulled up outside the home and secret workplace of autistic genius David Stringer at Tranton Road Bermondsey south east London.

Thirty five year old Richard Willows was a broad shouldered man standing at six feet with short blonde swept back hair and cold piercing blue eyes.

He wore a pale grey suit with a white open necked shirt and on his feet he wore brown Italian leather shoes.

With both hands now inside his trouser pockets he strolled up the short garden path where eventually he knocked on the white front door and waited.

Under normal circumstances the planning and logistics expert Willows was considered something of a ladies man but due the current situation regarding his sister, women were not on his mind.

He was being driven crazy at the thought of what could be happening to twenty two year old Sasha right now and he was desperate to find her.

The former Captain of the elite British SAS regiment turned as the white door was unlocked from inside and now standing in front of him was his chubby friend David Stringer.

David was dressed in a plain black t-shirt with black knee length sports shorts and white ankle length socks on his feet.

Richard glanced into David's over magnified eyes and they both forced a smile.

"How are you holding up mate?" David asked.

He motioned for Richard to enter before the door was closed behind him.

"I don't have the luxury of falling apart Dave, I have to stay focussed and hold it together." He quietly replied.

David sighed and nodded his head.

"Well I have made some progress, I definitely found the traffickers but it's getting knee deep." He told Richard as he climbed the stairs.

Richard followed him up and into the office bedroom where David had prepared a presentation so that Richard could fully grasp everything that he had discovered over the past two days.

David sat down in his usual black leather office chair and pointed toward the opposite side of the room.

"Grab yourself one of the chairs and bring it over, I have a big show for you." He said.

He then began to type on the keyboard that was attached to monitor one.

Just like before the monitor displayed the bland green and brown homepage of Jane Chapman's dating website.

David then pulled from beneath the desk a pale blue card file that he handed to Richard.

"That giant ship is Spanish and it's called the Indigo." He announced.

Richard opened the file and studied the colossal vessel from satellite imagery.

"She's one thousand two hundred feet long with a width of one hundred and sixty feet and her depth or draft to you land lubbers is nearly fifty feet." David explained in his usual mocking tone.

When he glanced across Richard broke into a wry smile for the first time as soon as he saw Stringer's over magnified eyes seemingly blink in slow motion.

"Do you get out on your own ship much, Skipper Dave?" He asked.

David nodded but in truth he had never been to sea in his entire life.

He hardly ever left the house.

His joviality was a natural mechanism for dealing with uncomfortable situations such as the one that he was about to create.

Jane Chapman's image suddenly appeared on monitor two on the right side of the bland green and brown website home page.

Then on monitor three the same internal banking details appeared displaying the cash transactions to and from the website.

The sequence of monitor images were exactly as David initially discovered them two days ago.

He pointed with his forefinger at the third monitor that showed the vast cash transactions.

"Most of the payments from all of these eastern European banks actually start from that big ship." He began.

The same forefinger now pointed at the aerial photograph in Richard's hand of the Indigo that was two days ago anchored off the coast of Syria.

Richard stared down at the satellite image.

"So somebody on this boat is taking payments from various banks all over Europe?" He asked.

He always had trouble keeping up with the genius seated beside him who was now rigorously nodding his head.

"And they're then sending on large quantities of it to this dating website." David replied.

He once again pointed to the banking details displayed on monitor three.

"This site has an online bank account that is almost impossible to track." He explained.

"Are you keeping up Willows?" He asked with a chuckle.

Richard nodded in silence.

"But almost two thirds of the cash received is being transferred out to two other accounts that I haven't been able to track down yet." He added.

Richard glanced at the dating site on monitor one and then down at the image of the Indigo in his hand.

"So what you're saying is that this ship is indirectly making all of those massive cash payments to that dating site?" He asked to confirm.

"You're so smart." David replied with a sarcastic chuckle.

Richard stared at monitor two.

"So who's the woman?" He asked.

He studied the DVLA photographic image of Jane Chapman.

"All of this was built by her." David replied.

"She's Jane Chapman a thirty six year old web designer living at Watford." He added.

"Take into account that the site is just a few weeks old and it's taken more than two million pounds already and isn't even registered on a single search engine." He continued.

"That massive amount of money can't possibly be from membership fees." He continued.

"You have to know and physically type in the web address to find it."

Richard nodded as his blue eyes danced from monitor to monitor.

"I understand that's a hell of a lot of money going into a dating site but how do we know for certain that she's involved with the disappearing homeless?" He asked.

David again logged into the 'Administration' area using monitor number four and Richard watched as three hundred and twenty six miniature jpeg images started to upload.

Before they finished uploading David clicked his mouse and onto the same dark haired sleeping beauty that he viewed two days ago after he initially tracked down the site.

"Why do they pose like they're asleep?" Richard asked with a chuckle.

David searched beneath the wooden work surface for remnants of last night's pizza.

"Why do they do what?" He asked.

Richard pointed to the screen.

"She looks like she's sleeping Dave." He pointed out.

David rummaged through what remained of last night's takeaway.

"That got me the first time too." He replied.

"But she definitely is asleep."

He reached out the red pizza box toward Richard and he promptly declined.

"I'll give that a miss thanks mate." He chuckled.

He then pointed to the fourth monitor.

"So how do you know that she's actually asleep and where's this all going?" He asked.

David clicked on a second image of another sleeping woman.

"I didn't see it at first either." David said.

Richard studied the image of the second woman.

"You didn't see what?" He asked as he scrutinised her.

David now clicked on and enlarged a third image of yet another woman that appeared to be sleeping.

He had to show Richard in the exact same sequence that he had made the discovery himself.

"Can you see it yet?" He asked.

The hairs suddenly stood up at the back of Richard's neck as he slowly nodded his head.

"They've all been photographed on the same floor." He replied.

David confirmed with another nod.

"Correct and it's some kind of industrial concrete floor like in a warehouse or something."

David now pointed to the sleeping blonde's face.

"Can you see the chloroform burns?" He asked.

Richard studied her before David clicked back to the second woman who showed exactly the same very faint marks as the first.

"Prolonged use of chloroform causes burns to the sensitive areas of the nose and mouth." David recited.

Richard nodded again as he continued to study.

"I know mate." He quietly replied.

There was a deftly silence as Richard digested everything that he had seen today.

Eventually he pointed to the image of a beautiful Italian woman with long dark wavy hair that was walking on a beach somewhere.

"Hold on, so what about her?" He asked.

"She's not unconscious."

David nodded as he ate cold pizza.

"That's the scariest part." He started to explain with a mouthful of cold pizza.

Again he pointed to one of the opened images of the unconscious women.

"See the digits below the images?" He asked.

Richard nodded.

"That's the price." David explained.

He then pointed back to the image of the beautiful woman walking along the beach and pointed to the similar digits below her picture that now displayed 00085000.

He turned to stare into Richard's eyes.

"You can buy her for eighty five thousand pounds or Euros I'm not sure which yet." He explained.

Richard's eyes widened as the hairs once again stood up on the back of his neck.

"And when I say that's the scariest part I mean it." David continued.

"That woman is walking about doing whatever she likes and doesn't have a clue that people are currently bidding to buy her."

"She is at some point in the not too distant future going to become the bought and paid for property of another person"

Richard had learned over the past couple of years that David Stringer had the uncanny ability to place himself into somebody else's shoes.

He could determine everything that they would more than likely do next and his predictions always seemed to happen with alarming accuracy.

Richard had also learned to trust that judgement and right now David Stringer was walking Jane Chapman's path and she had absolutely no idea that he even existed.

There was another deftly silence as Richard contemplated everything that David had shown him and he slowly allowed it to digest.

Eventually he turned to his friend again.

"So do you have any idea of how to find Sasha from all of this?" He asked.

David stared back at him for a few moments and seemed to be afraid to answer but eventually he sighed.

"Going by the dates I would hazard a guess that she's actually on the Indigo right now mate." He finally replied.

"I'm thinking that because the payments are all coming from there it's actually the transporter and I'm watching it every step of its journey." He added.

Richard nodded with frustration.

"If she is on it Richard I'll see her when she's eventually taken off." David assured him.

"Thankfully she wasn't taken off at Syria."

There was another lengthy pause before David pointed to monitor two and the DVLA driving licence photograph of Jane Chapman.

"Richard you can't go anywhere near her until we find Sasha." He pointed out.

Richard immediately nodded because he knew and he understood why.

"The moment she knows that we're onto her she'll shut down and disappear and this new trail goes as dead as a post." David added.

Again Richard slowly nodded.

"I know mate."

Fourteen
Monday August 7th 2000

It was pouring with rain when twenty nine year old Detective Inspector Nicola Garwood stepped through the brown double doors at the new task force headquarters building at Commercial street Whitechapel central London.

She closed her black umbrella and shook it inside the door before she stepped through secondary doors into a bustling wide hallway where she saw many uniformed police officers walking to and from all directions.

Her long straight blonde hair was pulled into a ponytail and she wore a black suit jacket with a white open necked blouse beneath it and black denim jeans with white training shoes on her feet.

"So this is me for the next god knows how long." She quietly uttered.

She scanned the busy scene in front of her.

This was the building acquired by Sir Christopher Dwyer and allocated to the recently assembled task force to investigate what seemed to be a very highly organised human trafficking ring operating within the city of London.

The truth of the matter was that nobody really knew how long it had been operating right under their noses in the city's manically busy streets with a population of more than six million people.

She understood from the briefing that she and Sam Henning attended at John Islip Street Westminster with Sir Christopher that the building was currently being prepared.

The ops room (Operations room) where she and Sam would be based was on the first floor so she headed toward a wide staircase directly in front of her.

When she reached halfway up the staircase a booming deep voice called out to her.

"Excuse me madam!"

Nicola turned to see a tall and bald uniformed policeman staring directly up at her.

"Can I ask who you are?" He enquired.

He then pointed toward the top of the staircase.

"That's a restricted area." He informed her.

"And it's out of bounds to members of the public and of course to members of the press." He added with a smile.

Nicola grinned mostly to herself as she headed back down the stairs where she reached into her inside jacket pocket and produced her warrant card.

"DI Garwood." She informed him.

He took the card and examined it.

"And your name is?" She asked.

"PC Michael Meadows ma'am but me mates call me Mick." He replied with a very broad London accent.

Nicola smiled again.

"Well done Mick." She replied.

She took her card from between his thick fingers and turned to continue to walk up the stairs as he watched her.

But when she reached halfway up the staircase for the second time she stopped and turned again.

"That's exactly how it needs to be around here Mick." She told him.

Meadows nodded with agreement.

"Then please keep your warrant card on display when inside the building ma'am." He suggested.

Nicola smiled again.

"Ops room is at the top of the stairs and the first door on the right ma'am." He informed her.

Now he smiled but mostly to himself.

At the top of the stairs on the right just as Mick Meadows described there was a single brown wooden door.

On the right side of it an engineer was busily fitting an electronic swipe card machine onto the wall.

She walked past him and through the door.

"Wow!" She quietly uttered to herself.

Nicola now stared wide eyed.

The huge open space in front of her had twelve rows of tables and they all ran the entire length of the room toward a far end.

All of them had unassembled CCTV systems that were being prepared for connection by technicians for more than seven hundred tiny hidden cameras that would be secretly installed onto the manically busy streets of London.

She stepped inside and watched the bustling room full of uniformed officers, technicians and engineers that would eventually transform this huge room into a working spy centre watching almost every street corner of London.

A man of average build that stood at around five feet eight inches with a mop of curly black hair and dark brown eyes approached Nicola.

He was wearing a black suit and a white shirt with a grey tie and his warrant card was displayed.

"Can I help?" He asked her.

Garwood smiled at him.

"I don't know, can you?"

He smiled back at her.

"Ok, let's begin with, who are you?" He enquired.

Nicola again took the warrant card from her inside jacket pocket and handed it to him.

She watched as he studied it before his facial expression suddenly changed.

"Sorry guv." He uttered.

He handed back her card and Nicola leaned forward and read the card that was clipped onto his jacket breast pocket.

"That's ok Detective Sergeant Jacob Saunders." She sarcastically replied.

Nicola was in fact his new boss.

A vaguely familiar voice called out from a small cubicle office behind her.

"We're in here Nik!" Sam Henning called out as he appeared in the opened doorway.

Nicola waved to Sam before she returned her attention to Saunders in front of her.

"Let's see just how resourceful you are Jacob Saunders." She told him.

Saunders raised his eyebrows.

"Find me a cup of coffee, white with three sugars. She said.

He nodded with a grin.

"Yes of course guv."

Nicola headed toward the cubicle office and turned to see Saunders still standing in exactly the same place.

"And I'll have it in there." She told him.

She pointed toward her new office where Sam Henning disappeared inside.

Jacob Saunders stared for a few moments and looked somewhat confused.

"Three sugars guv, really?" He asked.

Garwood nodded.

"Three sugars Jacob."

He then watched her disappear inside the cubicle office.

Nicola walked through the door to find Sam Henning sitting behind a desk in the left corner while a technician finished preparing a computer on top of it.

In the far right corner was her own new desk and there was a computer ready to use on top of it.

The three square windows to her right that looked out at the vast ops room were concealed by white horizontal blinds.

She strolled to her new desk and sat down before she glanced across at Sam.

"So what's on the agenda?" She asked.

Sam sighed.

"Not much today." He replied.

"Over the next two weeks the seven hundred cams will be hidden all over London." He began.

"And the first of the safe houses will become available at Hounslow tomorrow." He added.

"And one of us has a scheduled meeting with the Chief Inspector in..." Sam looked at his watch.

"Ten minutes."

Garwood mocked a frown.

"Well I have coffee coming so the meeting's definitely yours." She chuckled.

Sam laughed too.

"It's actually me he wants to see and specifically not you." He informed her.

Nicola stood up and walked toward the concealing blinds where she bent one with her finger and peered out to the ops room.

"I heard he doesn't approve of me." She said.

Sam nodded.

"You're nothing but a jump start fast tracker I understand." He replied.

They both chuckled again.

She turned to Sam and then nodded her head out toward the busy ops room.

"At some point we'll have to address this lot." She said.

She was referring to the newly assembled team that were busy putting together the monitors and other technical equipment.

Sam sat back in his chair.

"Actually I was thinking of not stepping on your toes." He replied.

"I was looking at getting my teeth into all of these recent missing person reports." He added.

Sam then climbed to his feet.

"I'm obviously here but why don't we try with you running the homeless cases while I work on the missing person reports?" He asked.

"I have a theory on it." He added.

Nicola shrugged.

"As long as we remember that we're working together I don't mind how we go about it." She replied.

She watched Sam as he walked toward the door.

"Where are you going?" She asked.

He grinned again.

"I'm going to try to convince our new boss that you're the best thing around here since sliced bread." He replied with a chuckle.

"Good luck with that." Nicola quietly uttered.

A short while later Sam Henning sat inside an office on the ground floor opposite their new boss Chief Inspector Martin Roberts.

"How are you settling in upstairs?" The chief asked.

Sam nodded.

"We'll get there Sir, there's just so much going on at the moment with everything being installed." He replied.

Roberts nodded with full comprehension of the mania that was currently occurring up on the first floor.

The chief ran his thin bony fingers through his thinning dark swept back hair and stared out of the window on his right as the heavy rain continued to fall.

"Do we have any of these safe houses ready yet?" He asked.

Sam shook his head.

"The first one is available from tomorrow at Hounslow Sir." He replied.

"And DI Garwood will plot the rotations to supervise them as we won't have enough officers to man every house." Sam added.

Roberts nodded again while seemingly deep in thought.

He returned his attention to Sam.

"Well hopefully we'll get an injection of manpower over the next few weeks but in the meantime I want to know everything as it happens." He said.

"I mean everything right down to which safe houses are manned and which are unsupervised."

At first Sam found this strange until the chief openly explained.

"I don't want to get caught with my pants around my ankles in the middle of a press conference." He informed Sam.

"When safe houses open and become manned or unmanned I want to know with a fully comprehensive but private report."

Sam nodded as he considered the additional work that the Chief Inspector was handing out.

"I want a weekly report on the hidden camera situation too." Roberts continued.

"And I understand that they'll be moved around when necessary?" He asked.

Sam nodded again.

"Yes Sir if we're having no luck with a particular cam or if it's discovered we'll resituate with discretion."

Roberts again stared directly at Sam.

"I'm a hand's on type of fellow Henning." He explained.

"I want to know what's happening when it's happening and it's your job to make sure that I get every single scrap of information as it comes through."

When Sam later headed back up the wide staircase toward the ops room he considered what he had just learned about his new boss.

It was exactly as he was warned.

Roberts was a control freak with an agenda to advance his own future political career.

It was why he somehow manipulated somebody at Westminster to put his name at the top of the list to head this newly assembled task force.

Fifteen
Friday August 11th 2000

It was just after six on a warm sunny evening when Claire Grover casually strolled along Churchbury Lane at the town of Enfield Surrey on the outskirts of north London.

Today was her twenty second birthday.

She turned left into St Andrew's road where she shared a rented house with her two best friends when a long silver security van turned left into St Andrew's road in front of her.

Claire made very brief eye contact with the man seated in the passenger seat but she paid it and him very little attention.

She was a curvaceous five feet seven inches tall and she had straight shoulder length reddish brown bobbed hair but her most striking feature was her beautiful piercing very light green eyes.

Her two best friends were twenty six year old Veronica Willard and twenty four year old Sara Crossly and they waited for her in the living room of their shared house.

As soon as Claire stepped inside the loud congratulations began as birthday gifts and cards were handed to her.

After one or two glasses of wine the girls began with the mad rush of getting ready for that evening's celebrations that would begin with a stretch Limousine that was jointly paid for by Veronica and Sara.

It would arrive at eight sharp to take them on a one hour sight-seeing drive around the Enfield area and then onto their favourite night club in the neighbouring town of Barnet.

At almost 8pm Sara Crossly sat in the living room ready for their night out.

Her long blonde wavy hair was down, her make-up was applied and she wore a tight fitting black mini dress and up inside her bedroom Veronica Willard was almost ready too.

Her shoulder length straight blonde hair was down and she wore a black sparkling sleeveless top and a pair of skin tight black leggings with shiny black platform shoes on her feet.

"Claire, are you ready yet?" She called across the landing.

Claire sat in front of her own mirror wearing a short red sleeveless mini dress.

Her shoulder length reddish brown hair was perfect as was her make-up and those incredibly beautiful pale green eyes stared into the mirror as she applied lip gloss.

"Have we really got a Limo coming?" She called back.

Veronica grinned.

"Yes and apparently you're not allowed to be sick in it later." She replied with a giggle.

At just after eight the three women stepped outside to see the long wheel based black shiny Limousine with blackened windows.

In the driver seat was their Chauffer for the evening dressed in a black suit and he even wore a black peaked cap.

They all walked toward the car giggling as a long silver security van slowly passed behind it but in the excitement of the moment Claire Grover didn't even notice as it passed her for the second time.

The Limousine took the three girls sight-seeing around Enfield although with three bottles of Champagne in the car nobody really saw many sights outside of the darkened tinted windows.

It was close to ten that evening when they were finally dropped off right outside the night club in the town of Barnet.

The Limousine would return to pick them up and take them home at around 2:30am.

After a night of heavy drinking and dancing the three women literally staggered out from the night club and clambered into the back of the Limousine at 2:23am.

It would return them straight to St Andrew's road Enfield minus the sight-seeing tour and that was something that by now they were all more than happy about.

It was almost an hour later when the same silver security van quietly parked just up the street from the house.

The occupants inside the van watched as the girls retired to their respective beds as the lights were switched off one by one.

When it was decided that everybody inside was asleep which wasn't long after considering that they were obviously all very drunk, the van drove the short distance across St Andrew's road and pulled up directly outside the house.

The man in the passenger seat produced a printed photograph that he showed to each member of his team of former elite Spanish soldiers.

"Este antes de cualquier otro." Major Abran Delgado said in his usual quiet tone.

'This before any other.'

Everybody inside the vehicle nodded with acknowledgement as they studied the picture of beautiful twenty two year old Claire Grover.

She was the only target.

This somewhat arrogant Spanish team considered that they were not only elite soldiers but within the Indigo organisation they were far and above elite compared to the Romanians Turkish and Albanians.

This small group of former elite soldiers had already trained the other teams for the missions that had been carried out and for more in future with the exception of the Turkish, they were to begin their training soon.

It was however a fact that the Spanish and their performance were of a much higher standard as far as soldiering was concerned.

Major Delgado turned to the two soldiers in the back of the van.

Thirty year old former explosive expert Teo Cruz and six feet one inch Olinda Garza who was twenty nine and the only woman within any of the teams stared back at him.

Olinda Garza more than held her ground.

The former Spanish army Sergeant had taken part in numerous undercover operations during her military service.

After a few moments of specific instructions and continuous reminders that would ensure performance improvements within his team Delgado watched as Teo Cruz took less than seven seconds to pick the lock of the front door.

St Andrew's road was now very quiet and still.

He pushed the door forward as far as he could because Veronica Willard had somehow remembered to slide the security chain across.

What Delgado and his driver thirty five year old Fabio Gomez watched next was quite an incredible sight.

The tall athletic Olinda Garza leaned closely into the back of Cruz and wrapped her long arms around him.

She then took the two ends of the brass chain between both thumb and forefingers allowing Cruz to silently cut it while she prevented the separated ends from dropping and making any sound at all.

Cruz slowly and carefully ducked away allowing Olinda to move in closer where she placed the two separated ends at a rest.

There wasn't a single sound and it took them less than a minute.

She silently entered the hall and scanned the carpeted floor before she signalled to the Major that it was safe for them to enter.

As Major Delgado and the driver quietly entered the property Olinda Garza signalled to him using at first two fingers and then a single finger that pointed to the opened living room door on her right.

'One secondary target is in this room.'

He acknowledged with a nod before he indicated with his own hand to Fabio Gomez.

'You will remain here and watch this one.'

He referred to Sara Crossly who had fallen asleep in the living room.

Her two friends had gone to bed and left her on the sofa in a drunken state.

The Major silently headed up the staircase followed by Olinda Garza and Teo Cruz.

When they reached the landing at the top of the stairs Delgado calmly surveyed the environment.

He reached into the right breast pocket of his black tactical outfit and handed a thin black metal strip first to Olinda Garza and then to Teo Cruz.

All three placed the clips across the bridges of their noses and squeezed essentially sealing their nostrils.

He then took from the pouch on the left side of his belt two white paper masks and handed them to his two soldiers.

Delgado stood outside a closed bedroom door that was nearest to the bathroom on the right.

He slowly turned the handle before he pushed open the door to see Claire Grover the main target, sleeping still fully dressed on top of her bed.

"Ahí estás." He whispered.

'There you are.'

He turned and glanced at Olinda Garza and showed her a thumb instructing her that it would be ok to enter the room opposite where Veronica Willard slept.

Olinda very slowly and silently opened the door and saw Veronica closer to unconsciousness than sleeping thanks to the vast quantities of alcohol that she had consumed also fully dressed and on top of her bed.

In the doorway where Teo Cruz now stood and where Claire Grover was fast asleep inside the Major took from another pouch a small brown bottle and unscrewed the cap.

He carefully poured a small quantity of clear liquid into the white paper mask and watched as Cruz slowly swirled it and allowed the liquid to saturate into the mask.

Cruz then very quietly crept into the room toward the sleeping Claire Grover.

Major Delgado walked across the carpeted hall toward Olinda Garza.

He poured a small amount of the same liquid into the mask that she held and immediately she entered the bedroom of Veronica Willard.

Not a single sound had been made.

In Claire's bedroom Teo Cruz knelt beside her in absolute silence.

With a completely steady hand he held the white paper mask just an inch from her face and allowed her lungs to fill with vapour.

Within three minutes he gently lifted her head and fitted the two white elastic straps around and fastened the mask to her face without her waking.

Claire was now unconscious not sleeping.

Major Delgado reappeared in the doorway and indicated to Cruz to tie her using the black plastic cable ties that all of his team carried.

Claire Grover was the prime target of this operation.

Anybody else would now be an additional financial bonus but only Claire featured on Jane Chapman's auction site.

She was already part bought and paid for.

The Spanish team could have quite easily taken her without Veronica or Sara waking up and could have left them.

There was however additional money to be made here because they were also attractive young women.

Veronica Willard slept on her right side and faced Olinda Garza.

Olinda held the mask with a completely steady hand just two inches from Veronica's face and allowed her to breathe in the vapour just as Claire had across the hall.

But Veronica suddenly coughed in her sleep.

Her face touched the white paper mask and Olinda Garza cringed at the unavoidable contact.

"Mierda!" She whispered to herself.

'Shit!'

Veronica slowly opened her blurred eyes and for a very brief moment she stared into the masked face of Olinda Garza.

Olinda eyes widened as she actually smiled back at her and suddenly Veronica's eyes filled with absolute terror.

The Sergeant quickly leapt up and turned the much smaller and much weaker disorientated Veronica onto her back.

Her gloved hand then covered the dazed confused Veronica's mouth and she was temporarily silenced.

Olinda then climbed on top of Veronica and using her knees she pinned the blonde's arms by her side.

With her free hand she ripped one of the strips of black shiny duct tape from her own right thigh and firmly pressed it over Veronica's mouth.

Veronica instinctively tried to scream out.

She struggled to move any part of her body but with the much larger and heavier woman on top of her it was impossible.

Her muffled screams would only wake Sara Crossly downstairs in the living room because Claire Grover across the hall had already been dealt with and was rendered completely unconscious.

Olinda picked up the mask from beside Veronica's head and pressed it down firmly over the helpless young woman's face and forced her to inhale the chloroform.

There was absolutely nothing that Veronica could do to stop it from happening as she squealed from behind her duct tape gag.

It wasn't from any sadistic pleasure that Olinda grinned as she stared down at Veronica but because with the mask now sealed over her face she knew that the intoxicated woman would fade much faster than she would have if she was sober.

She was right because within seconds Veronica's eyes started to close and in her weakened state she kicked out with no real force and those muffled screams turned to quietened whimpers.

Olinda glanced back toward the open door and saw Major Delgado standing with his tranquiliser gun at the ready.

There was no need for it.

Before he left he shook his head with disappointment.

Downstairs in the living room Sara Crossly suddenly opened her eyes.

The house was completely dark and eerily silent.

Because the central heating was switched on she hadn't suddenly woken from feeling cold.

Sara sensed that something was wrong but she didn't know what it was.

She sat up on the sofa and stared around the darkened room.

She made out objects that she recognised like the TV and the dining table at the other side of the room.

The room itself was spinning from the effects of the alcohol and she heard the clock ticking loudly on the wall above her.

Eventually she convinced herself that everything was fine.

"I'm never doing that again." She croaked.

The living room door to her right was opened but there were no lights on in the hall or any light from upstairs and eventually she called out.

"Claire?"

When Sara eventually stood up the light brown leather sofa creaked in the otherwise completely silent house.

She steadied herself on her feet and still heavily intoxicated, she very slowly and cautiously staggered out to the hall.

Sara held onto the bottom bannister rail and stared up the staircase where she saw and heard absolutely nothing.

Again she knew that something wasn't quite right but she also understood that she was very drunk.

What she hadn't yet figured was that there was no snoring breathing or anybody turning in their beds which were the sounds that she didn't realise occurred all of the time.

They were signs of life.

Everybody still conscious inside the house remained silent and waited.

That was why it was just too quiet and she knew it but her intoxicated brain simply couldn't figure it out.

Suddenly in the dead quiet her attention was for some reason drawn toward the open kitchen door on her left.

Her night vision was grained and things looked to be dancing including things that couldn't possibly move.

Something drew her attention to that direction and she sensed that something or someone was inside the darkened kitchen.

"Ronnie?" She quietly called out to Veronica Willard.

Sara stared into the kitchen.

She turned to look at the closed front door to see that the security chain hadn't been pulled across.

That too was a trick of the grained effect and darkened hall combined with the effects of alcohol because she didn't realise that the chain now had two loose ends instead of just one.

When she stared back at the kitchen door frame she made out a dark shape almost halfway up from the floor.

Her heart started to heavily pound against her chest until she eventually realised that she was staring at the black metal latch.

She sighed.

"Calm down Sara." She quietly told herself with a tremble in her tone.

Her heart now started to slow down.

She then stared back up toward the landing at the top of the stairs.

"Claire?" She called out again.

She would receive no reply from Claire Grover.

Her eyes were fixed upon the lampshade at the centre of the landing upstairs as she waited for something, anything.

"Ronnie?"

She would also receive no reply from Veronica Willard.

For some reason Sara's attention returned to the open kitchen door.

Again she fixed her gaze as she tightly held onto the bannister rail and swayed.

Her heart pounded again and her breath was short as she stared at the door latch on the right side of the frame that seemed to dance with the grained effects of her very poor alcohol induced night vision.

Sara squinted and then she rubbed her deceiving eyes as a second latch appeared just above the first.

Now another larger shape seemed to appear from behind the wall on the right.

'This is ridiculous, how can there be two latches?' She asked herself.

She blamed her poor night vision on the vast quantities of alcohol that were still in full disorientating effect.

But she suddenly realised exactly what she was staring at.

Everything suddenly caught up.

That second the larger object that had just appeared was definitely a person.

It was a large person, too large to be Veronica Willard or Claire Grover.

Sara was now frozen to the spot.

"H…Hello?" She nervously uttered with the same terrified tremble in her tone.

A bright red dot appeared just above the upper dark shape that had initially confused her as a second latch at the door frame.

Sara slowly glanced down and saw that a bright red beam created a red dot directly onto her chest.

She slowly glanced up.

There was just enough time to hear a 'CLACK' as Fabio Gomez pulled the trigger of his tranquiliser gun.

At first Sara felt nothing but a light thud.

She stared back down and saw the dark feather of a dart that was imbedded into her chest.

Everything slowly caught up again and after she realised what had happened she slumped to the floor.

Suddenly from the upper landing Major Delgado appeared and climbed down the staircase.

"Demasiado lento Fabio." He scowled at Gomez.

'Fabio too slow.'

Sixteen
Wednesday August 16th 2000

Inside the new task force headquarters at Commercial Street Whitechapel London, Detective Inspector Sam Henning sat alone inside the cubicle office.

Nicola Garwood was out for the day and Sam was left with a large pile of folders on his desk.

He meticulously read through them because he believed that he might be onto something new, something that everybody else had somehow missed.

After reading the latest file he glanced up to the wall at Nicola's laminated detailed map of London.

Again everything that he had just read occurred inside the blue belt that completely encircled the city of London.

That blue belt was the M25 Motorway.

The files that engrossed him were missing person reports over the past twelve months and seemingly unrelated to the case of the abducted homeless.

But in comparison to the previous year the report statistics revealed an eighteen percent increase.

It was far higher than the rise of missing persons for even the highest previous years and also much higher than the seven percent projected by Sir Christopher Dwyer.

Sir Christopher's statistics represented the city of London and didn't include the surrounding areas.

But he wasn't a Detective.

Sam Henning however was and a highly experienced and respected one.

Sam had just read the report of a missing woman from Greenford south of Wembley and before that a missing woman from Bromley Kent, both still inside that blue M25 belt but outside the city of London itself.

He also discovered that the eighteen percent increase only occurred inside this border of the Motorway that could be viewed from any standard road map.

'Could it be that simple?' He wondered.

Detective Sergeant Jacob Saunders knocked on the cubicle door and opened it.

Sam glanced up.

"Guv I thought you'd like to know that the first mini camera is live." Saunders informed him.

Because there had been a long delay with the start of the camera installations Sam breathed a sigh of relief.

"At last!" He uttered.

He stood up and walked toward the door where Saunders still stood.

"Can I ask you a question?" Jacob asked.

Sam smiled.

"Of course, what's up?"

Saunders seemed apprehensive as he ran his fingers through his curly black hair.

"Why is DI Garwood out on the streets installing cameras with the Engineers?" He asked.

"I mean we have them to do that surely her job here is more important?" He asked.

The two of them stepped out to the din of the bustling ops room.

Sam glanced at Jacob and smiled.

"It's called dedication." He replied.

He stared the Detective Sergeant in the eye.

"When she goes home tonight she knows for a fact that wherever she's been is exactly as it should be." He added.

"It's pure dedication."

Then he grinned and winked at Saunders.

As the two men walked down one of the aisles of camera monitors Sam stopped and turned to Saunders again.

"Jacob she's on our side and she's a part of this team." He pointed out.

Saunders nodded.

"I understand that guv, it just seems a waste of a valuable resource having a Detective Inspector outside helping to install cameras when she could be here doing the really important things." He replied.

Sam smiled and again he stared into Saunders eyes.

"Is making sure that a secret camera is installed in secret and having the Engineers know that she's out there not important?" He asked.

Saunders nodded again.

"Yes of course guv." He replied in a quieter tone.

Sam paused for a moment and thought of how to choose his next words.

"We're on her side too we're not hoping and waiting for her to cock this up." He eventually added.

"Now that would be a waste of valuable resources wouldn't it?"

Saunders half smiled.

"I get your point guv." He conceded.

They reached the only live camera monitor where Sam saw Detective Inspector Nicola Garwood wearing a bright yellow rubberized raincoat with the hood up standing outside in the pouring rain.

He chuckled to himself and took the telephone from his inside jacket pocket and dialled her number.

He watched the monitor as Nicola fumbled through her pockets until she found her ringing telephone and answered it.

"How's the weather in Lewisham?" Sam asked with a chuckle.

Nicola stood on the corner of John Penn Street at the junction with Lewisham road that was partially closed.

The traffic was diverted due to bogus gas mains work so that the secret camera could be installed.

"I'm watching you as we speak." He informed her.

Nicola smiled and waved into the camera lens and Sam grinned.

He then watched her look to her left and he heard her call out.

"Come on Reg hurry up and I might treat you to a cup of tea somewhere!" She yelled.

Sam glanced around the ops room for a few moments before he spoke again and decided to keep his next comment as short as possible.

"Listen I think I've stumbled across something but I'll explain when you get back later." He told her.

Nicola responded by nodding toward the camera lens.

Of course she wouldn't be present for the installation of every single hidden camera.

Many roads were closed across London over the next few weeks but on that first day a total of fifty six tiny hidden cameras were installed and became operational.

The newly assembled task force could now begin to watch the busy streets of London.

At Tranton Road Bermondsey, David Stringer sat on the right side of his converted bedroom and slowly spun on his office chair to see Nicola Garwood flicker onto one of his monitors at the other side of the room as the camera went live.

"Hello!" He said.

He stared at the monitor with a smile although of course Nicola couldn't hear him and she had absolutely no idea that he could see her.

But he could.

Seventeen
Saturday August 26th 2000

It was a warm and sunny Saturday morning when twenty seven year old Clive Henderson and his long term partner twenty four year old Bridget Oaks travelled on the London underground railway network.

They recently bought their first home at Norton road Wembley.

They travelled to Charing Cross in the busy city centre and then walked the short distance to the National portrait gallery among other places before they stopped for lunch at a small café near Trafalgar Square at around mid-day.

Clive was five feet eleven inches tall with a stocky build and he had short dark brown hair and today he wore a new white replica England Rugby shirt with blue jeans with black training shoes on his feet.

His beautiful partner of three years Bridget was five feet six inches tall and she had straightened shoulder length dark brown hair and brown eyes.

She worked as an investment manager for the same bank and also the same branch which was where they first met.

She wore a pale yellow t-shirt with tight fitting burgundy corduroy jeans and white designer training shoes on her feet and slung over her right shoulder was a black leather bag.

When they walked onto Trafalgar square amongst hundreds of tourists and thousand of pigeons Bridget produced Clive's new digital camera from her bag.

"Stand in front of the Lion." She told him.

She pointed to one of the four black statues that surrounded Nelson's Column with his camera in her hand.

Clive walked toward the black Lion where he turned and mocked a pose with his hands on his hips that made Bridget giggle as she stared through the view finder.

"Will you behave?" She giggled.

Bridget actually wanted a picture of him to mark this time as they had just purchased their own house together.

Eventually Clive struck a natural pose with a smile and Bridget clicked on the button to capture the moment.

"Let me take one more." She insisted.

This time Clive sat on a concrete plinth and he smiled again before Bridget took a second picture.

"There's a pigeon to your left shush it away." She told him.

Clive glanced to his left and saw the pigeon that stared back up at him and he chuckled.

"Do you mean this one?" He asked.

He pointed a thumb toward the grey bird as he stared toward the camera with a grin.

Bridget took another photograph and she giggled again.

"If you get it to move another two will only take its place." A voice said from behind Bridget.

Bridget turned to see a woman.

She had straight shoulder length reddish brown hair and green eyes and she was dressed in a short faded blue denim jacket with a pale pink blouse beneath and tight fitting faded blue jeans.

Around this woman's neck was the wide black strap of what looked like a very expensive state of the art digital camera.

"The trick is to throw half a tonne of bird seed that way." The woman added with another chuckle.

She looked at Clive through her own view finder as she pointed her thumb behind her.

Bridget laughed again.

"Ah, an expert speaks."

The woman looked back at her with a grin.

"I'm not so sure because the bloody things seem to follow me everywhere I go around here." She replied with a giggle.

She took a very natural picture of Clive who appeared to be talking to the pigeon that still refused to budge.

"I take pictures of tourists when I come here and email them on." She informed Bridget.

She then pointed her camera at the dark haired beautiful Bridget and clicked on the button.

"That one's for free." She insisted.

Bridget gave her an apprehensive nod.

"We're not tourists." She replied with a smile.

The photographer grinned as she took another picture.

"I know I can spot them from a mile away." She replied.

She then lowered her camera.

"Go and sit with him and I'll take one of you together." She said.

Bridget glanced over at Clive.

He seemed to be holding a conversation with the pigeon and she glanced back at the woman.

"How much do they cost first?" The astute investment manager asked.

The photographer again glanced up from her own view finder and smiled.

"Don't be silly." She replied.

"Just give me an email address to send them to before I leave." She added.

"I make three hundred a day from the tourists, this one's a freebie."

Bridget smiled.

"Are you sure?" She asked.

"I don't mind paying if it's not ridiculously overpriced."

The photographer grinned back at her.

"It is ridiculously overpriced when you have to pay but you don't so just get over there." She insisted again.

Bridget laughed before she walked toward the black Lion statue where Clive was still seated.

"Oh god how much will this cost?" He asked in a very quiet tone.

Bridget linked her arm through his as she looked over toward the woman who stood patiently with her camera.

"Nothing she's just going to email the pictures over to me later." She assured him.

"So stop complaining, look at the camera and smile."

The photographer took three more shots of them together before she walked to where they both stood.

She looked directly at Bridget as she handed her a small note pad and a pen.

"Just scribble your email address and I'll send them to you by tomorrow afternoon." She said.

As Bridget wrote her email address Clive smiled at the photographer.

"This is really nice of you." He told her.

She smiled back at him.

"It's no big deal."

She then nodded toward his camera that Bridget still held.

"You know it doesn't cost anything, I can just delete them once they're uploaded onto the PC and start again." She added.

"And besides I've already had a good day with the tourists."

Clive beamed a smile as he reached out his hand.

"I'm Clive Henderson and this is my partner Bridget Oaks."

The photographer shook his hand.

"Lisa Moore." She replied.

Bridget handed back the note pad with her email address scribbled on the top page.

Lisa read out loud the email address for Bridget to confirm.

After, Bridget also shook hands with her.

"I'll get them uploaded tonight and then email yours over tomorrow." Lisa told Bridget again.

She then beamed another smile.

"Just remember me if you two decide to get married and need a photographer." She laughed.

Bridget giggled too.

"You're top of the list!" She replied.

Clive and Bridget watched the photographer disappear into the crowd of tourists before he turned to Bridget.

"It's nice to see somebody that isn't always about making money." He told her.

Bridget nodded with agreement.

"It is." She replied.

"What a lovely lady."

Lisa Moore would later take her camera to Glade Road Watford where most of the pictures including those of Bridget and Clive together would be deleted.

The initial picture of the incredibly beautiful twenty four year old Bridget Oaks that was taken by Moore while they chatted was uploaded onto Jane Chapman's hidden auction website.

The bidding would begin with immediate effect and the opening price was seventy thousand pounds.

Bridget Oaks was now walking around and temporarily free and ignorant of the fact that she was for sale to the highest foreign bidder.

Lisa Moore didn't possess the technical understanding to track an IP address to the tangible residential street address of Bridget Oaks.

But the former talented web designer Jane Chapman most certainly did using Bridget's provided email address.

Eighteen
Thursday August 31st 2000

At just after 2pm local time the colossal cargo vessel the Indigo anchored in the Flores Sea nine miles south of the Indonesian island of Sulawesi.

The South African *Madagascar* sailed out from the disused isolated south western port of Bontosunggu to rendezvous with the mega vessel.

The Madagascar weighed considerably less than The Indigo at a mere 107,000 tonnes and her length of just 956 feet, width of 106 feet and draft of 40 feet meant that she could sail into the shallower waters of most of the island's southern ports.

Fifty eight minutes after departing Bontosunggu the South African vessel lowered her anchors just thirty three feet south of the Indigo.

The telescopic poles were manoeuvred across from the Spanish giant to prevent the two colossal ships from colliding and they were securely latched into position.

The crew of the Madagascar had performed this clandestine operation many more times than the British Candlelit Queen and it showed.

Her huge extendable orange crane already started to turn before the long poles were latched into position.

When the crane reached the deck of the Indigo the Spanish crew immediately secured the four chained clasps to a red rusty forty feet long steel container and it was almost immediately hoisted into the air.

The crane gently turned anti-clockwise toward the rear of the Indigo until it was clear.

At first the giant extendable crane slowly retracted gently pulling the huge container toward The Madagascar.

Her slow anti-clockwise turn continued until the large red container was gently lowered onto her own deck and the transfer was completed.

The steel poles were then released and retracted toward the Indigo before the anchors of the Madagascar were raised and she immediately started her return to the island.

From the moment that the Madagascar lowered her anchors to the time that she raised them to return to port was less than eighteen minutes.

Fifty three minutes later she moored at the southern port of Bontosunggu and as usual without any challenge whatsoever from the Indonesian authorities thanks to kick backs.

The delivered red steel container was immediately opened and a large green battered former Serbian military truck slowly drove out and began the long drive north along the island's western ridge.

It would eventually pass through the white painted gates at the military base just south of a small town called Mamuju.

At Tranton road Bermondsey the autistic genius David Stringer sat on the left side of his converted spare bedroom and watched the entire process via overhead passing Russian and Chinese spy satellites.

At the not so secret base at Mamuju he saw what he had been waiting for when the unconscious Sasha Willows was lifted from the back of the green truck and carried into a long windowless red brick building.

David now had the unenviable task of informing Richard Willows that he now knew exactly where Sasha was.

The twenty two year old was inside a heavily armed supposedly secret military base on an Indonesian island half way around the world.

Nineteen
Tuesday September 5th 2000

Many of the surrounding borough councils of London had by this time provided the use of various properties that were for one reason or another vacant.

There were several meetings with high ranking government officials that fabricated a story.

The story was of an outbreak of a non-fatal infection that had started to spread amongst the homeless population of London.

It was directed toward all of the council officials from the surrounding boroughs with an urgent plea for help from the House of Commons.

According to this fictitious report the fake minor outbreak was now isolated and the people that were to be temporarily housed inside the vacant properties had been given a clean bill of health.

They were also isolated from the main to ensure that none of them contracted the bogus infection that had been caused by the recent spell of poor weather.

They even had medical paperwork to back up their story.

The government scam worked and it seemed to be completely believed.

Fifty five currently unoccupied three and four bedroom houses were temporarily released with minimal rent along with council tax and amenity bills courtesy of the British tax payer.

More importantly as a result almost three hundred of London's homeless community in the most vulnerable areas such as soup kitchens refuges and known hideaways would now be safely placed inside with immediate effect.

Some houses were to be managed by on-site supervising police officers but due to the limited manpower available to the task force many properties remained unmanned.

The homeless people deemed most responsible or less likely to cause damage were initially placed in the unsupervised properties.

The temporary residents with drug or alcohol related issues were of course prioritised to be supervised.

Inside the cubicle office shared by Sam and Nicola and joined by Jacob Saunders there was a discussion regarding how this had come to be.

"The councils actually bought into this?" Nicola asked.

Sam nodded but Jacob Saunders interjected.

"As a rule the masses generally believe what they're told if it's official, guv." He informed her.

Sam glanced up at the large map on the wall that was marked with many small sticky coloured circular and triangular labels.

"How many cameras have we got live now?" He asked.

Nicola glanced up at it too.

"We've got two hundred and fifty five of seven hundred left to install." She proudly replied.

Jacob Saunders continued to ponder on the subject of the safe houses.

"It's amazing that they can suddenly find all of these empty houses when they need to isn't it?" He asked.

"Which means those homeless people could've been housed before." He added.

Neither of his senior officers replied.

"When do the rest of the cams go into operation?" Sam enquired.

Nicola shrugged.

"We always knew that it couldn't be done in one go." She replied.

"We have to close roads to stop people from seeing them being installed and if you close down three or four hundred roads at once some little smart arse in a radio station helicopter will blab the locations over the air."

Sam nodded but Saunders still pondered on the subject of houses before he then joined in on the subject of hidden cameras.

"But the Engineers don't have any kind of security clearance so what if they go blabbing to their mates?" He asked.

Nicola shrugged with a sigh.

"We'll never be able to completely hide them unless the three of us install them ourselves." She replied.

"This has always been about minimisation but the fewer people that know about it the less chance there is of it becoming public knowledge." She explained.

"And the Engineers all signed an adaptation of the official secrets act and know they can be prosecuted for passing on information of their whereabouts."

Saunders suddenly looked surprised.

"Hang on are you saying that only the three of us know the locations of all of the safe houses and secret cams?" He asked.

Garwood nodded.

"Individual Engineers only know the locations of the cams that they personally installed and they've all come from different areas outside London." She replied.

"And with regard to the houses, none of the borough councils know anything about properties allocated by other councils so basically yes because the collective information never leaves this room we are the only people with access to absolutely all of it."

Sam glanced up at the map on the wall again.

"And the sooner that information is transferred onto our computers the sooner it can come down off the walls Nik." He pointed out.

She agreed before she glanced across at Saunders.

"That'll be a Jacob job." She grinned.

After a few moments of staring back at her Jacob slowly nodded.

"Gee thanks." He sighed.

There was a knock on the cubicle door and Jacob spun around to see a pretty young uniformed police woman standing behind him.

WPC Samantha Pilkington was twenty three and one of several officers that operated the information and response desk where Sam earlier paid a visit.

He asked to be notified of any recent non-homeless missing person reports within the landmark borders of the M25 Motorway.

Pilkington looked directly at Sam.

"Sir we discovered a triple missing person's report that was filed at Enfield." She informed him.

Sam glanced at Nicola and then back to the WPC.

"Three?"

She nodded.

"Yes Sir three girls from the same house at St Andrew's Road." She continued.

"They all had jobs but none of them turned up for work on Monday morning."

She went on to explain that yesterday Enfield police were called after several work colleagues of the three girls visited the house.

The officers gained entry to discover that they were missing but clothes jewellery and personal belongings like phones passports driving licenses and some bank cards were all still inside the house.

Sam thanked her for bringing him the information.

After she left the room and closed the door Sam stared across at Nicola.

"I think Sir Christopher Dwyer's right and it's not just the homeless being taken." He said.

He then revealed all of the information that he had gathered including the eighteen percent increase in missing person reports within the land area inside the M25 Motorway that encircled the city of London.

Garwood stared back at him.

"Are you saying that there are two groups of abductors?" She asked.

Eventually Sam shrugged.

"I'm not saying anything yet." He replied with a sigh.

Nicola stood up and walked toward the door where Jacob Saunders was standing.

"Where are you going?" Sam asked.

She stopped and turned to face him.

"To get the address of the house in Enfield and then I'm going to Enfield." She replied.

"Coming?"

Sam sighed again.

"Nope I have a meeting downstairs with the boss in half an hour." He told her.

"He wants updates."

Nicola nodded.

"Yep that's definitely your department." She grinned.

"Jacob and I will go to Enfield."

Saunders suddenly stared at her.

"We will?" He asked and Nicola nodded.

"So go and find us a car you're driving."

Twenty
Wednesday September 15th 2000

It was late afternoon at Alpha grove on the Isle of Dogs east London where thirty four year old Carmen Richardson quietly closed the back door.

Her six inch heels echoed as she casually strolled across the black and white tiled floor in the otherwise silent hallway as she headed toward a swinging brown kitchen door.

From behind a long jet black wavy mane of hair swayed down past her incredibly tight fitting shiny black creaking leather corset.

She also wore tight fitting black leather hot pants and black fishnet tights that disappeared into a pair of shiny black patent leather thigh high boots.

In her left hand she carried a short black leather riding crop that she gently tapped onto the top of her boot while she hummed a tune.

She reached out with her right hand and gently pushed open the swinging door to step into a spacious and brightly lit kitchen.

She saw her oldest friend right back from secondary school standing at the far end of the kitchen with her back to Carmen.

Thirty four year old April Marsh was in comparison chubby and she stood at just five feet three inches with similar dark brown wavy hair.

April wore a long black knitted cardigan and a pair of blue denim jeans with white fluffy slippers on her feet.

She turned to see Carmen enter the kitchen.

"Has Lord Whatshisname left?" She asked.

She returned to continue with what she was doing.

Carmen walked to a small circular wooden dining table on her left where she pulled out one of the chairs and sat down.

"He went out through the back door to where his driver usually waits." She replied.

She then pulled off her long black wavy wig to reveal her real dark brown shoulder length pinned back bobbed hair.

April walked across and placed a cup of hot coffee onto the table beside Carmen's discarded wig before she headed back to the kitchen work surface.

"That's you done for the day Car." She announced.

Carmen nodded in silence at first as she began to very carefully remove one of her long black false eyelashes using tweezers and a small hand held mirror.

"I know." She eventually replied.

When the false eyelashes were removed from her left eye Carmen glanced across at April.

"Who's in with Jade?" She asked.

April turned to look back at Carmen and a wry grin appeared before she returned her attention to her coffee making duties.

"It's the council official from Hounslow." She replied with a chuckle.

Carmen grinned.

"Oh god the parking ticket fiasco?" She asked.

April nodded.

A few moments later they both heard heavy footsteps that seemed negotiate the hard wooden staircase.

They grew louder clicking as they then crossed the black and white tiles in the hall as they neared the kitchen.

Jade Harris entered the kitchen through the same swinging wooden door and her high heels clicked across the kitchen floor toward the dining table.

Her hair was real and similar to Carmen's although Jade's shoulder length bob was reddish brown in colour thanks to her Irish ancestry.

She had bright green eyes and across her nose there were many brown freckles and just above her upper lip on the right side was a small dark brown mole.

Although standing at close to six feet Jade was in fact just an inch taller than Carmen at five feet nine.

She wore a far too tight fitting white cotton blouse and a far too short grey pleated skirt with very shiny black patent leather knee high boots that had a four inch heel.

Twenty nine year old Jade sat down directly opposite Carmen and watched her friend carefully removing the last fake eyelash.

Their eyes met as Carmen looked back at her over her small circular mirror.

"How long have you been working for me?" She asked.

April walked across and placed a second coffee onto the table for Jade.

"Since I was twenty, why?" Jade asked in response.

She watched as Carmen very carefully peeled away the last thick long dark lash.

"Why?" Jade asked again.

Carmen shrugged.

"I never noticed you had so many freckles."

Jade started to giggle.

"They're painted on Carmen you twat." She explained as she covered her mouth with her hand.

"It's the council official from Hounslow." She added.

"He likes to be spanked by girls in a school uniform and with freckles remember?" She asked.

Carmen nodded and again glanced over her mirror to study Jade's face and could now see that they only real blemish was the small dark brown mole just above her lip.

Carmen grinned as she now started to strip away the layers of caked on make-up.

"And how's that going today?" She asked with a chuckle.

Jade sighed and Carmen glanced up again.

"Has he left now?" She asked.

Jade shook her head.

"I'm getting to that." She replied.

There was a pause.

"Is it ok if I give him an extra half an hour for free?" She finally asked.

Carmen shrugged again.

"Will it end this bloody parking ticket fiasco?" She asked.

Jade nodded and displayed a broad grin.

"Well until I park there again."

Carmen shrugged again.

"It's your time honey." She replied.

She continued to concentrate in front of her small mirror and Jade nodded.

"I'm still going to ask Car, it's your business after all." She replied.

April Marsh sat down between the two high class prostitutes with a small dark blue tin in front of her.

"How much have we taken today?" Carmen asked.

April opened the tin and removed a very large wad of cash.

"About eight grand I suppose." She replied.

Carmen nodded.

As soon as April started to count they all heard a faint knock on the front door.

Both Carmen and Jade glanced at April who looked up, first at Carmen and then at Jade.

"Oh shall I go and see who it is then?" She sarcastically asked.

Jade and Carmen laughed as Carmen slowly shook her head with disbelief.

"You've been working for me for over ten years and you still haven't grasped this maid role, have you?" She asked with a chuckle.

"We do the clients." She said.

She pointed her finger toward Jade and then at herself.

"You do the door and appointments." She added as she now pointed to April.

"And you make the coffee."

April attempted to stare down Carmen but it was something that she had never been able to do in the twenty years that they had been friends.

She wasn't about to win today.

Eventually she stood up and pushed away the chair with her foot.

"I suppose the only real lady of this house really ought to go anyway." She said.

She walked out of the kitchen and headed toward the front door and Carmen again glanced over her small mirror at Jade.

"Where have you left the council official?"." She asked.

Jade displayed a wry grin.

"He's tied face down on the bed with his own white frilly knickers stuffed in his mouth." She replied.

"Like I said I thought it best to come and ask you first."

It was around five minutes later that April returned and informed Carmen that the caller was another man from the property developers that had already bought many of the properties at Alpha grove.

The developers intended to flatten all of the existing houses and replace them with a huge shopping complex.

"He left a hand written letter for you." April informed Carmen and returned to her seat.

"I left it on the second step." She added.

Two hours later Jade and April had already left when Carmen walked from the kitchen into the front hall.

She was now dressed in a thin white pullover and blue denim jeans and had brushed out her straight shoulder length dark brown bobbed hair.

She stared at the white security alarm panel on the wall and from the corner of her left eye she spotted the letter that April earlier told her about.

She reached down and picked it up.

She studied it for a few moments and saw that April was actually right for once.

It was hand written supposedly by the CEO of the multi-million pound property development company that had already bought up much of the Isle of Dogs, not only Alpha grove.

She placed the envelope inside her dark brown leather shoulder bag before she entered the alarm code into the white box on the wall and then left the house and headed toward her plush flat at the King's road Chelsea.

Twenty One
Wednesday September 20th 2000

On a warm and sunny evening PC Chris Williams walked through the brown double doors at task force headquarters.

He was five feet eight inches tall and a just little overweight with short dark thinning hair and one of those natural likeable always smiling faces.

The thirty one year old father of three was liked by everybody that he worked with mostly because he always had a smile on his face and never had a bad word to say about anybody.

Chris always kept his personal opinions to himself and his great sense of humour helped in an environment where a man worked alongside the same people on a daily basis.

Every manager needed somebody like Chris Williams on the team.

He walked through the corridor and from the canteen on his right stepped one of his colleagues twenty four year old WPC Kerry Whittaker.

Kerry's long dark hair was pulled back into a ponytail and she carried a polystyrene cup of coffee.

She turned to respond to somebody behind her and just as she did Chris Williams relieved her of her coffee and he proceeded to climb the wide staircase toward the ops room.

At first Kerry stared up at him with disbelief.

"Bring my coffee back here!"   She demanded.

Williams continued to climb the staircase and a little more than halfway up he turned and grinned.

"Get your own."

Kerry stood with her mouth open and watched as he walked away with her coffee.

Eventually she laughed because everybody liked Chris Williams including Kerry Whittaker.

He headed toward the third aisle of monitor stations where he would relieve his buddy PC Chris Breslin who had manned the Shoreditch monitors since six that morning.

Williams arrived a little early to get his friend away.

"How's Shoreditch been today?" He asked.

They discussed events that occurred over the course of the day including a minor car accident where nobody was hurt.

Breslin eventually thanked Chris for arriving early and it was just after 5:35pm when he headed out of the ops room and home for the evening.

Chris Williams settled down in his chair in the middle of aisle three with twelve camera operators to his left and nine to his right.

There were nine rows in front and two behind Williams where he would monitor the Shoreditch area of London for the next twelve hours.

It was 9:06pm when Chris watched her from his chair.

He had seen this young girl on camera every night for the past week and as more cameras were installed and went live, the more he saw of her and now knew her routine by heart.

He picked her up as usual from a tiny hidden camera at the corner of Cremer Street overlooking Hackney road where she headed south.

Chris knew exactly where she was going because she took this same walk every night at around this time.

He decided that she was a *'Sarah'* although he had never met her and hadn't learned her real identity.

He gave her the name because it was something that he habitually did with frequent visitors to his monitoring stations.

Her real name was Amy Hadlow.

She was eighteen and lived in a squat at Pritchard's road not far from Cambridge heath railway station where she had just walked from.

Amy ran away from home more than three years ago when her mother brought a new man into her life.

He was a man that Amy despised for no particular reason and at almost fifteen she ran away from their home in Sheffield and headed for the bright lights of London in search of something better.

She wore dirty dark blue denim jeans, equally dirty white training shoes and a white jacket that appeared even on Chris's monitor as if it had seen better days.

'Sarah' had short blonde spiked hair.

When she reached the end of Hackney road Chris watched her turn left onto the A10 Shoreditch high street.

He knew that she would head south until she reached the fuel station on the opposite side of the busy main road.

She would then cross before taking a right and head north-west on Great eastern street until she reached Curtain road and there she would take another left to meet her dark haired friend who was around the same age Chris guessed.

The two girls would then head back up to Great eastern street and take another left where they would walk up to Old street underground railway station and spend the evening begging for small change from passing commuters.

Chris Williams knew their routine.

A little more than an hour after he initially picked her up from Hackney road, 'Sarah' and her friend disappeared from his monitoring area as they walked onto Old street itself and out of his jurisdiction.

"See you in a few hours Sarah." He said to his monitor.

He watched the two girls disappeared.

Williams continued to monitor most of Shoreditch for the next five hours until Amy Hadlow and her dark haired friend reappeared on his screens at 1:03am.

"Right let's get you home." He told the girls on his monitor.

Of course they were completely unaware that he was watching them.

Amy Hadlow was a prime candidate for abduction at this time in London because she was young slim pretty and of course technically although she lived in a squat she was homeless too.

Chris knew where she would go each step of the way back to her home or at least back to Hackney road.

The girls walked down Curtain road and then took a right into Luke Street where her dark haired friend lived before Amy headed back toward Great eastern street alone.

At the junction of Curtain road and Great eastern street she would take a right and head south east back to Shoreditch high street.

From there she would take a left and head north toward Hackney road and then home.

When Amy was temporarily out of view at Curtain road Chris rushed down to the canteen and made a hot strong coffee with three sugars and hurried back up to his station where he caught her re-entering Great eastern street.

He sipped his hot coffee and waited for her to turn right as she always did but for the first time Amy crossed Great eastern street instead of taking her usual right turn.

"Where the bloody hell are you going?" He yelled at his monitor.

Kerry Whittaker sat two rows in front of Chris and she turned.

"You ok?" She asked.

Chris nodded.

"Sarah decided to go sight-seeing." He replied.

He shook his head as he continued to stare at the monitor.

Kerry Whittaker turned again and continued to watch her own monitors with a grin.

"Ok stalker!" She whispered beneath her breath with a giggle.

Chris watched as Amy stood on the corner of Great eastern street and the upper side of Curtain road that passed through it and he hoped to see her head right as she paused for a few moments.

He quickly checked the viewpoints of the area on another monitor before he glanced back at her.

"Ok, you can go straight ahead up to Old street and then take a right and cross over into Hackney road or take a right now and walk down Great eastern like you always bloody do." He told her.

Amy Hadlow stood outside a closed deli.

Williams checked the map again and then turned to the information that detailed his camera coverage before he returned his attention to Amy.

For the very first time since he started regularly watching Amy she started to walk north toward Old street instead of her usual route of right and back down Great eastern street.

Chris checked his camera coverage again.

"Ok, we're good as long as you don't take a right into New Inn Yard, everywhere else is covered." He told the teenager that couldn't hear him.

Amy headed north toward Old street until she reached the junction with New Inn Yard on her right.

She stopped and stared down the darkened road that was one of the very few in Shoreditch with no camera coverage whatsoever.

"Don't you dare do it!" Chris quietly uttered to his monitor.

Amy then took the right and headed into New Inn Yard.

"Why the bloody hell did you do that?" Chris yelled.

Amy disappeared into New Inn Yard, the only street within the immediate vicinity that Chris Williams couldn't view.

He returned to his detailed map of the area and saw that it should take her around ten minutes to reach the other end.

She should reappear at Shoreditch high street next to the all night fuel station and take a left and then head toward Hackney road.

After around a minute Chris noticed at the top left of his main monitor a black Jaguar car that turned left into New Inn Yard from upper Curtain road where Amy had just walked from.

"Oh this is great!" He uttered.

Kerry Whittaker turned again.

"Chris is everything ok?" She asked.

He glanced up at her and shook his head.

"It would be if she went where she's supposed to bloody go!" He replied.

He returned his attention to his monitors.

There were no turnings off New Inn Yard that he could see on his map so Chris knew that she had to reappear within the next eight or nine minutes at Shoreditch high street.

Half way down New Inn Yard was a large overhead railway bridge and as Amy approached it she heard the sound of a car from behind her.

She turned to see a black car heading in her direction just as she began to walk into the very dark area beneath the bridge.

When she reached roughly halfway through the black Jaguar slowed and the front passenger window slowly lowered.

"Young girl why are outside so late?" A deep voice asked from inside the car.

Amy completely ignored him and continued walking.

The car crawled beside her.

"I am Russian diplomat on my way home." He told her from inside his car.

"It's very dangerous for you to be outside in London at this time." He added.

Amy stopped and stared into the car.

"Whatever you're after mate I'm not interested so piss off!" She snapped.

The man inside the car chuckled.

"I am very happily married man on my way home from playing very bad poker at the casino." He assured her.

"I have children and want you to be at home with your family."

Amy stopped and stared inside the car again.

It looked warm and very posh with all of the chrome and cockpit lights.

"If you even think about touching me I'll call the coppers, got it?" She asked.

Vladimir Kolov smiled and nodded.

"I will never sleep if I am not sure that you are home safely." He told her in his genuine Russian accent.

Amy opened the car door and climbed in.

As the black Jaguar pulled away Kolov picked up the in-car mobile telephone and dialled a number.

"Inna I am on my way home but I have found a young lady who is alone." He told his wife.

"I am taking her home because London is a very dangerous place at this time." He added.

His wife responded before he ended the call.

Amy immediately felt more relaxed because this large foreigner called his wife to explain that she was in his car and she watched him place his phone next to the holder on top of the wide centre console.

On the windscreen of his car she saw the parking permit that validated his earlier claim to be a Russian diplomat at Kensington palace gardens.

He glanced across at Amy.

"Where do you live?" He asked.

Amy told him of the squat at Pritchard's road.

She thought that maybe if he felt a little sorry for her he might give her some cash to add to the small amount that she shared with her friend Gemma Clifford at Old street underground station.

Vladimir Kolov glanced across at her and smiled.

Everything that Kolov said or did was a very clever distraction to make Amy feel relaxed.

As the Jaguar approached the orange flashing lights of road works near the end of New Inn Yard he pressed his foot hard onto the brake and his phone dropped onto the floor between Amy's legs.

He immediately stopped the car.

He started to lean his huge frame over to pick up his phone but stopped as it was between Amy's feet.

"Would you mind?" He asked.

Amy then leaned down to pick up the phone.

As soon as she did Kolov removed from his inside jacket pocket a small black rectangular device that he pressed onto the back of her exposed neck and immediately pressed a red button.

There was a single squeal from the eighteen year old as the intense pain jolted through her entire body after Vladimir saw the electric blue spark from the device.

She was conscious but saw nothing but blinding bright white.

Her stiffened body remained in the same crouched position as Kolov edged the car forward to the junction of New Inn Yard and Shoreditch high street.

As he turned left his arm pushed down onto the back of Amy's neck to ensure that she remained out of sight.

He drove past not only the hidden task force camera on the left but also a yellow traffic speed camera on the right side of Shoreditch high street.

Kolov innocently stared straight ahead.

Inside the ops room Chris Williams watched the black Jaguar exit New Inn Yard and head north along Shoreditch high street.

He saw when he immediately played back a single occupant inside the car and breathed a sigh of relief on Amy's behalf.

"You should come out in a couple of minutes." He told her.

He returned his attention to the junction.

A short while later Vladimir Kolov glanced to his right as he drove through the cross junction of Old street on his left.

But he stared at Hackney road on his right where Amy would have eventually walked if she hadn't climbed into his car.

He picked her up purely by chance.

Amy Hadlow was never a target.

She was young blonde slim and very pretty and she was also alone in the only road remaining at Shoreditch that had absolutely no camera coverage.

Vladimir Kolov was aware of all of those facts.

Eight more minutes passed and Chris Williams saw no sign of Amy the girl he called 'Sarah' and he was now very anxious.

All around Chris could see and feel it.

"Ok she's not coming back out." He said.

He turned in his seat.

"I need a car to New Inn Yard right now!" He yelled to the entire room.

He stood up with his eyes still fixed upon his monitors.

The entire ops room was suddenly a buzzing hive of manic activity around Chris Williams.

After a short while he watched a marked police patrol car turn into New Inn Yard from upper Curtain road.

"Be there, be there!" He quietly uttered.

Four minutes later he saw the same police car at the exit as it turned left onto Shoreditch high street.

The police officers inside the car reported that there was nobody walking at New Inn Yard.

Amy Hadlow's disappearance was the result of a series of opportunistic events.

If she had turned right at the junction of lower Curtain road and headed down Great eastern as she usually did, she would never have met Vladimir Kolov.

Twenty Two
Wednesday September 20th 2000

At Croydon road Caterham Surrey the main road that runs through the small town on the outskirts four women were moved into one of the secret safe houses allocated to the task force a week ago.

It was the same night that Amy Hadlow disappeared from Shoreditch.

Linda Edmunds Denise Ruane Deborah Franklin and Jane Carey were temporarily resituated from a women's refuge at Lower road Rotherhithe south east London, an area where many of the initial abductions took place.

The four women were deemed safe to remain unsupervised because none had any kind of drug or alcohol related problems whereas many had issues with either or both.

The necessity to supervise them was deemed greater than those fewer non-users and addicts.

The reality was that they had probably already been noticed and were possibly targeted.

In addition these four women had been placed in a small almost rural and reasonably quiet town especially at night on the outskirts of London with no protection and they were very much at risk.

All four of them knew and felt it.

From their own viewpoint the people that were taking the homeless people were highly organised.

They were obviously structured in some way just due to the fact that more than eight hundred members of the homeless community were now missing and there was no clue leading to their identification.

It was 2:23am and the small town of Caterham was as usual very quiet.

Linda Edmunds Deborah Franklin and Jane Carey were sleeping in their beds and it was twenty seven year old Denise Ruane that drew the short straw.

Tonight was her turn to remain awake.

None of them were naïve and the gossip had travelled around as to why they had really been moved not just out of Rotherhithe where they felt safer in numbers but completely out of the city into this quiet town on the outskirts.

They all personally knew some of the people that were now missing and they sat down together on the day that they arrived at Caterham.

"They've dumped us out here to fend for ourselves." Linda Edmunds told her three friends.

As a result tonight it was Denise Ruane that would remain awake throughout the night so that everybody else woke in their beds in the morning.

Denise was curled up in front of the living room window fully clothed beneath a blanket where only her head and shoulder length blonde hair remained visible.

She sat in silent darkness and that alone considerably heightened her senses.

It also increased her awareness of things that were not there as her night of lonely self-induced terror began.

A short while ago she heard a vehicle that slowed almost to a stop outside.

When she discretely spied through a tiny gap in the curtains she saw a marked police car that checked the safe house and would visit every two hours incidents elsewhere permitting.

She was already nervous because in the dark and the silence her mind and eyes played tricks and hearing the car outside only added to her already heightened levels of anxiety even after she discovered that it was in fact a police car.

Denise tried to think positively and reminded herself that at least she was too terrified to fall asleep on her watch.

She heard another car slow down outside and turned in the chair again.

Still wrapped in the blanket she used her thumb and forefinger to carefully ease back the slight gap in the curtains to see a red car as it turned right into the road directly opposite and again she sighed with relief.

"This is going to drive me up the wall all night!" She told herself.

She then released her grip of the curtains.

This happened a few more times and Denise scared herself more and more as several cars slowed down outside.

They mostly briefly stopped before moving on or turning off and with the sounds of the house creaking as it cooled and the clock in the hall ticking in otherwise silence her imagination continued to run wild.

It wasn't long before her nerves were in absolute tatters.

Denise suddenly opened her eyes.

She had no idea of how long she had been asleep and no recollection of how or when she drifted off.

"Oh shit!" She uttered to herself.

She became cold in the dead of night and made herself more comfortable for the long night ahead and that's precisely how she fell asleep.

She jumped up in the chair as everything suddenly came back to her.

She was the one on watch.

'How the hell did that happen?' She asked herself.

She considered herself lucky because at least she was still sitting in the chair and hadn't been abducted.

She considered walking to the kitchen to make a strong coffee to ensure that it didn't happen again.

Denise slowly turned in her chair and checked through the tiny gap in the curtains and saw a parked silver security van outside.

She breathed a sigh of relief.

"I feel better already!"

Obviously she knew that she had fallen asleep.

She was however yet to learn that she was woken by twenty nine year old former Romanian soldier Emil Hagi when he picked the lock of the front door.

She was also unaware that during her brief nap the latest police drive-by from the patrol car occurred ten minutes ago.

It was watched by the Romanians and they knew that it wouldn't return for another two hours.

She didn't know any of this but she did know that now something wasn't right inside the house.

She didn't know what it was but this was different to before when she was scaring herself half to death.

Something else, something unknown was now doing that to her.

She also had no idea that less than twelve feet in front of her behind the wall were four Romanian soldiers in the hall.

They however knew exactly where she was as Hagi just watched her waking.

Denise stared out toward the hall through the open door with the Romanians to the left of the door frame but she still had no idea that they were there.

She could sense that something was wrong but at least the security van was outside and that gave her a sense of security.

Of course it was a very, very false sense of security.

She could see the white painted bannister rail with her grained effect vision where everything moved if she concentrated hard enough on any specific object.

There was now a more deftly silence inside the house that wasn't present before.

It was quieter than earlier.

Denise stared out toward the hall gripped with sheer unexplainable terror.

"There's nobody there, there's nobody there, there's nobody there." She whispered to herself.

Her breath was short and her heart pounded even though there was no sound coming from the hall or anywhere else for that matter.

Denise knew that something was wrong and that whatever it was had happened as she slept.

It wasn't just quiet.

Like Sara Crossly discovered at St Andrew's Road Enfield on the eleventh of August.

It was too quiet.

A small dark object suddenly appeared in what seemed like slow motion near the floor to the left of the door frame.

Denise knew for a fact that it has just appeared and definitely wasn't there before.

She knew that this wasn't some kind of darkened illusion.

She wanted to scream as loud as she could.

She knew that she had to scream out but she couldn't.

She could only stare at whatever was definitely moving just twelve feet in front of her.

Denise was gripped with sheer terror and unable to even move.

A larger object slowly appeared near the floor just above the first and she realised exactly what that second object was.

Her eyes widened as her heart pounded even faster.

Denise breathed very heavily.

Her heart was ready to explode as she stared into the eyes behind the balaclava mask of the Romanian driver Lucian Banica.

Suddenly a small bright red light appeared from the lower object that settled steady below his staring eyes.

Banica was against the wall and had slowly manoeuvred himself into a position where he could fire his gun as he lay dead still.

He was completely focussed as he gently eased back the trigger.

Denise stared back at him frozen with fear before she heard the echoed CLACK just a split second before the device thudded into her.

It hit her on the left side of her neck from Banica's viewpoint.

50,000 volts instantly jolted through her body rendering.

Denise sat completely immobilised and violently shaking in the chair.

She was fully conscious as the four men then entered the living room and headed toward her as her body trembled in silence.

Eventually the bright white turned to darkness when she slipped into unconsciousness.

However that wasn't before she lay on the floor vaguely aware that she had been turned over onto her front as her wrists and ankles were bound together with black plastic cable ties.

Linda Edmunds Deborah Franklin and Jane Carey were also taken but never woke from their sleep and knew nothing of what happened to them.

Denise Ruane knew everything.

Around an hour and twenty minutes after the silver security van left Caterham a marked police car slowed to a stop outside the house before it continued with its patrol.

The house was in complete darkness therefore all of the occupants inside were obviously sleeping.

It was just after eight that morning during daylight hours when a routine visit was made by a uniformed police sergeant from task force headquarters.

He discovered the house completely empty and found that the solid brass security chain on the front door had been cut.

Denise Ruane Linda Edmunds Deborah Franklin and Jane Carey had become the latest casualties on a rapidly growing list of names.

These four women were deemed least likely to require police supervision on the basis that none of them had alcohol or drug related problems.

The management at task force headquarters now realised that they needed to re-evaluate their priorities and they needed to do it right now.

This one could have and should have been prevented.

However the silent question that was on everybody's lips was more urgent.

How could this have happened at one of the safe houses?

Twenty Three
Thursday September 21st 2000

The operations room at task force headquarters was in complete silence.

Chief Inspector Martin Roberts stood in the centre of aisle three and watched the recorded disappearance of eighteen year old Amy Hadlow at Shoreditch during the very early hours of the same morning.

Her identity was revealed by the local police.

They issued a caution to her and her friend Gemma Clifford some weeks earlier and the officer that confronted them at Old street mainline station identified them from the CCTV footage.

It was the same CCTV footage that Chief Inspector Roberts viewed.

After Nicola Garwood interviewed Amy's friend Gemma Clifford when the scene was initially investigated, nineteen year old Gemma who was seen on the same CCTV footage identified her friend as Amy Hadlow who was originally from Sheffield.

Behind the chief in the completely silent operations room stood Detective Inspector Garwood wearing a black suit jacket black denim jeans and flat black shoes and her arms were folded in front of her.

Beside her was Detective Inspector Sam Henning in a dark suit with a white shirt and a dark blue tie.

After viewing the police patrol car leaving the junction of New Inn Yard onto Shoreditch high street the chief turned to the Detective Inspectors but his main attention was directed toward Nicola Garwood.

"Does your naive incompetence know no bounds?" He asked her in a full room of silent police officers.

Garwood opened her mouth to speak but her boss hadn't finished.

"Why is that the only road no camera coverage?" He angrily asked.

She wanted to explain to him that there were genuine road works underway at one end of New Inn Yard and that they couldn't move into the area until the council employed workers were finished.

Garwood however considered that here and now in a room full of people was not the time for that discussion.

Ironically the work being carried out at the Shoreditch high street end of New Inn Yard was the installation of two cast iron bollards that would turn it into a pedestrianized street.

Vladimir Kolov would never have driven down there as an opportunist.

Garwood took the chief's criticism, it came with the job.

"Sir we need to talk with the driver of the only vehicle that travelled down that road at the time of her disappearance." She told Roberts.

Roberts walked away.

Nicola glanced at Sam Henning.

"Thanks for the back up!" She uttered.

She headed after the chief as he walked toward the door on his way out of the ops room.

"Sir, can we have permission to speak with Vladimir Kolov?" She called out.

There was complete silence as Roberts stopped and slowly turned.

"Are you insane?" He asked.

"He's a Russian diplomat with full immunity!" He reminded her at the top of his voice.

Nicola took in a deep breath.

"Sir, his rented car was the only vehicle to travel down New Inn Yard at the time of her disappearance." She reminded him.

Roberts stared into her eyes.

"I want you Garwood, to pay full attention to what I'm about to tell you." He began.

"I'm not going to use a phrase that you might hear in a movie that you'll be directing traffic if you go within fifty feet of Vladimir Kolov." He continued.

"I'm warning you that you'll be unemployed and unemployable if you go within five feet of him!" He snapped.

The chief turned again and this time he left the room leaving Garwood standing in the same spot while the entire ops room stared at her in silence.

She eventually walked into the cubicle office and slammed the door behind her.

Sam walked in followed by Jacob Saunders.

"You ok?" He asked.

Nicola nodded with a sigh as she sat down at her desk.

She wasn't particularly angry with Sam.

Her outburst was a result of her frustration and the fact that Amy Hadlow had been taken from right under their noses in the only road in Shoreditch that was yet to be installed with secret camera coverage.

She explained this to Sam.

"There's something not right here Sam." She told him.

As Nicola took in a deep breath he agreed with her.

"I'm beginning to think that this wasn't pure coincidence." He replied.

Nicola looked up at him.

"But how could they know?" She asked.

Now she glanced at Saunders and then back to Sam.

"Only the three of us know the locations of every camera." She reminded him.

Nicola suddenly turned her attention to Jacob Saunders.

"Please tell me that you haven't been down the pub blabbing!" She said.

Saunders appeared stunned.

"Of course I haven't!" He snapped back.

"Well I'm more than certain that DI Henning and I haven't told anybody Jacob so that leaves just you!"

Nicola's paranoia was now in full overdrive thanks to her encounter with the chief.

Saunders assured her that her new found distrust of him was misplaced.

"How many people have made passing remarks to it in the past seven days?" She asked.

Saunders took in a long deep breath and then exhaled it.

"None guv if you recall it was *you* that told me to get all of the information off the walls and onto the computer system." He reminded her.

"That's what I've been doing every night this week." He added.

Sam attempted to diffuse the volatile confrontation but Nicola was adamant.

"We're still the only three people that have seen the whereabouts of everything!" She reminded him.

For a few moments there was silence as everybody cleared their heads and calmed down.

Suddenly Sam looked across at her.

"Hold on a minute!"

He reached into his desk drawer and pulled out a single sheet of A5 paper before he again turned to Nicola.

"Got a blunt pencil over there?" He asked.

Nicola tossed over a yellow pencil that Sam used to scribble over the page to turn it from blank white to a solid grey etching.

He then stared at it for a few seconds before he looked up and hand it to Saunders.

"Pass this to Detective Inspector angry knickers over there will you?" He asked.

Jacob took the sheet of paper and studied it before he handed it to Nicola.

She studied it for a few moments.

"What's this?" She asked.

Sam told her what she already knew.

That of course wasn't the real question because she already recognised it as some of the list of the concealed micro cameras and their exact locations.

She stared at Sam and he stared straight back at her.

"There are four not three people who know the exact locations of everything Nik." He told her.

He then revealed where the sheet of paper came from.

It was Chief Inspector Martin Robert's own note pad.

Nicola continued to stare at Sam.

"And I get called insane?" She sarcastically asked with a chuckle.

Jacob Saunders interjected.

"There is nothing more deceptive than the obvious fact." He said.

Sam Henning grinned.

"Did you just think that up?" He asked.

Saunders smiled back at him.

"No guv Sherlock Holmes did."

A short while later there was a knock at the cubicle door and a middle aged police woman with dark brown shoulder length wavy hair stepped inside.

She looked at Henning and then at Garwood before she spoke.

"We lost four women last night." She eventually informed them.

It was obvious to both of them that she waited to add more.

Sam stared at her.

He somehow knew what she was about to tell them.

"Was it an unmanned safe house?" He asked.

The WPC nodded.

"Yes Sir, Croydon Road in Caterham."

The task force actually lost five women last night.

One was watched as it happened on camera at New Inn Yard Shoreditch and four were taken from inside one of their own safe houses.

"Now tell me that they don't know everything that we're doing." Nicola quietly uttered.

Twenty Four
Monday September 25th 2000

At just after ten in the morning thirty four year old Carmen Richardson sat in the plush reception area on the fifth floor of a building owned by Balcombe and Webb property developments at Kensington west London.

The letter that April Marsh left on the second step at the brothel that Carmen owned at Alpha grove on the isle of Dogs was it seemed handwritten by Mr Arron Balcombe himself.

Balcombe was the CEO of the company.

He invited Carmen to private negotiations and according to the handwritten letter she was invited to meet with him in person with regard to the possible purchase of her four bedroom house.

In contrast to the tight leather corset today Carmen looked the complete professional in a very smart pale lilac business suit and a white satin blouse with beige leather shoes and on the floor beside her feet was a beige leather handbag.

Occasionally she would glance across from the brown leather sofa at a young receptionist that sat behind a desk beside a brown door that displayed a brass plaque.

Mr A Balcombe CEO

The young woman behind the desk was called Monique and she had long dark brown hair that had been fashioned with clips on top of her head to an oriental effect.

Carmen guessed that Monique was in her early twenties.

Monique glanced at her again and Carmen guessed that the young secretary knew of her chosen profession.

She also guessed that she was more likely thinking the worst taking into account that she was the PA to the very wealthy man inside the office to her right

Carmen paid her glances little attention.

She was already in fact a millionaire twice over herself.

Her clients more often than not paid around five hundred pounds for an hour of her specialist time and she had been providing the service for over fifteen years.

She believed in investments and owned the house at Alpha grove, a plush flat at the Kings road Chelsea and an eight bedroom mansion on the Greek island of Kefalonia where she planned to retire one day.

Her own opinion was to hell with what people thought of her and that included the pretty young upstart that sat across the reception area.

These two women came from completely different backgrounds and continued to exchange glances.

Both smiled warmly.

Neither smile was genuine.

Suddenly Carmen's attention turned to the brown door on Monique's right as a tall man of average build with short greying blonde hair in his late forties Carmen guessed, stepped out.

He wore a well fitted grey suit and expensive brown Italian leather shoes.

He glanced across at the attractive high class prostitute with a smile before he turned his attention to Monique.

He and the PA spoke very quietly but Carmen could only make out that her name had been mentioned when Monique motioned in her direction with a forefinger.

The man in the suit turned and smiled.

"Carmen Richardson?" He asked.

Carmen climbed to her feet and held out her hand for him to shake and he continued to smile.

"Arron Balcombe, CEO of Balcombe and Webb." He announced.

Carmen smiled back at him.

"I'm going to be completely honest Mr Balcombe, I'm intrigued and nothing more." She informed him.

"The CEO of the company sending me hand written letters?" She asked.

"Whatever would the neighbours think?"

Balcombe's face slightly reddened.

"Well it got you here didn't it?"

He then ushered Carmen toward his office door.

"Were you going somewhere?" She asked.

She guessed that he had no idea that she had been sitting in his reception area for the past twenty five minutes.

Monique interjected.

"Mr Balcombe, I did send you an internal memo informing you that Mrs Richardson was here." She informed him.

It was now Carmen's turn to interject.

"It's Ms Richardson not Mrs" She corrected Monique.

Balcombe smiled again.

"My day is just getting better." He joked.

He ushered Carmen into his office and turned to Monique.

"Could you organise refreshments?" He asked.

He then followed Carmen into his office and closed the door behind him.

His office was the former penthouse suite from when ten years ago the building was an exclusive Kensington hotel.

Today it was converted into offices for the group of companies that he owned.

His office was thirty feet by twenty feet and had a complete glass frontage that led out onto a balcony with black painted rails overlooking a picturesque park.

The first thing that Carmen noticed was a very old original painted portrait of a man with grey swept back hair posing from what was seemed to be his own very old fashioned office in the background.

She pointed up to the ornate framed portrait.

"Is that your dad?" She asked with tongue in cheek.

Balcombe flashed another smile.

"How old do you think I am?" He asked with a chuckle.

"He was my great grandfather." He replied.

"He was the founder of Balcombe and Webb." He added.

Carmen nodded.

"I see and what happened to Webb?"

Balcombe ushered Carmen toward a beige leather sofa that was situated in front of an unlit real log fire on their right.

"Webb was my great grandmother's maiden name, his wife." He revealed.

As they walked toward the sofa Carmen spotted the gold wedding band on his finger.

"Do you have children Mr Balcombe?" She asked.

He nodded.

"I have a daughter."

As they both sat down Monique entered the office.

"Ms Richardson would you like tea or coffee?" She asked.

Balcombe interjected.

"We do have something stronger if you'd prefer." He told Carmen.

She shook her head.

"Coffee would be fine Mr Balcombe." She replied.

Carmen directly replied to him purposely ignoring Monique to play her game of superiority.

She then glanced behind the sofa as Monique left the office.

"You have a water feature in your office?" She chuckled.

Balcombe laughed.

"I can't take responsibility for that, we had an interior designer in." He assured her.

Carmen found that one difficult to believe.

There was a pause before Balcombe spoke again.

"So, shall we talk business?" He asked.

Carmen raised her eyebrows.

"I told you I came here purely out of intrigue." She reminded him.

Balcombe again paused with a smile.

"Let me explain why I'm so keen to buy your house." He told her.

Carmen sat back.

"Please do Mr Balcombe." She replied.

He smiled again.

"Please, call me Arron." He insisted.

Carmen smiled again.

"Stop flirting and tell me why you're so keen to buy my house." She said in jest.

Balcombe chuckled again.

Carmen knew precisely how to work this business situation because she came with a plan.

Carmen Richardson always had a plan.

Balcombe explained that he had already purchased most of the properties at Alpha grove and in fact all four of the houses that formed the terrace where she owned the property where she worked with Jade Harris and April Marsh.

"The block of flats behind your house will eventually come down and that entire area will become a huge shopping complex providing over fourteen hundred jobs." He boasted.

Carmen nodded with a smile.

"You mean it would if I sold you my house?" She asked.

Balcombe smiled back at her.

"So could we at least discuss it as a possibility?" He asked.

Carmen grinned.

"Keep talking." She told him.

There was a short pause.

"Arron." She promptly added with another grin.

Monique re-entered the office with a silver tray holding two coffees, cream in a small jug and a sugar bowl that she placed onto the rectangular glass table in front of Arron Balcombe.

Carmen glanced up to her.

"Thank you dear." She said in a patronising tone.

It brought a wry grin to Arron Balcombe's lips as he realised what was going on between the two women.

When Monique left Arron made an informal apology on her behalf.

"Monique can sometimes be..." He began.

Carmen suddenly finished his sentence.

"A stuck up little bitch?" She asked.

Balcombe chuckled.

"I was going to say a little bit of an elitist but you obviously get the gist." He added with another chuckle.

"But she makes good coffee."

Arron Balcombe already worked out that the woman seated on his sofa was in fact here to discuss business but she was incredibly smart and even more devious.

He now knew that she had an astute brain for business.

Meanwhile despite being the guest Carmen started to organise the coffee.

"I'm dying to know why a hand written letter?" She asked.

Balcombe shrugged.

"You're not stupid, I can see that and until you sell me your house I can't even obtain full planning consent and I have everything else ready to move." He honestly confessed.

"The truth is that I need your house."

Carmen recognised and appreciated his honesty.

"Ok here's my next question. She began again.

"I'm taking into account that you're going to create more than fourteen hundred jobs not including the demolition and reconstruction." She continued.

"How much does that little lot realistically cost?" She asked.

Balcombe shrugged his shoulders.

"We're investing an initial thirty five million into the project."

Again Carmen nodded quite un-phased by the vast quantities of cash that he was talking about.

She sipped her coffee before she continued.

"And if I were to sell you my little house you could begin work almost immediately?" She asked.

Without going into the technicalities theoretically she guessed correctly and that was how Balcombe explained it to her.

He picked up his own coffee and appeared calm but Carmen knew that if he looked that way it was because he was trying to.

"I'm going to surprise you now." He said.

There was another pause.

"What if I offered you two million pounds for your little four bedroomed House?" He asked.

Carmen seemed to ponder on his offer for a few moments.

"With that sort of money you could easily find another house to continue providing the services that you do." He added.

That was Arron Balcombe's first wrong move.

Not wrong because he showed her that he was aware of her profession but that he described it as seedy and underhanded.

Carmen considered it very differently.

She paid her bills and taxes for her entire adult life and she owed nobody a penny.

She raised her eyebrows as she seemed to ponder.

"I'm going to surprise you now Arron." She finally responded.

"How about we begin at four million and work our way up from there?" She asked.

She knew that at least thirty five million was already invested and that would have been Balcombe's version not the accurate one.

She also knew that his project was on hold until he owned her property.

He was visibly shocked but eventually he regained his composure.

"Who taught you to conduct business?" He eventually asked.

Carmen smiled once again.

"Life did Arron." She replied as she sipped her coffee.

Twenty Five
Thursday September 28th 2000

There was a cold crisp breeze in the air at just after five in the morning at the coastal town of Folkestone Kent south east England.

Fifty year old Italian Giovanni placed the silver furniture outside his coffee shop on a cobbled street called Sandgate road in the town centre.

At around six he said good morning to the regular postman and handed him his free takeaway cappuccino and sat down outside his shop to relax before the Friday morning rush that would begin in around an hour.

Across the street from Giovanni was a closed down former high street superstore that was completely covered with white painted wooden boarding on the ground floor to protect the full glass frontage.

From beneath the ground inside the closed down store brown eyes watched Giovanni as he quietly enjoyed his coffee.

It was considerably warmer three hours later when two women in their mid-thirties sat at the exact same table where Giovanni had enjoyed his morning coffee.

The woman on the left had long straight blonde hair and her blue eyes were protected by large dark designer sunglasses.

She was dressed in a white blouse and white denim jeans with beige sandals on her feet.

Seated at the same table was her friend with straight shoulder length dark brown bobbed hair and she wore a plain white cotton t-shirt beneath a short black leather jacket and blue denim jeans with black leather boots on her feet.

The dark haired woman glanced across at the white boarded former high street giant superstore.

"Have you heard about what's going to happen to that place?" She asked.

She nodded in the general direction of the closed down store across the street.

"Please tell me it's not another bloody discount shop." The blonde uttered with a sigh.

Her dark haired friend nodded her head.

"That's what I heard."

From across the street those same brown eyes that earlier watched Giovanni slowly opened and saw the two women.

At the back of the store a long green electronic gate slowly opened while a black convertible Mercedes car waited to enter the former staff car park and loading area.

When the gate was fully opened the black car drove inside and parked outside a dark blue metal roller shutter door where huge trucks used to reverse inside to unload their deliveries.

The driver of the black Mercedes climbed out and watched over her large dark designer sunglasses as the sliding green gate closed.

She reached into her black leather designer shoulder bag and removed a large key bunch before she walked toward the smaller blue steel door beside the roller shutter and unlocked it.

Once inside she locked the door behind her and walked to the right side of the building where she opened a white plastic box on the wall and tapped in a four digit code to silence the alarm activation warning.

She then placed the key bunch back into her bag and removed her phone from it and dialled a number.

"Barak it is I, Inna." She said with a Russian accent.

"I am inside the store now." She added.

"I will call you when she is gone."

Twenty nine year old Inna Kolov was five feet eleven inches tall and had long straight dark brown hair and beautiful brown eyes behind her designer sunglasses.

She wore a thin white knitted top that draped over her right shoulder to reveal a hint of white bra strap and skin tight blue designer jeans with white designer training shoes on her feet.

The once bustling warehouse area at the back of the store was now still and silent as Inna casually made her way toward the front of the store through clear plastic strip curtains that divided the main shop floor and the storage area.

The former Russian catwalk model pushed through the white plastic strip curtains and stepped onto a sticky burgundy nylon carpet where she stared directly ahead at the darkened inside of those white wooden boards that covered the glass frontage at Sandgate road.

On the other side of the boards sat the two women outside Giovanni's coffee shop.

Inna walked down the right side of the shop floor along a pale grey tiled walkway that led to an alcove that in turn led to a flight of stairs up to the offices of the former high street giant.

Inna walked straight past the alcove and stepped back onto the burgundy carpet where she headed for a small square shaped silver framed trap door.

She bent down and lifted it and saw eight narrow wooden makeshift steps that led down into a darkened basement area.

She searched for a white cord that was apparently on the left side.

Inna had never been here before.

She removed her sunglasses and cautiously climbed down the first few steps where she pulled on the white hanging cord that switched on a single dimly lit bulb at the basement ceiling below her.

When she reached the bottom and put both feet onto the dusty grey concrete floor her eyes scanned.

She saw two unconscious young women that lay bound and gagged on the floor and between them were three empty used syringes.

"This is so terrible." She uttered to herself.

She slowly walked toward an arch beneath the ground floor and carefully stepped over one of the women and into an adjoining alcove.

A woman stood with her back to Inna.

She had long wavy matted dark brown hair and she was around five feet six inches tall and dressed in nothing but filthy peach coloured underwear.

Her arms were pulled high above her head where her wrists were chained over a thin metal pipe that ran across the ceiling from wall to wall.

Her legs were tightly tied together at her ankles and also just above her knees.

Several layers of sticky black duct tape were firmly presses across her mouth and tightly wrapped around her entire head to prevent her from making a sound.

On the floor by her tightly tied ankles was yet another empty used plastic medical syringe.

But that was used quite some time ago.

Twenty three year old Dawn Sheppard slowly opened her brown eyes and now saw in front of her an incredibly beautiful woman wearing large dark sunglasses on top of her head.

Inna Kolov smiled at her.

"Can you wake for me?" She asked in a warm caring tone.

She studied the shiny black duct tape that was pressed firmly over the bound woman's mouth.

Dawn's exhausted eyes stared back at her.

"When the Doctor came to see you he found that you have the disease." Inna informed her.

The quantities of Heroin that had been injected into Dawn over the past month had taken their toll.

She had now been denied it for the past three days since this discovery was made by a twenty two year old medical student that Inna described as a Doctor.

Inna smiled again not really sure if what she was telling this young woman was sinking in.

What she did know was that because of this detected case of Syphilis Dawn could not be sold to the brothel that she had been destined for.

Therefore no more of the drug would be wasted.

She studied Dawn for a few moments.

"This is not good for me but of course is good for you." Inna smiled.

"Because I cannot use you now and must allow you to leave this place."

Again Dawn slowly opened her blurred brown eyes and saw over this woman's shoulder the two women that sat outside the coffee shop across the street through a tiny gap in the concrete.

She envied them so.

The former Russian model stepped behind Dawn where she reached down to an old wooden stool and picked up a roll of black duct tape and tore off a long strip.

She placed it between her perfectly straight white teeth.

She reached into her black leather bag and produced a large thin clear plastic bag and without hesitation she pulled it over Dawn's head and then pulled it tightly around her neck.

She removed the length of black tape from her teeth and sealed it completely around Dawn's neck.

Inna then casually walked back toward the adjoining basement and eight wooden steps to the sounds of Dawn's muffled squeals.

She carefully stepped over Heroin laced syringes and unconscious bound and gagged women as Dawn Sheppard's body twisted and turned from her arms that were chained to the metal pipe above her.

Eventually Inna pulled on the white cord and switched off the single basement light before she climbed out onto the shop floor again and closed the hatch.

She started to make her way back toward the warehouse at the rear of the store.

As she walked she removed the phone from her black leather bag and dialled the same number as before and waited for the recipient to pick up.

"Barak it is I Inna." She began.

"Yes it is done." She replied to his question.

"Barak there are syringes on the floor down there." She pointed out.

"I could be hurt and they must be picked up when you come to take her away."

When Inna left the building she looked up at the beautiful clear blue sky with a smile as she replaced her sunglasses and then climbed back into her black Mercedes.

After the long green sliding gate fully opened she drove out of the car park and headed toward Dover road and then onto the M20 Motorway northbound toward the city of London.

Outside Giovanni's coffee shop the two women climbed to their feet.

"It looks as though it's going to be a beautiful day considering it's the end of September doesn't it?" The blonde haired woman asked.

Her dark haired friend nodded with agreement as she picked up her bag.

Across the street the brown eyes of Dawn Sheppard no longer stared with envy.

They just stared.

The case of Syphilis diagnosed by the medical student was in fact a simple case of mouth ulcers caused by borderline malnutrition.

Twenty Six
Wednesday October 4th 2000

Twenty four year old banking investments manager Bridget Oaks was an incredibly smart and beautiful woman.

She stood at five feet six and had shoulder length wavy dark brown hair and beautiful brown eyes with a tanned complexion.

It was around eight in the evening when Bridget took a shower followed by a bath before she spent the rest of the evening watching TV.

She knew that she needed to get an early night because tomorrow she was to give a presentation to the board of Directors at work.

Bridget's partner Clive Henderson was away for three more days at a business seminar and Bridget was incredibly bored and in truth a little lonely.

At just after ten thirty she decided to call it a night and threw out her cat before she climbed the staircase and went to bed.

Their brand new three bedroom house at Norton road Wembley was peaceful and quiet.

Everybody in the cul-de-sac nodded and smiled to everybody else and every resident was a professional in one way or another.

Bridget and Clive had found their own idyllic little corner of heaven.

It was just after one thirty in the morning when Romanian Emil Hagi very quietly picked the lock on the front door in about the same time that he had at Love lane Micham.

The ever anxious Captain Abel Barbu entered the house followed by Hagi and Dorin Christescu while the thirty year old driver Lucian Banica remained inside the van.

This one was to be no mass abduction like the last when they took six squatters from the house at Love Lane then owned by the late Stanley Morton.

This was just a single woman.

Her photograph featured on Jane Chapman's website thanks to Lisa Moore who spotted Bridget with her partner at Trafalgar Square on Saturday August 26th.

As soon as Bridget's picture was displayed on Chapman's auction site the bids started to flood in due to her exceptional beauty.

Bridget was photographed alone in front of Nelson's column Trafalgar square and it was the first photograph taken by Lisa Moore that day that featured on the auction site.

All other photographs of Bridget and Clive taken on that day were immediately deleted and removed from Moore's camera.

David Stringer in fact viewed Bridget recently but amongst the hundreds of women featured on the site she was even to him just another beautiful woman.

David however did know that she hadn't yet been abducted because she was in his words *still walking around*.

The three men formerly of the Romanian army performed a stealthy search of the ground floor of the house before they quietly made their way up the stairs.

Captain Barbu knew that because Bridget was home alone and that she lived in the house with only her partner that she would be found in the master bedroom.

According to the blueprint drawings of the house it was at the top of the stairs and on the left next to the bathroom.

Barbu motioned both Hagi and Christescu toward the closed master bedroom door where they all armed their electronic pistols in otherwise silent preparation on the darkened landing.

The three men stood in front of the white panelled door.

Bridget Oaks lay in her bed with absolutely no idea that just a few feet away inside her own house were three professional soldiers that prepared to abduct her.

Suddenly one of the spare bedroom doors behind the three men opened.

A young woman stepped out wearing pale pink pyjama bottoms and a white t-shirt.

She turned to her right still half asleep and came face to face with the Captain and Barbu appeared to be more shocked than her.

Not for the first time Captain Barbu froze to the spot.

His electronic pistol dropped to the floor.

The dark haired woman in the master bedroom was supposed to be alone.

Three days ago when her partner left for his business trip she most certainly was alone.

It was all that Barbu could think about as he stared wide eyed into this second woman's eyes.

Hagi turned to see her still standing there because his commanding officer was frozen.

As Olivia Fletcher opened her mouth to scream Hagi fired his pistol.

CLACK!

A small projectile thudded into her chest.

Olivia fell to the floor and her body violently trembled from the effects of his shot but not before she half screamed with terror on the otherwise silent darkened landing right outside Bridget's bedroom door.

Dorin Christescu had also turned to see what had happened and looked up to his Captain to see that he had dropped his gun and not for the first time he was frozen to the spot in such a situation.

Christescu then watched his friend Emil open fire and saw this unknown woman drop to the floor but not before she screamed as the device connected.

He was certain that she had woken the target woman inside the bedroom.

Without hesitation Christescu opened the bedroom door and saw that Bridget stood beside her bed and had already pulled on her black dressing gown.

She suddenly turned to see three figures dressed in black, two kneeling and one that stood by the opened door.

Bridget then made eye contact with Christescu.

Her eyes widened and her mouth opened to scream as she saw her friend Olivia slumped on the floor behind them.

Dorin Christescu suddenly fired his shot that thudded into Bridget's chest.

Emil Hagi immediately moved toward the semi-conscious Olivia Fletcher and rolled her over onto her front.

He knew that she was probably fully aware of what was happening as she had not yet slipped into unconsciousness.

Not all of them did.

From the left breast pocket of his black tactical jacket Hagi took two thin black plastic cable ties and pulled Olivia's arms behind her back and fastened them tightly together at her wrists.

Christescu looked up at his still frozen Captain and shook his head before he moved into the bedroom and glanced down at Bridget Oaks.

Her body continued to convulse and her eyes flickered from the effects of 50,000 volts that had just jolted and surged through her.

He knelt beside her as he pulled two cable ties from his left breast pocket and recalled the Captain freezing once before when they were enlisted soldiers of the Romanian army.

Thankfully on that occasion it was during an exercise.

But this wasn't an exercise, this was real.

Christescu knew then that something had to be done about their leader.

Not just because he had once again quite clearly panicked under pressure but also because this house should have been monitored from the moment that the instructions came through to take this woman.

Not these two women.

Barbu didn't have the house under surveillance for three days prior to their arrival for this abduction.

Christescu feared that at some point his lacklustre approach would surely backfire on them.

Today was that point or at least it could have been if not for the quick reactions of Emil Hagi.

Olivia Fletcher was a close friend of Bridget Oaks.

They spoke earlier on the telephone because Bridget was in need of some company and Olivia offered to come and stay while Clive was away at the seminar.

She was simply a victim of circumstance.

She just happened to be there.

Earlier on the day that Bridget and Olivia were taken, Olivia developed a migraine.

It was a common occurrence for her and she had learned over the years that the only way to relieve it was to close her eyes in a fully darkened room.

Olivia Fletcher however arrived at the house twenty four hours after Abel Barbu last checked the address and nobody at Indigo was even aware of her existence.

Twenty Seven
Sunday October 8th 2000

Jade Harris who worked at the high class brothel owned by her friend Carmen Richardson stepped outside the bustling Sloane square underground railway station.

It was just ten minutes walking distance from Carmen's plush flat at the busy Kings road Chelsea.

The painted on freckles across her nose were gone and the only visible blemish was the small dark brown mole just above her upper right lip.

Today she wore a thin cream coloured knitted pullover and tight fitting faded blue denim jeans with brand new white designer training shoes that had a pale pink trim and motif.

Jade grinned as April Marsh followed her out from the station wearing a black leather coat that was too big with blue denim jeans and black flat heeled sandals.

The reason for Jade's grin was the cigarette between April's lips as she tried several times to light it.

"I thought you'd given that up!" Jade said.

April finally lit it and glanced up at her.

"I have so don't you go snitching to her ladyship." She replied.

She referred to thirty four year old Carmen Richardson.

The two women very slowly walked down the Kings road so that April had time to smoke her cigarette and then remove the smell tobacco from her breath using a large bag of peppermint sweets that were hidden inside her jacket pocket.

When they finally reached the junction with Blacklands terrace April dropped her cigarette onto the floor and stepped onto it.

"Remember if she asks you I don't smoke!"

Jade giggled at her short friend's antics.

"Why don't you just tell her that you smoke?" She asked.

"Or actually give it up for real?" She suggested.

As April pressed her finger onto the doorbell she looked up at Jade again.

"I have given up." She replied.

Jade's thin perfectly shaped eyebrows raised.

"I can see that!"

Suddenly the brown door opened and in front of them stood Carmen Richardson dressed in a thin white denim blouse and white denim jeans with the dark brown fluffy slippers that April gave her for Christmas last year.

Carmen immediately glared down at April.

"Have you been smoking?" She asked.

April appeared absolutely horrified that Carmen could even suggest such a thing.

"If I wanted to smoke I would tell you that I smoke and as I don't want to smoke I have nothing to say."

She then pushed past Carmen in the doorway and headed up the narrow staircase.

Carmen stared at Jade.

"She's been smoking hasn't she?"

Jade chuckled.

"I'm pleading the fifth on the grounds that it will definitely incriminate me!" She replied.

Jade then followed Carmen up the stairs.

Inside Carmen's spacious flat she and Jade sat down opposite each other on twin cream coloured leather sofas that were separated by a circular glass coffee table.

April as usual made the coffee in the small kitchen on Jade's right.

"So why have you invited us over for dinner?" Jade asked.

Carmen glanced across at her and smiled.

"I'll explain all later."

April entered the living room with a brown tray with three cups of coffee placed on it.

"What are we having for dinner?" She asked.

"There's nothing cooking in the kitchen and I'm starving!"

Jade giggled while Carmen stared April down.

"If you must know I'm taking you both out to dinner, mouth almighty!" Carmen announced.

"Why not smoke a cigarette while you're waiting?" She sarcastically asked.

Jade suddenly looked disappointed.

"We're going to a restaurant?" She asked.

Carmen nodded.

"I wish you'd said something before we came over?" She sighed.

She tugged on her thin cream coloured pullover but Carmen shrugged.

"You look fine and I'm going like this." She replied.

April now raised her eyebrows.

"You're such a tramp." She told Carmen.

Again Jade started to laugh but Carmen ended the battle of words.

"I'm also paying for it if you'd like to stop digging that hole."

April suddenly had nothing more to say.

A couple of hours later the three women sat inside a restaurant at the other end of the Kings road where they had just finished eating when April announced that she needed some air.

"Don't forget to take your mints." Carmen reminded her.

April again displayed a look of absolute horror that Carmen didn't believe that she had quit smoking.

They had already finished their second bottle of white wine and Carmen ordered a third when Jade looked down at her plate as she pushed the remnants of her food around.

"So what are we celebrating?" She finally asked.

"We're obviously celebrating something."

Carmen was a little drunk and she reached across and squeezed Jade's hand.

"You don't miss a trick do you?" She asked with a giggle.

Jade looked up at her.

"I've got a good teacher." She replied.

Carmen smiled again as she stared back at Jade.

"When the old battle axe comes back I'll make the announcement ok?" She asked.

"I'm fine Car, I just wondered." Jade replied.

"I'm curious more than anything."

Again Carmen squeezed her hand.

"I promise that it's all good news."

But then Carmen watched Jade as she started to giggle.

"What's so funny?" She asked.

Jade looked up at her.

"It's you." The twenty nine year old replied.

"You're such a prat when you're pissed." She laughed.

Carmen's eyes widened.

"You bitch!"

Around ten minutes later April returned to the table and saw that her two friends were laughing.

"What's so funny?" She asked.

They both stared at her.

"There's cigarette ash on your coat." Carmen replied.

April instinctively looked down to see that there was in fact no evidence to incriminate her at all and she looked back up at Carmen.

"If you're not smoking why are you looking for it?" Carmen calmly asked.

She watched April's face redden.

Suddenly Carmen and Jade started to laugh again as April sat down and shook her head.

"I've told you one hundred and seventy six times that I do not smoke." She assured them both.

Jade had of course just a couple of hours earlier walked down the Kings road with her while she puffed away on a cigarette.

When the laughter finally subsided Carmen reached into her beige leather shoulder bag and took out two white unsealed envelopes.

"How do you two feel about quitting the game?" She suddenly asked.

There was a silent pause before Jade looked up at her.

"Are you serious?" She asked.

Carmen nodded with a wry grin.

April continued to stare not quite believing what she had just heard.

"And what else would we do?" She finally asked.

Carmen paused for a few moments before she spoke again.

"Do you remember the letter that you left on the step from the property developer?" She asked.

April shrugged.

"Vaguely, do you mean the hand written one?" She asked.

Carmen nodded.

"Well I went to a meeting with the man that wrote it." She informed April.

April raised her eyebrows.

"I didn't think you wanted to sell up." She reminded Carmen.

Carmen shrugged with a sigh.

"That's never really been the case because if they bought everything but our house I'd end up with a compulsory purchase order and I've always known that." She explained.

"And that would've come with a minimum price for the house at Alpha grove whereas my plan has always been to get the maximum for it."

Jade now glanced up from her half empty plate.

"So what's going to happen now?" She asked.

Carmen grinned back.

"I'm glad you asked." She replied.

"I've already sold them the house at Alpha grove."

Jade glanced across at April before she returned her attention to Carmen.

"So I'll ask again, what happens now?"

Carmen sipped her wine before she continued.

"I'd like to come out of the game and start a brand new legitimate business venture." She said.

"And I've already sort of started it." She added.

Jade nodded without looking up at her best friend.

"To be honest I've been thinking of coming out of the game myself for a while now." She confessed.

Again April raised her eyebrows.

"You have?" She asked.

"And when were you going to tell us?"

Carmen glared across at April.

"When she had decided for definite I would imagine, mouth almighty." She replied on Jade's behalf.

Jade looked up with a smile.

"I've been thinking of opening my own clothes shop." She told Carmen.

Carmen beamed another smile, mostly from relief.

"Well before you decide to go ahead with that why don't listen to what I have to offer you?" She asked.

Carmen explained that she had struck a business deal with Arron Balcombe from the property development company that bought the house at Alpha grove along with just about every other property in the area.

The bizarre business arrangement involved not only the sale of her house at Alpha grove but he also offered her a position in management running her own business in partnership with Balcombe & Webb Property Developments.

Hers was on the renting and leasing side of the business.

He also offered her offices with a plush apartment above at the exclusive area of Mayfair.

Jade chuckled although she remained quite un-phased by this huge deal.

"I dread to think how you did all of that." She commented.

She then received a playful light punch on her upper arm from Carmen.

"You cow!"

"The problem that Arron Balcombe has or rather did have was that his own giant company has a reputation of swallowing up entire areas." Carmen explained.

"They have hundreds of single properties that they have trouble renting and leasing all over London." She continued.

"C R Properties will be taking over that side of things on their behalf." She added.

Jade raised her eyebrows.

"Who are C R Properties?" She asked.

Carmen grinned and then again squeezed Jade's hand.

"That's us baby, try to keep up." She chuckled.

Eventually she continued.

"Why don't you come and work for me in the properties market?" She asked.

Jade was already shaking her head before Carmen had finished asking.

"But you have a talent like no other." Carmen assured her.

Jade once again looked up into her eyes.

"I do?" She asked.

Carmen broke into a broad grin.

"You could charm the knickers off a nun!" She laughed.

Jade laughed but after a few moments she shook her head.

"If it's ok with you I'm going to go for it with my clothes shop idea." She said.

Carmen smiled again.

"And we'll support you every step of the way." She assured her.

April now nodded with full agreement.

Carmen now glanced across at April.

"You have to come with me because if I don't keep an eye on you, you'll smoke yourself to death!" She said.

April sighed.

"How charming are you?"

April now looked to be quite thoughtful as Jade and Carmen chatted about Jade's clothes shop idea.

"So how much did you sell the house at Alpha grove for?" April eventually asked.

Carmen glanced over at her.

"Did you suddenly become my financial advisor?" She asked.

April poked out her tongue.

Carmen slid one of the unsealed white envelopes across the table to April and she immediately opened it and found a cheque from Carmen's account made out to her for the sum of one hundred thousand pounds.

Carmen watched April's eyes widen.

"So what's this for?" She asked.

"Call it severance pay." Carmen replied.

She then slid the second envelope in the direction of Jade.

Jade again glanced up at her.

"Car what the hell do you know about property development?" She asked.

She slid the envelope back.

"It's your money, it was your house I'm ok." She insisted.

"I did ok." Carmen whispered.

Again she reached into her beige leather shoulder bag while Jade displayed a look of confusion.

She looked up at Jade again.

"Arron Balcombe is of the firm belief that he'd prefer to have me on his side and not as his competitor." She explained.

Jade nodded.

"But my question still stands, what do you know about property development?" She asked.

April Marsh nodded in agreement with Jade.

Carmen smiled again as she showed Jade and April her little black book that contained the details and information of every client that she had ever had over the past fifteen years.

"I know nothing of the property business." She replied.

"Well not much anyway." She added.

"But I have these people." She continued.

She gently tapped the tip of Jade's nose with the little black book.

"And between them they know everything about everything and if they don't, you can bet that they know somebody that does." She said with a beaming grin.

Jade stared into Carmen's eyes and eventually she grinned.

"You're such a devious bitch!" She chuckled.

Carmen winked with a grin.

She then slid the envelope back toward Jade.

"I got four million for the house at Alpha grove." She discretely whispered.

Jade raised her eyebrows.

"Shut up!" She whispered back.

Carmen still grinned as she slowly nodded her head.

April also stared wide eyed after hearing what Carmen had just revealed.

"And I only get a lousy hundred grand?" She asked.

Carmen and Jade both turned and stared at April.

"Unbelievable." Jade uttered with a chuckle.

Twenty Eight
Monday October 9th 2000

Russian Vladimir Kolov sat inside the study at his rented house at Oakland's avenue Ponders end.

He wore a white open necked shirt and blue denim jeans with black slippers on his feet.

He ran his thick fingers through his bushy beard as he read yesterday's edition of his Russian newspaper.

His beautiful and much younger former model wife Inna who was solely responsible for the murder of Dawn Sheppard inside the basement beneath the closed down high street giant store at Folkestone Kent appeared in the opened doorway.

She watched her husband for a few moments until the dark haired beauty eventually spoke.

"Vladimir, when do you take these girls away from our house?" She asked him in English.

Vladimir and his wife only spoke in English regarding the true purpose for them being in the UK because their two small children that were just at the kitchen table spoke and understood only their native Russian.

He looked up from his newspaper.

"The doctor comes to see them tomorrow and after I will have them taken to the warehouse." He promised.

Inna sighed.

"It is wrong to keep them in the same house as the children." She told him.

Again he looked up from his newspaper.

"Inna the children are in the kitchen are they not?" He asked.

Inna didn't respond she only stared back at him.

"The women are in the basement, do you remember to keep the basement door locked always?" He asked.

She nodded.

"But still I don't like them here Vladimir." She told him again.

Again he nodded.

"When the doctor has been, I will have them taken to the warehouse." He assured her again.

He stared back down at his newspaper.

Inna stood up straight from the door frame and said nothing as she headed back toward the kitchen to play with their two children.

Outside the house stood a parked silver Ford car and the two occupants in the front seats stared directly toward the house.

"Not really what you'd expect for a Russian diplomat is it?" Detective Inspector Nicola Garwood asked.

Detective Sergeant Jacob Saunders shook his head with agreement before he turned to Nicola.

"Can I just point out again that we're strictly forbidden to approach Vladimir Kolov?" He asked.

Nicola glanced at him with a half-smile.

"Run this by me one more time Jacob." She began.

She opened her notepad.

"Describe the only car at New Inn Yard at the time of Amy Hadlow's disappearance at approximately one thirty six on the morning of Thursday the twenty first of September." She said.

She prompted Saunders to respond.

Jacob sighed and without looking up from the floor of the car.

He pointed toward the rented black Jaguar that was parked on Kolov's drive.

"It was that one." He finally replied.

Nicola smiled.

"So we're just going to knock on the door and be really polite and just speak to him, ok?" She asked.

"Stop worrying I have everything under control." She assured him.

As she opened the driver side door and climbed out she stopped and again smiled across at Jacob.

"Look, we just going to ask a couple of informal questions and it won't even be brought to anybody's attention."

That gave Jacob no more confidence with what he was about to do.

They were about to disobey a direct order from none other than the Chief Inspector of the entire task force, Martin Roberts himself.

"I think I might travel Europe." Jacob uttered.

"As soon as we're both fired that is." He added beneath his breath.

He then climbed out of the car too.

Kolov opened the front door of the rented house and saw a man and woman standing on his doorstep and he immediately knew that they were police officers.

Nicola smiled.

"Good morning Sir." She began.

She showed him her warrant card and Saunders reluctantly briefly did the same.

"We're in the area conducting door to door enquiries." She told him.

Kolov raised his eyebrows with a warm smile.

"How can I help you Detective Inspector?" He asked.

Garwood courteously smiled at him again.

"Well Sir we checked out the car on your drive and discovered who you are and what you do for a living." She began.

"And a Russian diplomat obviously isn't involved in the reason we're knocking on doors in the area." She continued.

"We're looking for a missing young girl." She added.

"Somebody called the station to say that they thought that they saw her just around the corner at Oakland's drive so we're knocking on all of the doors in the area to see if anybody can verify this claim."

Nicola held the same courteous smile.

Kolov raised his eyebrows again.

"Do you mean that a missing girl has been walking around here?" He asked.

Nicola nodded.

"Not actually here at Oakland's avenue itself but around the corner in Oakland's drive sir." She lied again.

Kolov broke into another smile.

"Please, come inside." He insisted.

Garwood smiled again as she passed him in the doorway followed by a very reluctant Detective Sergeant Jacob Saunders.

As they followed Kolov into the living room he turned to face them.

"How did you know that I was diplomat?" He asked.

Garwood smiled again.

"Earlier this week we were following a different lead at New Inn Yard at Shoreditch." She replied.

"Your car was seen by a speed camera at Shoreditch high street leaving the scene and at that time the vehicle registration was taken but we've since solved that case." She lied again.

Jacob Saunders watched Kolov's body language and reaction to Garwood's lies.

Nicola glanced back at Saunders before she continued with her untruthful explanation to the huge Russian.

"We had no idea about the issue at New Inn Yard but when a check was carried out on your car when we arrived this morning we were informed that it was there at that time." She told him.

"But like I said the missing girl at Shoreditch was found." She lied again.

Kolov offered them both a seat before he called out to the kitchen for his wife.

Inna entered a short while after and she smiled at Garwood and Saunders.

"Can I offer you tea or coffee?" She asked.

They both declined.

"Then please excuse me I must stay with our children because they are very young." She told them.

She smiled once more before she returned to the kitchen.

Vladimir Kolov was more than aware of the real reason for their visit.

He purposely called his wife in to meet them just to make her aware of their presence because of course they only spoke about business in front of their children in English.

He didn't want her to walk into the room and ask the same question that she did in the study a short while ago at the study.

Regardless of the fact that Garwood was being very warm and courteous toward Kolov there was still an incredibly tense atmosphere inside the room.

Inna Kolov stood just beside the kitchen door and listened.

Garwood started to explain to Kolov that they were from the recently assembled task force investigating the case of now over one thousand missing homeless people.

"But the young girl that you must have passed at New Inn Yard Shoreditch was found." She explained again.

Although confused, Vladimir Kolov smiled.

"The girl in New Inn Yard was found so again I'd like to point out that this is a completely unrelated case." She told him yet again.

She continued to refer back to the particular night in question while completely vindicating Kolov, keeping him on his guard at all times because she knew that was how mistakes were made.

Garwood was hoping for just one slip of the tongue, one error, because something just didn't feel right here.

Kolov looked thoughtful for a few moments.

"This girl at the New Inn Yard she had, how do you say this word?" He began.

He looked to be asking himself and then glanced up at Garwood.

"Her hair was the same colour as yours." He said.

Garwood took her long blonde ponytail in her hand and showed him.

"Do you mean blonde?" She asked.

Kolov nodded.

"That is right blonde I am afraid that my English is not so good." He told her.

Garwood smiled.

"Yes her hair was blonde." She replied.

Kolov knew that they knew that he must have at least seen Amy Hadlow at New Inn Yard that night.

"Yes I remember this girl." He said.

"She was talking into her telephone when I drove past her." He continued.

"I don't like to stop because London is very dangerous place at night." He added in his new found broken English.

Garwood agreed with him.

"Yes it is."

There was a short pause of silence before she began again.

"Just out of curiosity, was she alone or with somebody?" She asked.

"When we finally found her she was with three friends." She lied again.

Kolov seemed to recall the night in question and decided to now choose his words carefully.

"I do not recall." He eventually replied.

Nicola thanked him again for his time and apologised for any inconvenience that they may have caused but Kolov shook his head.

"I am sorry that I cannot help you Detective Inspector." He replied.

"I hope that you find this young girl that you seek."

Five or six minutes later back in the silver Ford car Jacob Saunders made an observation.

"Guv I don't condone what we just did but he was lying through his teeth." He told Nicola.

She raised her eyebrows.

"What makes you say that?" She asked as she started the engine.

Saunders glanced across at her.

"His English got progressively worse." He replied.

Garwood nodded.

"He didn't want to have the ability to answer you properly." Jacob added.

Again Nicola nodded.

"I know."

"And he recalled seeing Amy Hadlow on her phone but he couldn't remember if she was standing with anybody." She reminded Saunders.

Now he nodded.

"Not forgetting of course that Amy's friend Gemma Clifford insisted that Amy didn't have a phone." He added.

"And Kolov just said that she was talking on one."

Again Nicola nodded as she slowly drove along Oakland's avenue.

As they headed back toward central London Jacob Saunders watched Nicola grin.

"What's so funny?" He asked.

Nicola turned to him.

"I'm just curious as to why he never mentioned his diplomatic immunity." She replied.

Saunders looked confused.

"Why would he want to if he was playing innocent?" He asked.

Garwood again glanced across at Jacob.

"Because my dear boy he isn't a diplomat and he has no diplomatic immunity." She revealed.

"And yet when I referred to him as a diplomat he didn't refute it."

Neither of them could have possibly known that Amy Hadlow and three more women lay on a cold concrete basement floor right beneath their feet bound and unconscious.

Nicola held a polite and civilised conversation with their captor Vladimir Kolov and his wife.

She was so close.

From high in the sky Nicola and Jacob were watched by David Stringer from Tranton road Bermondsey via several passing French spy satellites.

"Let's look into you then, comrade Kolov." David said to his monitor.

Twenty Nine
Friday October 13th 2000

It was just after six in the evening when Detective Inspector Sam Henning climbed off the packed underground train at Baker Street station.

He then walked for five or six minutes to the very heavily congested Marylebone mainline station.

Inside he stepped into a privately owned wine bar called Constantine's.

Constantine's was quiet in comparison to the mania outside in the mainline Marylebone station and Sam's eyes slowly scanned the spacious dimly lit bar with soft gold lighting and quiet pipe music.

He was looking for somebody in particular as he stood in the quiet din of multiple conversations from the thirty or so people that sat at tables around him.

Sam's eyes continued to search when a young woman with blonde hair that stood at around five feet five and wore a white cotton blouse and a knee length black skirt approached him.

There was a brief conversation between them as Sam's eyes continued to scan before he spotted the person that he was here to meet with and then he smiled down at the pretty young waitress.

"Can I have two pints of your best bitter and two whiskey chasers over there?" He pointed.

"Of course, I'll bring them over." She replied.

Fifty three year old Chief Inspector Keith Curtis sat alone at a small circular table in an alcove next to the dark tinted windows that looked out at the manically busy Marylebone station.

He was five feet eight inches tall and had a large round frame as a result of far too many meetings just like this one with Sam.

He had grey rapidly thinning hair and wore a dark grey crumpled suit with a lighter grey shirt with an open necked collar and as he finished his second pint of the hour he looked up to see Sam approaching.

"Hello guv." Sam grinned.

The two men shook hands.

"What the bloody hell are you doing on this task force thing with just a few months left until you retire?" Curtis asked.

Sam shrugged.

"It beats me guv." He replied.

"How's the yard?"

Curtis chuckled.

"I finish a month after you so they pretty much leave me alone."

Sam laughed too.

"I bet they do!"

It was no secret that throughout his long and quite illustrious career Keith Curtis had issues with people in general but in particular with those in positions of authority.

Especially with those directly above him.

Sam could testify to this as Curtis was his boss at Acton CID for eight years before he was promoted and transferred to the famous New Scotland Yard.

The waitress arrived at their table and placed onto it two pints of best bitter and two whiskey chasers and Sam handed her a twenty pound note.

He then stared at the small amount of cash that she gave him back as change.

Curtis immediately supped on his fresh pint as the waitress disappeared.

"So is this a social call or what Sam?" He asked.

Sam took in a deep breath and sighed.

"It's a bit of both really guv." He replied.

Curtis immediately grinned.

"So you're not only here just for my sparkling personality then?" He asked.

He mocked a grin and Sam chuckled.

Sam started by explaining everything that he discovered including the very private correspondence to and from Chief Inspector Martin Roberts back at the task force headquarters.

He went on to explain about the discovered etching on Robert's personal and private note pad.

"I know for certain that what he scribbled in that book left the building." He told Curtis.

He went on to note that on that top page was coincidentally the address and information regarding the safe house at Caterham where Denise Ruane and her friends were abducted.

Curtis pondered for a few moments before he stared back at Sam.

"Roberts is a slimy little bastard at the best of times." He said.

He continued to consider what Sam was implying.

"But involved in this human trafficking lark?" He asked.

"I can't see it mate."

Sam nodded with a sigh.

Curtis then drank his entire pint of ale while Sam responded.

"I can't see it either guv but there are four of us that know the exact locations of all the safe houses and the cameras including the one that was waiting to go up at New Inn Yard." He explained.

"And he's one of the four."

There was a brief pause before Sam continued.

"I was actually hoping that you might know of a way that I could eliminate him from suspicion." He said.

Curtis nodded with a sigh.

"I saw the New Inn Yard incident on the news." He said.

He then glanced down at his empty glass.

"I could probably think better with another drink."

Sam chuckled.

"I'll get them in."

He climbed to his feet and headed to the bar for his former boss's refill.

"This is just like the old days!" He uttered beneath his breath.

It was six or seven minutes before he returned to the alcove to see that Keith Curtis just ended a call on his phone.

He glanced up at Sam as he returned it to his inside jacket pocket.

"Ok listen up." He began.

"I'm finding you another safe house." He explained.

"When I get it in a couple of days you inform nobody but Roberts of its existence." He told Sam.

Sam visibly cringed at the thought of hiding this from Nicola Garwood and Curtis could see it on his face.

"And I mean you tell nobody Sam, not even that Garwood woman." He re-emphasised.

Sam nodded with a sigh.

"I know guv."

Curtis now leaned across the table.

"If you want Roberts properly eliminated from suspicion he has to be the only other person in the world that knows that this new house exists."

Eventually Sam nodded again.

"I understand." He replied.

Thirty
Monday October 16th 2000

It was just after nine on a dry but cloudy morning when the pale green Aston Martin that Carmen Richardson owned pulled up outside the new office building at Mount Street Mayfair that was supplied by Mr Arron Balcombe.

She sat in the driver seat for a few moments and stared at her large new building.

"Well here's to new starts." She quietly uttered.

Beside her sat April Marsh holding a large yellow plastic bucket and between her feet was another.

Both were full of cleaning detergents because to Carmen's dismay April insisted on cleaning this property herself as opposed to her own idea of employing a professional cleaning company.

Two days ago when Carmen merely suggested it April showed her a look of utter horror.

"Excuse me?" She asked.

"I can clean better than any bloody professional company!" She insisted.

Carmen sighed as she shook her head.

"You know something?" She began.

"You're right you're the best scrubber in London."

April didn't quite catch the gist of Carmen's snipe and she agreed with a smile.

"I know!"

Carmen stepped out from her car that was parked in her new allocated private space and began to climb the six stone steps up to the large dark green panelled door.

April was still back at the car unloading her two yellow buckets and she began to carry the heavy loads toward the steps.

At the top there were two large stone pillars and Carmen leaned against one as she scrutinised the key bunch because although she had been here twice before, on both occasions she was with Arron Balcombe.

She now pondered on which keys to use as there were two separate locks in the door but half a dozen keys.

At the bottom of the steps April stood holding her two heavy buckets and stared up at Carmen.

"You could help me if you like?" She suggested.

Carmen didn't take her eyes of the key bunch as she made her decision.

"I'm fine thanks." She called back.

She slipped one key into the upper lock in the green door and successfully turned it.

"That's one down and one to go." She quietly told herself.

April continued to stare up at her.

"What do you mean no?" She asked.

"This is your bloody building we're cleaning." She reminded Carmen.

Carmen turned and looked down at her friend still holding her two full and heavy buckets.

"What do you mean, we?" She asked.

"You wanted to clean the place to save money remember?" She asked.

"I'm not cleaning anything."

April's eyes widened as she stared up at Carmen with shock.

"Are you saying I've got to do this all on my own?" She asked.

Carmen grinned as she turned and slipped the second key into the lock and turned it and the door opened.

"No you could call a proper cleaning company and get them in to do it if you like."

She stepped inside leaving April to struggle up the stone steps toward the now opened green door.

Carmen deactivated the alarm system and as she climbed the steps April adamantly shook her head.

"Not on your nelly!" April uttered.

Carmen strolled down the long darkened corridor and she secretly grinned.

"Now you know why I keep you around." She replied.

April was now wheezing out of breath as she reached the top step.

She watched Carmen turning as she glanced around in the musty smelling hallway.

"So where are you going to live?" She enquired.

Carmen pointed one finger upward.

"There's an apartment right at the top." She replied.

April continued to stare at her.

"That's where we should start." She finally responded.

Again Carmen chuckled to herself.

"Why do you keep saying we?" She asked.

Not for the first time April sighed.

"Ok so where's the lift?" She asked.

Carmen turned to her.

"What lift?" She asked.

April suddenly dropped the buckets onto the floor and stared back at her.

"So I've got to climb god knows how many stairs to clean your poxy flat?" She asked.

Carmen nodded with a grin.

"You don't buy a dog and bark yourself do you?" She asked in response.

April's eyes widened at her remark.

"This is so not worth a hundred thousand!" She uttered to herself.

Carmen chuckled.

"Anyway, while you're busy here I'm going over to Walworth." She said.

April continued to stare.

"What do you want to go to Walworth for?" She asked.

Carmen turned to face her again.

"Jade's getting started on her new shop today and I'd like to go over and see if I can help clean it."

April shook her head with disbelief.

"So you won't help me clean your building but you're going to Walworth to help clean hers?" She asked.

Carmen nodded as she continued to glance around the hall.

"I have a funny feeling that for some reason it'll be much more peaceful in Walworth."

Again April's eyes widened and her mouth opened before she made her final comment.

"You bitch!" She uttered.

Carmen nodded with a smile.

"But it takes one to know one sweetie."

Thirty One
Monday October 16th 2000

The other former high class prostitute Jade Harris pulled up in her red Ford car at New Kent road Walworth south London.

She stared at the horrid brown coloured shop front across the manically busy road.

She had been here just once before with Carmen but they were talking when they pulled up on that day and walked straight into the shop.

Today Jade was paying more attention to the detail that she was staring at now.

"The first job on the list is to get somebody to sort out the shop front." She quietly uttered with disgust.

She glanced above the shop where there was a two bedroomed flat that came with it.

She would at some point in the not too distant future live there or at least start to move some of her belongings in.

Jade was dressed for a day of working in a short blue denim jacket and a pale lilac coloured t-shirt along with tight fitting faded blue denim jeans and pale blue training shoes on her feet.

She vaguely recalled the vast quantity of shelves on the walls inside the shop due to it being a pet supply store before its former owners went out of business.

Today she dismissed that dreadful image because she had specific plans.

When she climbed out of the car as heavy traffic sped past in both directions to and from the city of London she crossed New Kent road and headed toward a large dark brown door to the right of the glass shop front and unlocked it.

She opened the door and pushed it forward brushing a large pile of old mail into the wall.

She stared up at the threadbare burgundy carpet on the narrow staircase that led up to the flat.

Jade removed her phone from her back pocket and made a call to one of the suppliers that she researched.

"Hi am I right in thinking that you do shop front sign writing?" She asked.

She climbed the stairs toward her new flat.

"Good could you come and do an estimate for me?" She asked.

There was another pause as she listened to a response.

"I already know exactly what I want and how I want it thanks." She replied.

When she reached the top of the staircase she turned left onto a narrow musty smelling corridor with two closed doors on her right and three on the left.

The first door on the right was the darkened windowless bathroom and she remembered from her last visit that a new shower head was needed.

She opened the white door on her left directly opposite the bathroom and immediately recalled the small spare bedroom that was badly painted in yellow and grey with a dark brown carpet on the floor.

"Oh my good lord no!" She uttered.

She quickly closed the door again.

Eventually, after checking each room she found herself in the kitchen that was behind the only other door on the right.

She discovered that three pine cupboard doors hung from single hinges and the kitchen was in a better condition than the living room opposite from where she just fled.

Her new flat above the shop was worse than she recalled but Jade saw it as a start, a brand new start and she knew that it wouldn't look like this when she was finished with it.

An hour or so later Jade stood inside the shop below where she very slowly turned full circle and stared in disbelief at the vast quantity of short pine shelves that were very badly fixed onto every single wall.

"I'm sure there weren't this many!" She quietly uttered to herself.

She stood in front of the old serving counter and like the shop front outside the interior was decorated in a dark chocolate brown.

"What on earth were you thinking?" She asked out loud.

She stopped and looked past the serving counter toward the horrid small bright yellow kitchenette.

Past it was the toilet that she was too afraid to investigate today based on the fact that Carmen chose not to show it the last time that they were here.

However none of this really mattered to Jade.

She knew that this was going to be her initial reaction because when she viewed it with Carmen she saw it in this condition but she also saw the potential.

In Jade's opinion Carmen had chosen wisely.

There were two girl's schools in the area and her plan was to provide teenage fashion accessories and the latest fashion clothing for the discerning thirteen to seventeen year old girls of south London.

She spun around when the tiny bell above the door tinkled.

Carmen Richardson entered wearing a short brown leather jacket and white denim jeans with a turquoise blouse beneath the jacket.

"Well?" She asked with a smile.

Jade smiled back and nodded.

"I love it!" She honestly replied.

Jade looked beyond Carmen because wherever there was Carmen there was April but the plump short woman was nowhere to be seen.

"Where's the old hag?" She asked.

Carmen now slowly turned full circle while she stared at the vast amount of shelves and she also couldn't recall there being this many.

"Do those things mate and reproduce?" She asked as she pointed.

Carmen stepped toward the counter and placed her brown leather bag on top and removed her phone.

"Oh she's at my new place cleaning."

She dialled a number and then waited for the recipient to pick up.

"I made a point of pissing her off before I came here." She added.

She waited for an answer on her phone.

"You know what she does when she's pissed."

Jade nodded with a grin.

"She goes on a cleaning rampage." She replied with a giggle.

Carmen nodded as she spoke into her phone.

"Arron, could I be a pain and borrow one of your maintenance men?" She asked.

"I'm at Jade's shop at Walworth."

"No it's the shelves they're multiplying." She told Arron Balcombe.

Carmen then smiled.

"Why thank you, I'll see you at dinner tonight." She finished.

Jade stared and after Carmen ended the call she grinned.

"Now it's all beginning to make sense!" She chuckled.

Carmen smiled as she placed her phone back into her bag.

"How many times do I have to tell you?" She asked.

"It's not what you know or even who you know." She explained.

"It's actually what you know about who you know." She told Jade with a grin and a wink.

Jade shook her head with disbelief.

"And you think it's me that could charm the knickers off a nun?"

Thirty Two
Monday October 16th 2000

At Tranton road Bermondsey the roof of the large steel shed in the back garden slowly electronically opened.

From inside his converted office bedroom David Stringer scrutinised one of his monitors on the left side of the room as he finished the remains of last night's cold pizza delivery.

On the screen he watched a young girl that had just left the residence of Jane Chapman at Glade road Watford.

David had not seen this girl arrive at the house and he had been watching it for most of the morning courtesy of several passing overhead satellites.

"I wonder who you are."

He finally watched the girl arrive at nearby town of Pinner south of Watford.

At Pinner she delivered a paper note by hand at the door and then she left.

He watched her then board another bus and followed it as another of his computers identified the owner of the address at Pinner as freelance photographer Lisa Moore.

After detailed research David discovered that Lisa Moore previously worked as a photographer for the same web design company where Jane Chapman previously worked as a web designer.

"Well this is interesting, a new player." He said to himself.

He still had no clue as to the identity of the young girl that delivered the note but he had just learned of the existence of Lisa Moore.

The unknown girl wore a red coat which meant that she would be easy to pick up when she eventually climbed off the bus and her final destination could be the key to discovering her identity.

Stringer tied Jane Chapman to Lisa Moore and the fact that even he could find absolutely no electronic communication between them meant that this young girl was most probably acting as a runner, a message carrier.

"But where are you going now?" He asked.

He watched her second journey by bus.

It was more than forty minutes before the girl in the red coat climbed off the bus at Amersham just west of Watford.

She arrived at a second address where she handed over a second note but this time she entered the house.

Stringer patiently waited for her to leave the palatial house at Amersham.

After a while he concluded that she originally came from the plush address and lived there and that he had somehow missed her arrival at the home of Jane Chapman at Watford earlier.

He researched the house and learned that it was owned by Debbie Davies.

He couldn't link Davies to Jane Chapman in any way but after a short while found just what he was looking for.

She was linked to Lisa Moore.

She had been married to Lisa's brother but he and Debbie Davies divorced some years ago and she reverted back to her maiden name.

"So Lisa Moore brought you in?"

He stared at the DVLA photograph of Debbie Davies and he now knew that she definitely wasn't the girl in the red coat.

A short while later Stringer had what he called a black spot.

It was a period of precisely twenty three minutes that the current satellite passed out of range and he had to wait for the next.

Eventually he backtracked everywhere that he viewed before.

"Let's hope she didn't move." He said with a sigh referring to the girl in the red coat.

Most would have missed her not David Stringer.

He switched from the address at Amersham owned by Davies to the main bus station at Watford due to a hunch that this additional new player, the unknown girl in the red coat never arrived at the house of Jane Chapman to begin with that morning.

She had been there all along.

His hunch and perseverance paid off as he watched her climb off the bus at Watford and return to the very same address.

"So you live at Chapman's house?"

He had no idea who this girl was but did know how to find out.

David picked up his telephone.

"Hello mate, I need you to get me a DNA sample." He told Richard Willows.

"I can get the lab to tell me who she is." He replied to Richard's question.

Thirty Three
Wednesday October 18th 2000

Detective Inspector Nicola Garwood quietly closed the door after leaving the office of Chief Inspector Martin Roberts.

Jacob Saunders stood outside in the busy corridor.

"Are you ok guv?" He asked.

She nodded with a grin.

"It's not what you know Jacob it's who you know." She replied.

Jacob responded with a look of confusion.

Both Garwood and Saunders were called to the chief after ignoring his specific instructions to refrain from approaching Vladimir Kolov.

But the chief saw it as Garwood disobeying a direct order and a means to a productive end as far as she was concerned after he discovered that the pair had visited the home of the Russian.

Chief Inspector Roberts attempted to have Nicola Garwood suspended from duty pending disciplinary action.

Garwood however contacted Sir Christopher Dwyer at his office at John Islip Street Westminster on the morning of October 9th prior to visiting the Russian.

Today was nine days later and it gave Sir Christopher plenty of time to prepare for the oncoming storm from Nicola's boss.

Sir Christopher was already fully aware of Vladimir Kolov and his quite pointless role within the Russian embassy but more importantly he was also fully aware of Kolov's dealings in various other European countries.

He knew that Kolov's position did not offer him the same diplomatic immunity as a full diplomat.

When Nicola Garwood privately called him after her warning from the chief, Sir Christopher told her to go ahead and approach Kolov because he was more than interested to see just how this played out.

"It's not what you know Jacob it's who you know."

When Garwood and Saunders were initially called into the office Nicola insisted that Saunders was not inside the ops room when the chief categorically instructed her not to approach Kolov.

She also explained that Saunders was not aware that Kolov was a diplomat with full immunity which of course she knew that Kolov in fact was not.

Based on that information Roberts had no choice but to dismiss Saunders.

The Detective Sergeant waited outside for Nicola and heard the loud rants from the chief from outside in the corridor.

Garwood informed the Chief Inspector that she didn't realise that she was outside Kolov's house and knocked on his door just as she had other residents at Oakland's avenue and that it was a genuine mistake.

This of course had no bearing on what the chief wanted to achieve with regard to her and he knew full well that she hadn't once told him the truth as she stood in his office.

Earlier that morning when Roberts telephoned Sir Christopher himself and demanded her immediate suspension the well-versed politician won that debate too.

Sir Christopher was already fully aware of Kolov and his flimsy diplomatic status before his name had even cropped up in this investigation.

He was also aware that should this come to light the Russian embassy at Kensington palace gardens would very quickly disassociate from Kolov.

Saunders thanked Nicola for covering for him as they headed toward the wide staircase that lead up to the first floor.

"But I was ready to take one for the team guv." He told her.

Garwood nodded with a smile.

"I know that Jacob." She replied.

"Or I would've told him that it was all your idea."

Nicola continued to grin as she and Jacob headed up the stairs toward the ops room.

"Guv what's so funny?" Saunders eventually asked.

He swiped his card into the white box and then pushed the door open for her to enter.

Nicola stopped to face him.

"We both agreed at the time that Kolov was lying didn't we?" She asked.

Saunders nodded.

"I'm just wondering how the chief even knew that we'd been to Kolov's house." She continued.

"I already checked with the front desk and there's been no official complaint made by Kolov or his embassy." She added.

Jacob pondered on her question for a few moments.

"Could Kolov have told him personally?" He asked.

"Strange for somebody who was as keen to help as Kolov was, wouldn't you say?" She asked.

She continued toward the cubicle office leaving Saunders to ponder more.

"How does a Russian crook even know the number for the boss of the task force to be able call him Jacob?" Garwood asked as she walked away.

Saunders still stood and considered.

"Ok so where did Kolov get his number from then?" He asked.

Jacob hoped that she had the answer to the same question that she herself had just asked.

Nicola only turned her head and glanced back at him with raised eyebrows but she said nothing.

"Wait because that's absolutely insane." Jacob called out.

Inside the cubicle office Sam Henning had just been informed that two women were reported missing two days ago from Wembley.

He informed Nicola before she even sat down.

"Was it a squat?" She asked.

Sam shook his head.

"Bridget Oakes is a professional and she joint owns a brand new house at Norton road." He replied.

"She's exceptionally beautiful and it doesn't look like there were problems at home." He informed her.

Nicola sat down as Jacob entered the office and closed the door behind him.

"Who reported them as missing?" She asked.

"Her partner and he's been away at a business seminar and never left there at any time." Sam replied.

There was a pause before he continued.

"I think that we have one group of traffickers possibly taking two types of people." He suggested.

Nicola instinctively shook her head.

"I understand about the homeless because they're easy to take as most of them are either drunk or smashed out of their faces on drugs so that one makes a bit of sense." She pointed out.

"But why risk taking people from their homes that would be missed?" She asked.

"It doesn't make sense Sam."

"It makes sense if you truly believe that you're never going to get caught." Sam replied.

Saunders looked thoughtful for a moment before he spoke.

"Maybe we're looking at this the wrong way." He suggested.

Sam looked intrigued but Nicola was still dismissive of the theory.

"How do you mean?" Sam asked.

Saunders thought it through some more before he spoke again.

"Well guv if your theory is right maybe the pretty women are the real targets and the homeless are extra income or a diversion?" He suggested.

Sam pondered before he shook his head.

"The French Spanish Portuguese and Greek are all experiencing the same problem with their homeless so we know that's international." He replied.

Jacob nodded.

"And maybe so is the situation with the attractive women." He retorted.

"After all right now it's just a theory here and maybe you're right but maybe it's going on in other countries too but they're just not saying anything or haven't worked it out yet." He added.

"Let's face it we're not entirely sure either."

Sam glanced up at Nicola.

"Talking of theories can you do something for me?" He asked.

Nicola glanced up at him.

It was now Sam's turn to choose his words carefully.

He asked if he was correct in thinking that in a week's time she would change the pre-organised roster that determined what officers would supervise particular safe houses and which houses would be left unmanned.

Garwood nodded.

"It's next Wednesday why?" She asked.

Sam looked down at his desk.

"It's just a process of elimination that I'm working on." He replied.

"Is there a chance that you could revise it today?" He asked.

There was a pause before Garwood raised her eyebrows.

"You want it done today?" She asked.

Sam nodded with a hopeful smile.

"Could you?"

Nicola glanced across at Jacob and he nodded with anticipation of what she was going to say.

"I'll get started on it now." He said with a sigh.

Nicola grinned.

"Thanks Jacob."

It took Jacob Saunders over four hours to revise the supervision of the safe houses but it enabled Sam to walk downstairs later that day to the office of the still disgruntled Chief Inspector Martin Roberts.

"Sir I brought the revisions down." Sam said.

He handed over the new paperwork to the chief.

Roberts glanced up over his glasses.

"When will this revision come into effect?" He asked.

"The changes take place the day after tomorrow Sir." Sam replied.

He could see that the chief was still livid and he doubted that it was only because Nicola visited Kolov but probably more because she was still here and that his hands were politically tied.

Sam recalled that beforehand Sir Christopher made his own assurances to protect Nicola.

The chief waved the paperwork at Sam.

"I'll dispose of it correctly later and remember I want no electronic correspondence with these details attached." He reminded Sam.

"As soon as it goes out into the atmosphere there's no telling who can read it."

So far Sam knew that the chief had written the information on his notepad and it left the building for some unknown reason on the very first occasion.

He also knew that the chief had ensured that nothing pointed in his direction via emails and other electronic correspondence.

This meant that there was absolutely nothing evidential in black and white other than Sam's own handwriting.

This was precisely why he asked Nicola to bring the revisions forward a week early.

He laid bait for the chief to eliminate him from suspicion and now he waited for a bite.

It was a bite that he genuinely hoped would not be taken.

Sam needed to rule out the Chief Inspector of the task force from his enquiries however ridiculous that notion was.

But evidence and facts were evidence and facts.

Thirty Four
Wednesday November 1st 2000

Jade Harris had moved a few of her belongings into the flat above the shop at New Kent Road Walworth but nothing yet of any value.

Yesterday the sign writers finished after working for three days and completed the brand new shop front.

Now in place of the drab chocolate brown was a facia with her new shop name emblazoned in large shiny gold letters that protruded from a deep purple background.

Jasmine Fashions

She still had so much to do both upstairs inside her new flat and down in the shop where an employee from Balcombe and Webb had at least removed the one hundred and twenty six horrid pine shelves.

Jade had started painting but because she still had so much to do to open her shop and for it to be possible for her to live upstairs a local painter and decorator was due to start work at the beginning of next week.

She had at least now registered her company name and *Jasmine Fashions* was the name that she always intended to call her enterprise.

When the sign writers finished outside Jade stood for over an hour staring up at the new signage above and imagined what it would be like in a few months from now when business actually started.

She even considered a grand opening day but she was still undecided on that one.

"Just wait until you see this missy." She whispered.

She stared up at the new signwriting with a beaming grin.

New carpets already arrived and a deep burgundy was laid throughout the flat upstairs but she was still undecided on the floor downstairs inside the shop.

But up in the flat the kitchen cupboards had been replaced and for Jade this was a major victory because just being able to close them without them falling off was a major step in the right direction.

On the work surface was a booklet with samples of linoleum for the kitchen floor that she was also still undecided upon.

April loaned her a sofa bed that was in the living room and it would do for now but the sooner she had her flat the way she wanted it the sooner she could settle and maybe then she might be able to sleep properly.

Right now sleep seemed to be impossible.

It was 2:37am and Jade lay in her makeshift bed.

Her eyes were wide open because she had a hundred and one things running around inside her head and this was the third night that she experienced trouble sleeping.

Eventually she climbed out of bed and walked across the hall into the kitchen where she filled her new electric kettle with cold water and switched it on before she prepared a mug with instant coffee.

She walked back into her living room where she pulled on her long pink dressing gown and tied it around her waist before she pushed her feet into the pink fluffy slippers that April bought for her last Christmas.

Carmen was given the exact same slippers by April but hers came in dark brown.

She walked back into the kitchen and poured hot water into the mug and concluded that it really didn't matter that she was giving herself a stimulant because she already couldn't sleep.

She decided that she might just as well get on with something constructive such as the large box of short denim skirts down inside the shop that arrived a whole month earlier than planned.

She slipped her phone into her dressing gown pocket and picked up her key bunch with one hand and coffee in the other and headed down the hallway toward the staircase that led down to the usually busy New Kent road.

She hoped that it would be considerably quieter than during the hectic daylight hours.

When Jade reached the brown door at the bottom of the stairs she paused.

She knew that she had to get this right and not walk outside in her dressing gown and slippers to be seen by passing cars or worse a group of drunks staggering along New Kent road.

Her plan was simple.

She would slightly open the door and check both left and right for either of those possibilities and then make a run for the shop door and get inside before anybody could see her.

She bit down on the purple leather key fob and with her coffee still in her hand Jade slowly opened the front door just enough to peek outside.

She slowly pulled the door and looked outside where she checked first left and then right.

When she glanced to the right she saw bright vehicle headlights heading in her direction.

She quickly pushed the door closed and waited until she heard the approaching car pass.

When the sound of the passing car eventually disappeared into the background din of distant traffic Jade slowly pulled the door open again and looked to her left over parked cars to where the passing vehicle was headed in the direction of the city.

She turned to her right and glanced over the top of more parked cars and saw no headlights and more importantly no approaching drunks.

It was now clear for her to make a run for the glass front door of the shop and then quickly get inside.

Suddenly she heard a sound like the snap of a twig that came from directly opposite so she quickly pushed the door closed again.

"Oh for god's sake it's like Piccadilly circus!" She quietly told herself.

She leaned against the inside of the door.

"I could've been dressed by now!" She added and shook her head.

Eventually she slowly pulled the door again and took another look hoping that whoever was across the street was now gone.

She stared across and saw a silver security van that had been there all along but it was parked just like every other vehicle and she had automatically ignored it.

Indigo Security Services 'London's Finest' was sign-written on the side.

She noticed that the back doors of the van were now very slowly opening from inside.

"What the hell is going on over there?"

Now she saw a man across the street walking backward toward the back of the van.

With his back to her he didn't see Jade as she now peered through a tiny gap in the door.

It was only when he backed himself right up to the now fully opened back doors of the van that Jade saw why he was walking backward.

Beyond him from Jade's viewpoint was another man, shorter in stature and he walked forward.

Because the man walking backward was considerably larger Jade simply hadn't seen the second man.

But it was now that she realised that they were both carrying not something but someone.

Her eyes widened through the tiny gap in the door as she saw that the blonde girl between the two men had bound legs.

Jade started to realise exactly what she was staring at and her mouth slowly opened wide.

"What the…" She very quietly uttered.

She very quietly pushed the door and closed her eyes with a cringe.

The front door *'clicked!'*

Under normal circumstances that sound would have been very quiet in the darkened hall.

Because it was the early hours of the morning with no traffic and no other sounds and with her senses fully heightened that tiny click sounded like an earth shattering thud.

"Shit!" She whispered.

She leaned back against the door with her eyes tightly closed.

Jade's heart pounded and she was breathing very heavily almost to the point of hyperventilation.

"H…Holy shit I can't move!" She whispered to herself.

Her breath became heavier as she stood waiting to hear footsteps outside the door as her heart continued to pound.

"Get it together!" She whispered to herself.

She realised that her body was paralysed with fear.

She wanted to turn and slide the bolts across at the top and bottom of the door but she knew that she would make even more noise than she already had.

Eventually she found her nerve and made a staggered run for it back up the stairs where she ran straight to kitchen and fumbled inside her dressing gown pocket for her phone.

She waited for the recipient of her call to pick up and she eventually did.

"C...Carmen!" Jade blurted.

Eventually Carmen Richardson woke herself up and calmed Jade down to the point of coherent conversation before she listened.

"Those abductions we've been hearing about!" Jade blurted.

"I think I just saw one happen right across the street!"

Carmen had one simple question for Jade.

"Did they see you?" She asked.

Jade shook her head.

"N...No."

Carmen insisted that she didn't want Jade involved in any way.

"But Carmen I saw that poor girl!" Jade protested with tear filled eyes.

Carmen understood but her utmost concern was for the safety of Jade.

She then asked if the van was still there.

Jade took in a deep shuddering breath.

"Should I look through the window?" She asked.

Carmen replied with a defined no.

"I want you to stay on the phone with me, take another deep breath, drink some coffee and get dressed." Carmen told her.

"In half an hour discretely look through your living room window." She told Jade.

"And then get straight over to me!" Carmen insisted.

It was 4:46am when Jade left her flat and hurriedly climbed into her car that was parked directly in front of the brown door at New Kent road.

She was right that the abductors of the blonde girl had not seen her and they hadn't heard that earth shattering 'click' as the door latch locked back into position after she carefully pushed it.

The two Spanish spotters that sat three vehicles behind her car in a green Citroen however had seen absolutely everything.

Thirty Five
Friday November 3rd 2000

It was a cool slowly darkening early evening just two days after Jade Harris witnessed the abduction of a blonde girl opposite her flat and shop at New Kent road Walworth.

A black convertible Audi pulled into one of the vacant parking spaces outside a large warehouse building at the bank of the river Thames near north Woolwich pier and the mooring platform for the Woolwich ferry.

An attractive thirty two year old woman with long blonde wavy hair standing at five feet six inches tall climbed out of the car and closed the door behind her.

Tania Downing slowly turned to view her surroundings before she casually strolled toward a brown steel door in front of Unit 4B on the Stanley industrial estate.

She wore a red knitted pullover and figure hugging blue designer jeans with black patent leather high heeled shoes beneath an opened full length black leather coat.

Tania glanced around again before she rapped on the brown steel door and waited for it to open.

There was an eerie silence on the otherwise deserted industrial estate until she heard several large bolts being pushed across from the other side of the door and she turned to face it.

When the door opened she saw a tall thin man with olive skin who was eastern European with short dark cropped hair and a very thin moustache above his top lip.

He wore a smartly pressed white cotton shirt with black trousers and shiny black leather shoes on his feet.

Tania smiled at him.

"Hi whatever your name is I'm Mark Downing's wife." She began.

"Can I speak to my husband please?" She asked.

Her smile displayed nothing but contempt.

He looked her up and down.

"There is nobody here by that name." He assured her with his foreign accent evident.

Tania sighed.

"Just go and find him and tell him that his wife is here you idiot." She replied.

He closed the brown steel door and she heard the large bolts on the other side as they slid back into their locked position.

She shook her head.

"What a twat!" She uttered with another sigh.

It was around five minutes before Tania heard the sliding bolts from inside again and the same man reappeared but this time he displayed a smile.

"Mrs Downing please come in we must be very careful of course, you understand." He told her.

Tania stepped inside with nothing constructive to say to him.

She waited in a narrow white painted aisle with a red metal staircase on her left that led up to the offices of Indigo security services.

He finished re-securing the brown steel door before he walked across the aisle to blue wooden double doors that he unlocked.

Tania watched in silence for a moment until she eventually addressed him again.

"You haven't got a clue have you?" She asked.

Again he smiled.

"Please accept my apology Mrs Downing we must be careful of course." He explained again.

Tania stepped into an eerily silent dimly lit warehouse onto hard grey concrete floor that was once home to metal pressing machinery.

It was the same floor that David Stringer and Richard Willows had seen on the computer images of unconscious women.

But today the long windowless industrial space housed more than one hundred solid steel black barred cubes that measured four feet by four feet by four feet.

The cages were positioned in five straight rows of ten with an identical number stacked and bolted on top.

Tania had never seen a sight like the one now in front of her.

She casually strolled to one of the aisles without acknowledging that these large black solid steel constructions actually held unconscious but living and breathing human beings.

It mattered not.

Most of the cages held unconscious women although the need for enforced labour within the mines beneath Europe was still a hungry one.

It accounted for the twenty three unconscious men that were also abducted from the streets of London and currently kept here.

Tania continued to stroll down a particular aisle with the large black constructions on both sides mostly occupied by half naked women that wore white paper industrial face masks that covered their noses and mouths.

She headed down this particular aisle because she saw a man that she recognised.

He appeared to be working inside an empty cage at the far end.

Bill Jessop was forty two with greying red hair and he stood at around five feet nine.

He was dressed in a red and black padded lumberjack shirt over a dark blue t-shirt with blue denim jeans and he wore black steel toe-capped work boots on his feet.

He glanced up from his cleaning chores and saw Tania.

"Hello Tania, what are you doing here?" He asked.

He slowly climbed to his feet and wiped his hands with a red rag.

Tania smiled back at him.

"Hi Billy I'm looking for Mark, do you know where he is?" She asked.

Bill Jessop seemed to ponder and considered sending her in the right direction.

"Have you tried the bar yet?" He eventually asked.

Tania raised her eyebrows.

"You have a bar here?" She asked.

"It's no wonder he never comes home!" She uttered with a sigh.

Bill pointed to the far end of the aisle.

"Straight to the end and hang a left." He explained.

"Then keep walking until you reach an arch in the wall." He continued.

"Go through the arch and you'll see the bar."

Tania immediately started to follow his directions.

"Thanks Billy."

She walked past him and headed toward the far end of the aisle.

"You're welcome." He quietly uttered as he watched her walk away.

At the end of the aisle Tania turned left and directly ahead of her she could see the arch that was cut into a plasterboard wall that separated unit 4B into two halves.

Ahead in front of the very last row of cages on her left Tania saw another familiar figure seated on a blue plastic chair.

A woman with shoulder length blonde hair sat on the blue plastic chair and she was actually talking to two conscious women that were together locked inside a ground floor cage.

Tania considered this a bizarre sight because the two women were now cargo awaiting shipment and not really considered people.

Her sister explained this to her.

As Tania neared she decided against questioning this sight because she confirmed that the woman on the blue chair in front of the cage was in fact Debbie Davies.

As Davies turned to see her, Tania smiled.

"Hi Debbie have you seen Mark?" She asked.

Davies turned on the chair and smiled at Tania and shook her head.

She said nothing but she would have plenty to say later with regard to Tania using her name in front of the two women.

As she neared the home-made arch in the plasterboard Tania could see another dividing wall just the other side of it.

She saw that on the left side was a wooden home-made platform with similar blue plastic chairs placed in front of it and she concluded that this was the live auction room.

On the right side of the second dividing wall was a dimly lit room that was created to simulate a real bar with soft white leather furniture and small rectangular glass tables between them.

She also spotted the alcohol optics on the wall behind a constructed wooden bar.

"Unbelievable!" She quietly uttered to herself.

She headed right and into the bar area where suddenly she heard a very familiar voice.

"Tania?" Her husband asked.

"What are you doing here?"

Thirty eight year old Mark Downing was a broad shouldered man and stood at just over six feet tall and he had short spiked blonde hair and bright blue eyes.

He stood up from one of the white leather sofas where he sat opposite another male work colleague.

He started to walk toward his wife.

Tania stood and watched him approach her.

He wore an unfastened white cotton short sleeved shirt over a pale grey t-shirt and blue denim jeans and because the floor of the mock up bar was fitted with a deep dark brown carpet he wore no shoes just black socks on his feet.

"Why are you here?" He asked again.

Tania angrily stared up into his eyes.

"Well you never seem to come home these days so I came here to see you and to find out what keeps you here so much." She explained.

She glanced across at the bar.

Downing smiled.

"I know but we have an auction in a few weeks so it's been pretty manic around here." He replied.

Tania nodded but her angry facial expression remained the same.

"Does everybody else go home from work at the end of the day Mark?" She asked.

"I haven't seen you for three days!"

He leaned forward and kissed Tania on her cheek but she didn't move and her facial expression remained the same.

"I'll be home tomorrow I promise." He assured her.

He leaned forward to kiss her on her cheek again but this time Tania backed away from him.

For a few more moments she stared back at him because she could tell when her husband of seven years was lying to her.

"I had lunch with my sister today." She eventually replied.

"And she doesn't know why you don't come home either."

The first statement caught him completely off guard.

"You saw Jane?" He asked.

His wife, the younger sister of Jane Chapman continued to stare back at him and she slowly nodded.

Suddenly and without warning Tania turned on her heels and began to walk back toward the warehouse.

"Be home tonight Mark or come and pick up your belongings tomorrow." She called back without turning.

"They'll be on the front garden path!"

With widened eyes Downing watched Tania before she disappeared into one of the cage aisles as she headed back toward the exit.

"Tania, hold on!" He called after her.

After a few moments and no response he headed in the same direction but he chose a completely different aisle to the one that his wife stepped into.

Half way up the aisle that Downing purposely chose he stopped where Bill Jessop was cleaning.

Again Bill stood up from a vacant cage and Downing smiled at him.

"Billy I need you to do me a favour." He said in a half-whisper.

Downing's eyes scanned several of the occupied cages in the vicinity until he saw what he was looking for.

"There she is that one." He whispered.

He pointed to one of the upper cages.

"Can you get her down and take her into the bar for me?" He asked.

Bill shrugged and nodded.

"Sure."

Downing winked with a wry grin.

"And bring her round a little bit, not too much though." He said.

Bill Jessop slowly nodded his head again now that he realised exactly why Downing wanted her brought down.

"Thanks mate." Downing said with another grin.

He started again toward the exit.

"Tania, wait up!" He yelled again.

Thirty Six
Sunday November 5th 2000

It was 1:53am when a silver security van slowed to a silent stop outside a new shop at New Kent road Walworth south London.

Jasmine Fashion

In the driver seat was thirty nine year old Atif Rahman the best friend of fellow Turkish immigrant Barak Yazici.

They both stared up at the flat above the shop.

There were long conversations throughout the day by way of planning between Yazici, the driver Atif Rahman, forty year old Doruk Gezmen who owned a kebab takeaway at Finsbury Park and taxi cab driver forty two year old Firat Alican.

Alican was in fact the only member of the group to ever serve as an enlisted man within the Turkish Army.

Nobody else inside the van had been anything more than a two year national conscript with very limited training.

The Spanish Major Abran Delgado protested that the Turkish were given this assignment and proposed that the Spanish carry it out but his request was denied.

This left the group that Delgado considered *'the Turkish idiots'* to perform this potentially dangerous task.

It was to be their very first abduction.

The woman that lived in the flat above the shop witnessed an abduction just under a week ago across the street and although there had been no police reports there could easily be a trap lying in wait.

The Spanish team would immediately know whereas the Turkish probably would not.

The Turkish leader Yazici instructed his friend Rahman to remain in the van while he took Doruk Gezmen and Firat Alican up to the flat.

"Onun sadece tek bir kadın." He told Rahman.

'It's just one woman.'

Rahman nodded with agreement.

The team waited for the two cars half a mile to the left and half a mile to the right to position themselves as spotters for the task ahead.

This was something that should have happened before the van arrived but this was their first assignment and there would always be minor glitches along the way as they learned their new found trade.

Yazici smiled to himself as he smoothed over his thick black moustache.

His planning had gone well and he was about to take *his* team in for their first real mission instead of hearing tales from the other teams.

It was *his* turn at last.

It took Doruk Gezmen some eleven minutes to pick the lock on the brown door as his three friends waited patiently inside the silver van and ushered him away whenever traffic approached.

Yazici's worst fear was now that they returned to the Stanley industrial estate empty handed because they couldn't gain access to the flat.

Eventually Gezmen gained access and pushed the door closed from inside when the last car passed before his two colleagues joined him in the darkened hallway.

Eventually Yazici quietly led his men up the stairs and at the top they turned left to face a long hallway that had two closed doors on the right and three on the left.

Now the question was simple.

'Where is this sleeping woman?'

There was absolute silence as everybody's senses became extremely heightened.

Yazici's heart pounded heavily against his chest.

He quietly checked the first door on the right in the pitch black hall to discover that it was the bathroom.

Slowly the three men then turned to face the closed door that would eventually become a spare bedroom.

They had no idea of what any of these rooms were used for.

Yazici slowly pushed down on the handle and in the dead of night every sound was intensified as he peered inside to find an empty half painted bedroom.

He stared ahead and could see that at the end of the hall on the right side was a very slightly opened kitchen door and the next two doors beside this one on the left were closed.

She *had* to be inside one of these two rooms on the left.

There was a high pitched buzz as Gezmen armed his electronic pistol and pointed it upward in front of him as the team of three moved forward to the next closed door.

It was the main bedroom.

After a few moments all three men stood outside and again Yazici slowly and as quietly as possible pushed down onto the handle and slowly opened the door.

He looked back at his two friends as they all stared into yet another empty room.

All eyes slowly turned to the last door on the left directly opposite the slightly opened kitchen door because she *had* to be inside there.

From outside the living room Yazici very slowly opened the door where all three peered inside to see her sleeping beneath the covers on a small sofa bed.

Yazici motioned with his hand for Firat Alican to move inside and for Gezmen to follow.

He would himself wait and stand guard by the door.

A few moments later Alican approached the bed of soundly sleeping Jade Harris who they knew witnessed a team that took not one but three girls from across the street almost a week ago.

Yazici took in a long deep shuddering breath as he considered that tonight the plan was basic and straight forward with minimal risks.

Shoot this woman in the chest using a tranquiliser gun and get straight out with her and leave the Spanish clean-up team to do the rest.

That was the plan.

Alican was quietly followed by Gezmen whose gun was armed and ready for use.

Gezmen would be the shooter.

Barak Yazici changed his mind and decided to follow and he moved between his two friends in the eerily silent dark living room.

Alican very slowly reached down to the covers and pulled them back to discover a line of positioned pillows.

She wasn't there.

When he glanced up at Gezmen with confusion his eyes suddenly widened with sheer terror.

Gezmen stared back at him with confusion.

'*What is this?*' Doruk wondered.

From behind the door dressed in her long pink towelling dressing gown Jade Harris silently emerged wielding a heavy full sized solid wooden baseball bat.

She bought it on the morning that she witnessed the abduction from across the street.

Firat Alican was frozen to the spot as he watched her very quietly approach Gezmen from behind.

Doruk Gezmen had absolutely no idea that she was there.

Obviously Gezmen also saw the line of positioned pillows and now he saw the fear that gripped his friend Firat as Jade Harris silently approached from behind him.

Gezmen very slowly turned in the dark to see just why Alican was so terrified.

It was the sight of Jade Harris with her solid wooden baseball bat raised high above her head waiting to strike.

She then did without any hesitation and with all of the force that she could possibly muster.

There was a heavy sickening thud as the heavy bat connected with the side of Gezmen's head with an additional crack!

The crack was the sound of Gezmen's skull as it fractured from the impact of Jade Harris's solid heavy wooden baseball bat.

Gezmen didn't make a sound.

He dropped his stun gun onto the floor as Firat Alican watched with sheer terror in his eyes.

Alican instinctively knew in the back of his mind that his friend Doruk was already dead before his body slumped to the floor.

Blood then slowly trickled from his right ear and right nostril as he lay motionless.

It all happened so quickly for Alican.

He had no time to react.

Jade immediately reached right back and swung again as hard and as fast as she possibly could.

The tip of her bat brushed across Firat Alican's nose making enough of a connection to break it with a 'snap!'

Alican fell across the sofa bed and landed on the floor behind it.

Jade turned her attention to the leader Barak Yazici.

He was completely frozen to the spot.

She screamed as she swung her heavy bat in the direction of his head and Yazici instinctively raised both arms in self-defence.

He heard and felt the crack as it snapped his forearm and knocked him backward over a disconnected lampshade causing him to scream out from the intense pain.

But Jade wasn't finished with him yet.

Yazici continued to scream with pain slumped over the small white bedside cabinet clutching his broken arm.

He looked up to see her raise the bat high above her head as she prepared to smash it into his face as hard as she possibly could.

This was it.

Yazici knew that this time she wouldn't miss.

He instinctively raised his arms despite one of them being broken.

He covered his head and screamed louder as he waited for the sickening blow from her heavy bat.

Barak Yazici knew that he was about to die.

Suddenly there was a loud CLACK!

From across the room Firat Alican knelt beside the sofa bed and composed himself enough as blood still trickled from his nose.

He carefully took aim at the back of Jade Harris and pulled the trigger.

Barak Yazici waited for the thudding blow from her bat that still hadn't smashed down into his face.

He slowly peered up from behind his protecting arms and saw that her eyes had turned completely white and they flickered as the connection from the gun fired by Alican took its effect.

Jade's entire body violently shook as she stood over him.

She slowly dropped the bat from above her head and it fell to the floor behind her and then she suddenly slumped beside it.

Yazici stared across to the sofa bed where Alican now buried his face into the covers.

He then stared down at Gezmen lying in a spreading pool of his own blood.

Yazici could see that his friend Doruk wasn't breathing.

Doruk Gezmen was dead as a result of a fractured skull caused from heavy blunt force trauma.

He died immediately from the impact from a blow to his head with the heavy wooden baseball bat at the hands of Jade Harris.

Alican slowly looked up and glanced across at Yazici before he also acknowledged that Gezmen was in fact dead and then he slowly climbed to his feet.

"Biz birakmak gerekir!" He told the leader Yazici.

'We need to leave!'

Alican then stepped over the convulsing body of Jade Harris and headed toward the door.

Barak Yazici slowly climbed to his unsteady feet and stared down at his motionless friend Doruk Gezmen.

"Onun sadece tek bir kadın." Alican uttered as he left the room.

'It's just one woman.'

The spotters were eventually called in to carry out the clinical clean up inside the flat but by now this was no standard clean up and it took several hours after twenty nine year old Jade Harris was removed from her flat.

She was the latest abduction statistic.

Thirty Seven
Monday November 6th 2000

Sam Henning sat inside the cubicle office alone and read the case file of missing Bridget Oaks and her friend Olivia Fletcher when his phone rang.

Nicola Garwood was at the safe house at Caterham with Jacob Saunders.

It meant that Sam had the privacy that he needed for this incoming call from Chief Inspector Keith Curtis from New Scotland Yard.

"Thanks guv I'll get right on it, you're a superstar!" Sam said at the end of the call.

He immediately left the ops room and headed down to the canteen to find one of those dreadful cups of stewed tea while several things ran through his mind.

Technicians had been through the computer owned by Bridget Oaks.

They learned that the presentation that she had ready for the board of directors where she worked was finished on the exact same day that she disappeared.

The report was perfect and she had nothing to worry about with regard to it and her work colleagues all claimed that she was happy at work and without a doubt on her way up the corporate ladder.

Her partner Clive Henderson was devastated by her disappearance and told investigating officers that he and Bridget had spoken on the telephone on the evening that she disappeared.

His mobile telephone contract records confirmed that there was a call made at 8:54pm and lasted until 9:37pm and Bridget's phone contract confirmed this.

Sam was certain that Bridget had no reason to disappear of her own free will and the same went for Olivia Fletcher.

She was due to attend the wedding of her sister on the following Saturday where she was to be the chief bridesmaid.

Sam was more than certain that they had both been taken against their will.

But his priorities for now had just changed.

He had information to give to the chief and he needed to be completely convincing in his approach.

If this all went wrong Sam would find himself in more trouble that Nicola Garwood could ever hope to be in her wildest dreams.

It was something of a test of character for Sam because he was to retire in a just few months from now.

He could quite easily just sit back and allowed his remaining time to ebb past until then.

He was doing this because right now he was still a dedicated copper and it needed to be done.

He needed to be absolutely certain and for that to happen he had to eliminate the chief from suspicion because this ridiculous theory was now eating away at him.

He held the cup of stewed tea in his hand as he stood outside the chief's office and took in a long deep breath before he knocked with his free hand and then entered without waiting to be called.

"Good morning Sir." He said.

Roberts sat at his desk and looked up to see Sam's smiling face.

"Good morning Henning." He replied.

Sam closed the door and crossed the large space past the unmanned TV cameras on his right that were permanently placed for the purpose of press conferences as he headed to the chief's desk.

Chief Inspector Roberts watched as Sam walked toward him.

"What can I do for you?" He asked.

Sam reached into his inside jacket pocket and produced a slip of paper that he handed to the chief.

"Ilford council have just released a new safe house Sir." Sam informed him.

"You might want to add it to the new list that I gave you." He added.

"Lovely it's in Belmont Road." Roberts read out loud.

"Yes Sir." Sam replied.

The chief smiled.

"It sounds a little glamorous doesn't it Henning?" He remarked.

A grin appeared on Sam's lips.

"You've never been to glamorous Ilford then Sir?" He asked with a chuckle.

The chief however didn't get his joke.

Roberts held up the slip of paper.

"Of course I'll dispose of this in the usual manner." He told Sam.

"Yes of course Sir." Sam replied.

The chief looked thoughtful before he glanced up at Henning.

"So tell me, how long now before you retire?" He asked.

Sam grinned.

"I have just over two months left now Sir." He replied.

Roberts smiled with a sigh.

"It'll be a serious loss to the force Henning." He said.

Again Sam smiled.

Roberts now glanced to his right toward the large window.

"Tell me Sam who is the young fellow that I often see with Garwood?"

"That'll be DS Saunders." Sam replied.

"He's a good copper." He added.

Roberts nodded but he still appeared to be deep in thought.

He then looked back at Sam.

"I'm going to need new eyes and ears on the ground when you're gone Sam." The chief told him.

"Maybe you might have a quiet word with this Saunders fellow for me."

Sam shrugged.

"Of course, he's an honest hard working copper." Sam replied.

"I'll have a quiet word in his ear for you."

As Sam headed to the door Robert's studied the slip of paper before he looked up again.

"Sam?" He called out.

Henning turned to face him.

"Yes Sir?"

Roberts waved the slip.

"Good work on getting another house." He said.

"Thank you Sir, but it just came through and I had very little to do with it." Sam lied.

Roberts smiled again.

"Are we manning this one straight away?" He asked.

Sam frowned before he shook his head.

"I'm a little worried about it to be honest Sir." He replied.

Roberts raised his eyebrows.

"Worried?"

Sam nodded again.

"It's a very quiet road and they're placing four young unsupervised women in the house." Sam informed him.

"We don't seem to have learned anything from Caterham if you ask me."

But then he half smiled.

"But I think we have a better beat on things now and only half a dozen or so people even know of its existence unlike Caterham." He added.

Roberts nodded with full agreement.

"That Caterham episode was a diabolical shambles Henning." He replied.

"Yes it was Sir." Sam agreed.

Sam eventually climbed the wide staircase and headed toward the ops room where he removed his phone from his jacket pocket and dialled a number and when the recipient picked up he spoke.

"I've done it guv. He quietly said.

"He has all of the information." He told Chief Inspector Keith Curtis.

"He knows that the house goes live in two days and it'll be unmanned with four young women in it." He continued.

Sam then nodded.

"Yes guv now we wait and see." He replied.

Thirty Eight
Monday November 6th 2000

Thirty five year old former SAS Captain Richard Willows stood at a bus stop not far from the house owned by Jane Chapman at Watford.

"Are you sure that she's going to come today String?" He asked David Stringer.

No communication devices were visible.

David Stringer sat inside his spare bedroom at his home eating dry toasted bread because he ran out of butter again.

He stared at one of his monitors on the left side of the room wearing headphones with a microphone attached as he viewed from one of the usual overhead passing French spy satellites.

David nodded although Richard couldn't see him.

"If my theory's right she starts from there every Monday at around eleven." David assured him.

Richard nodded.

"That's fair enough." He replied.

Richard completely trusted the judgement of David Stringer.

He stood for another forty minutes and had already waved on three buses before David informed him that the girl had just left Jane Chapman's house.

"She'll be with you in about six minutes." David informed him.

"Ok mate, thanks." Richard replied.

"Remember that I can't answer you when she's here so none of your usual babbling and asking me random questions like is she hot?" He reminded David with chuckle.

David pondered for a moment.

"That's all well and good but if she is hot could you slip my number into her coat pocket or something?" He asked.

Richard chuckled again.

"That way you'll be able to work your magic won't you??" He asked.

"You got it." David replied with a grin.

He then winked at the monitor.

Richard now saw a young woman approaching.

"Blue jacket String?" He asked.

David confirmed that he was correct.

"Yep that's her."

It was a cold morning in Watford and Richard was dressed in a fully fastened thick black padded jacket and blue denim jeans with black leather shoes on his feet.

As the girl neared he had some immediate intelligence for David.

"She's Asian, Vietnamese I'm guessing."

"But that would probably mean that she was paid for and then brought here if she originates from there." David replied.

"Asia is like the human trafficking capital of the world."

She was now too close for Richard to respond to anything that David asked without looking as if he was talking to himself.

After Richard flashed her one of his smiles that had absolutely no effect he waited in silence for the bus to arrive.

He knew the exact bus to take because he also knew that she would be travelling south to Pinner before moving onto Amersham to the home of Debbie Davies.

David Stringer did his homework.

"Now remember Richard." He began to explain.

"A sample of her hair will give us something." He reminded Richard.

"But don't touch it with your bare hands use the gloves." He added.

Ten minutes later the red number 186 double decker bus trundled up the hill toward the bus stop where just Richard and the unknown Asian girl waited.

"This is your bus Richard." David said in his ear.

"I hope you remembered to take some money with you." He added with a chuckle.

His comment brought a wry grin to Richard's lips.

He politely motioned for the girl to climb onto the bus in front of him.

Richard even knew the bus stop where she would eventually climb off thanks to David.

After the young girl paid her fare Richard announced to the driver that he wished to go two stops down from where she had just paid to go.

"Can I have a single to Hatch End please?" Richard asked the driver.

He guessed that although she was within earshot the girl would have no idea of any road at Pinner other than her own destination.

He also noticed when she paid her fare that she spoke only broken English.

He watched her climb the stairs to the upper deck of the almost empty bus as the driver gave him his change.

Richard eventually followed her up the stairs where he saw that thankfully she sat at the very front of the bus.

He was grateful because if she sat anywhere else he would have had to take different action after she had climbed off at Pinner.

The bus already started moving when Richard sat down directly behind her on the otherwise empty upper deck as it headed southbound toward Pinner eight miles from Watford.

He immediately reached into his inside jacket pocket and took out a pair of blue latex medical gloves and discretely stretched them over both hands.

From the same pocket he removed a small clear plastic re-sealable bag and opened it.

"Tell me how hot she is when you get off the bus." Stringer babbled in his ear.

Willows grinned.

'You should come with a government health warning mate!' He thought to himself.

He then removed small silver scissors from the outer right side pocket of his jacket.

He tapped twice onto the right side of his own neck as a response to David's comment.

The young girl turned to glance at the blonde man behind her to see him staring out of the window to his left before she returned her own gaze to the front.

She wondered why he sat directly behind her considering that the bus was almost empty.

Using the thumb and forefinger of his left hand Richard ensured that the small clear plastic bag remained fully opened as with his right he slowly reached toward the back of her head with the small scissors.

He moved the bag a little closer just below the scissors and held it open using his latex covered thumb before he carefully snipped ten single black hairs from the back of her head that all individually dropped into the bag.

The girl turned for the second time to see him still staring out of the window at the countryside view while Richard re-sealed the bag with his right thumb and forefinger from behind the back of her seat.

His left hand slowly returned the small silver scissors to his pocket.

She saw absolutely nothing.

At no point did Richard make eye contact with her.

When she returned her gaze to the front he quietly peeled off the blue latex gloves and returned them too before he used a single finger to tap on his own neck twice to inform David that the samples were obtained.

Stringer still watched the bus from above and acknowledged.

"I've just seen your car at Hatch End." He told Willows.

Richard already drove this trip today and left his car at his destination point so that he could take the hair samples straight to Stringer.

David would then have them transferred to the undisclosed company laboratory that was situated somewhere within the city of London.

Three days later the lab results would eventually identify her as Kim Cuc Nguy.

Richard had correctly guessed her country of origin as Vietnam.

She was just sixteen years of age.

The ten hair samples that were obtained by Richard were not enough to identify her because she appeared on no database but her DNA did match a sibling.

She had an older brother studying Medicine at Holborn College London.

David Stringer would discover and tell Richard the story behind Kim Cuc and her brother Huy Nguy and how she found herself in the UK without her brother's knowledge.

It was thanks to Miguel Sanchez that nineteen year old Huy Nguy had the opportunity to travel to the UK where he legally obtained a visa as a student for the initial three years of study.

His younger sister Kim Cuc Nguy was approached six months later and offered passage to the UK with the promise of work.

Kim Cuc Nguy was from an incredibly poor background and she gladly accepted the offer with the promise of a better life and of course to be closer to her brother.

She was completely unaware that she had in fact been sold to Jane Chapman for the equivalent of forty nine pounds sterling.

The price was something that Chapman found amusing at the time and upon her illegal arrival into the UK the sixteen year old discovered the true purpose of her new residency.

She spoke very little English but understood Jane Chapman and Lisa Moore when they explained to her what would happen to both her and her brother should she ever stray from her instructions.

She was assured that her brother would find himself the property of a mine in Siberia while she would find herself in much, much worse working conditions or even worse than that.

She had no reason to doubt their threats.

Huy Nguy had absolutely no idea that his sixteen year old sister was even in the UK.

Kim Cuc Nguy was paid for and brought in to become pivotal to the secrecy of Chapman Moore and Davies.

They never used any form of electronic communication that would lead evidence toward them.

Whenever they communicated it was by way of sealed paper slips that were delivered by Kim Cuc Nguy.

It was simple but very effective.

There was a middle man for the transaction between Miguel Sanchez and Jane Chapman for the purchase of Kim Cuc Nguy.

His name was Vladimir Kolov.

Thirty Nine
Wednesday November 8th 2000

Detective Inspector Nicola Garwood glanced across the cubicle office at Sam Henning.

He was completely engrossed and convinced in his theory that there was an underlying case hidden by the press covered abductions of London's missing homeless.

Nicola stared across and knew that there was something wrong with him.

He had become withdrawn and distant from her and she couldn't figure out why because he continued to assure her that he and everything was fine.

But it wasn't only Nicola that noticed the change in Sam.

Jacob Saunders knew it too.

Nicola knew that Sam had become engrossed of late and she wondered or feared that he might be a little too attached to the files that he studied so meticulously or was possibly suffering from stress.

But of course those files were not the only reason that Sam had become so detached.

He had a secret that he kept from Nicola but there were so many implications to consider.

He tried to push thoughts regarding the possibilities to the back of his mind because it was now out of his hands and firmly within the grasp of his old boss Chief Inspector Keith Curtis.

If Sam's hunch was wrong and he hoped that it was, there would at some point be a budget analysis and of course it would include the team lying in wait inside the house at Belmont road Ilford.

Garwood would definitely question it or the chief would discover that he had been duped by Sam.

He was without a doubt in a no-win situation.

In fact the only good outcome for Sam would be that the chief was guilty and consequently discovered by Keith Curtis's secret armed team inside the house.

Sam knew in the back of his mind that this wouldn't be the case.

However until it was positively resolved this issue was holding up the investigation.

Sam studied and compared the eleven most recent cases of the non-homeless missing women within the belt of the encircling M25 Motorway.

He could clearly see that all of them were incredibly beautiful and in no cases could he find a reason for any of them to disappear of their own free will.

The uncomfortable silence in the cubicle office would be shattered within the next hour when Jacob Saunders would enter with the first real breakthrough of the case.

But for now Nicola climbed to her feet and glanced across at Sam still engrossed in his files.

"I'm going downstairs to get a coffee Sam, do you want one?" She asked.

Sam glanced up.

"Sorry?"

There was a pause while Nicola sighed.

"Look, why don't you just tell me what's wrong?" She asked.

"Did I do something to piss you off?"

Sam immediately shook his head and sat back in his chair not quite knowing how to respond.

He wanted to divulge but his secret was a covert operation and he knew that if he told her she would be one of two people who knew about the house at Belmont road as opposed to one.

He knew that couldn't tell her.

He glanced up at Nicola.

This time she was staying put until she got an answer.

"I promise we're fine Nik." He assured her.

That wasn't good enough for Garwood.

"Sam this is driving me insane." She told him.

"We as a team seriously can't function this way."

Sam nodded because he knew that she was right and now he really was somewhere between a rock and a hard place.

Eventually he sighed.

"I've got something to tell you that *must* remain strictly between us." He finally conceded.

Nicola stared at him.

"I'm listening."

She stood before him with her arms folded in front of her.

Just then the door burst open and Detective Sergeant Jacob Saunders entered the office.

It looked to Sam and Nicola as if he had been running for his life.

While he caught his breath Saunders looked to Sam but then focussed his attention on Nicola and took in another long deep breath.

"We've got a break!" He gasped as he still stared at her.

"What do you mean a break?" She asked.

"Somebody called in with a name." He replied.

Garwood immediately returned to her desk and moved the mouse to wake up her sleeping computer as she glanced up at Saunders.

"Where did the name come from?"

Jacob frowned.

"It was an anon guv." He replied with a sigh.

"It was a woman caller and we couldn't get a trace." He added.

Garwood nodded.

"Ok so what's the name?" She asked.

Saunders glanced over at Sam and then back to Nicola.

"She's called Jade Harris."

"And the caller said that this Jade Harris lives in New Kent road above a shop but the shop is just a front and isn't even open for business." He continued.

Nicola started to tap onto the keyboard of her computer.

"I already checked out the address guv." Jacob informed her.

"It is registered to her but only recently." He added.

Nicola stared into her computer monitor at a police photograph of twenty nine year old Jade Harris.

"She was arrested three times for soliciting but never charged." She told Sam and Jacob.

She read out loud the information from her computer monitor.

"She's been working out of an address at Alpha grove on the Isle of Dogs until recently."

Sam Henning suddenly looked up.

"She was working for Carmen Richardson?" He asked.

Garwood shrugged.

"Do you know her?" She asked.

Sam nodded.

"I've dealt with Carmen once or twice." He replied.

"Who's the suspect again?"

Garwood looked up at Sam from her computer.

"Her name's Jade Harris." She replied.

Sam logged into his own computer to take a look for himself.

"This doesn't sound right." He quietly uttered.

Sam stood up after a little more research on this new found suspect at the same time as Nicola.

She stared across at him.

"Where are you going?" She asked.

Sam searched for his mobile telephone.

"I'm going to pop out and see Carmen Richardson." He replied.

"Because I already know you're going straight down to New Kent road Walworth."

Nicola grinned.

"How did you know that?" She asked.

Sam headed for the door and then he stopped.

"Call it a copper's hunch." He told her and then winked.

"Let's meet back here in three hours."

Nicola glanced at Jacob.

"Well get the car started Jacob!" She instructed.

"Let's pop down to Walworth and speak to this Jade Harris."

Lisa Moore played something of a master stroke because Nicola Garwood now had a name other than Vladimir Kolov on her mind.

That new name was Jade Harris.

Sam Henning avoided confrontation and confession time with Nicola once again.

Forty
Wednesday November 8th 2000

A silver Ford Mondeo pulled up outside the shop at New Kent Road where Nicola Garwood immediately noticed the signage above the shop.

Jasmine Fashions

She then glanced up at the flat above the signage.

"This is it." She said.

Jacob Saunders stared too and he nodded.

"I just found out that it was rented to her by none other than her friend Carmen Richardson." He replied.

Nicola continued to stare up at the flat.

"Well like the caller said, the shop isn't open so let's see if our Jade is at home shall we?" She asked.

Saunders nodded again.

After they crossed the busy New Kent road they headed toward the shop where Nicola cupped her hands around her face and pressed it against the glass door.

She immediately noticed that the shop was still under some kind of reconstruction.

There were several unopened envelopes on the floor that were recently delivered and she also noted that one of the letters was addressed to Jade Harris.

"Well this place definitely isn't open for business." She informed Jacob.

They made their way to the brown door on the right where Nicola rapped her knuckles loudly several times and waited for a response.

She took a step back and stared up at the closed windows of the flat to watch for any signs of life, the twitch of a curtain or a moving silhouette in the background.

Jacob knocked on the door again and again to no response.

As Garwood stared up at the windows Jacob removed the black plastic credit card from his wallet and placed the wallet back into his jacket pocket and within just a few moments there was a quiet 'click!'

As he returned the credit card to his pocket he turned to Garwood.

"That's strange guv." He told her.

"The door just opened itself."

Nicola grinned as she watched his card disappear.

"Detective Sergeant Jacob Saunders I'm utterly ashamed of you!" She told him.

She pushed the door open and began to climb the staircase inside with a look of mock horror at what she had just witnessed.

Saunders followed her inside.

"Well I'm guessing that at some point you're going to get me fired so I might as well have something to do with it." He quietly uttered.

He then closed the door behind them.

Nicola called out several times before they reached the top of the staircase and after receiving no answer they turned left and began to check behind each door as they made their way down the hallway.

"It looks as if she was just moving in guv." Saunders commented.

Garwood nodded with agreement.

"It does."

Nicola stared into the kitchen and saw that there was an electric kettle, a new toaster and there was food inside the cupboards and she also discovered that there was milk in the fridge.

"But she definitely lives here." .

It was Saunders that opened the door to the living room and stared inside.

"Guv you had better come in here." He told Nicola.

She joined him and stared inside too.

"Is that what I think it is?" She quietly asked.

They both saw a broken lampshade and that there had definitely been some kind of struggle in the room.

What they were both most interested in was the large dark stain in the centre of the recently laid new carpet.

The brand new carpet was deep burgundy but a large darker patch was clearly visible.

"Does that look like blood to you?" Nicola asked.

Jacob shrugged.

"It's difficult to say guv." He replied as he slowly stepped forward.

Nicola glanced across at him.

"Remember Jacob you touch nothing!"

"This looks to be a crime scene." She added.

Saunders nodded with agreement.

"A fight definitely went on in here." He replied.

They both silently scanned the room for a few moments searching for evidence and clues.

Nicola Garwood's phone suddenly started to ring and startled both of them in the now very creepy and silent environment.

She sighed with relief when she looked at her screen to see that the caller was Sam Henning.

"Sam?"

Henning informed her that he had been to Carmen's flat at the King's road Chelsea where her neighbour directed him to Mount Street.

He now stood right outside Carmen's new office.

"There are no signs of life here." He informed her.

Nicola continued to scan the room while looking for evidence as Sam spoke.

"Ok my turn." She began.

"I think we're standing in the middle of a crime scene." She told him.

"There's no sign of Jade Harris but there is what looks to be a large pool of dried blood on a brand new carpet in her living room." She added.

There was a brief pause while Sam responded and before Garwood replied to his enquiry and she glanced across at Jacob with a wry grin.

"The front door was already open when we got here." She lied.

After she hung up Nicola took another glance around the room before she looked back across at Saunders as she returned her phone to her pocket.

"Jacob, get forensics down here now."

"I seriously think that's blood." She pointed.

Saunders nodded again.

"Guv I don't think this is just a crime scene." He told her in a quiet tone.

He stared across at her.

"I think this might be a murder scene."

After Saunders finished the call he returned his phone to his inside jacket pocket.

"Jacob it's starting to make sense now." Nicola began.

Saunders interjected.

"A forensics team is on the way here now." He informed her.

Nicola nodded.

"I think she knows that somebody grassed on her and she killed whoever it was right here and then did a runner." She suggested.

Saunders stared down at the blood stained carpet.

"We'll know more when forensics can confirm if that's blood and hopefully who it belongs to." He replied.

Garwood walked out of the door and headed to the bathroom where she took a long length of pale orange toilet paper from the roll and then she walked around the flat.

She opened doors and checked cupboards and drawers without touching anything else with her bare hands and eventually returned to Jacob in the living room.

"She's taken none of her clothes." She told him.

"I think she did whatever went on here and then left in a panic." She continued.

"But I can't find her passport."

Jade Harris had just become the new prime suspect in the case that she was actually its most recent victim.

Lisa Moore accomplished exactly what she set out to when she anonymously called the help desk at task force headquarters.

Detective Inspector Nicola Garwood finally had something or somebody other than Vladimir Kolov to sink her teeth into.

Forty One
Saturday November 11th 2000

Earlier this morning David Stringer contacted Richard Willows.

He informed Richard that he believed that he had made a breakthrough with regard to the rescue and recovery of Richard's younger sister Sasha who was taken from Lant Street Southwark on July 13th.

That was now close to four months ago.

Richard hurried his tasks that morning and arrived at David's house at Tranton road Bermondsey just after midday.

David had prepared for his arrival and he now stared at one of the computer monitors.

"I like helping you Richard." He told Willows.

Richard stared back at him.

"I doubt it's half as much as I like you helping me Dave." He replied.

David continued to stare into the monitor.

"You know when I work with other people?" He asked without taking his eyes from the screen.

Richard nodded.

"Yes I know when you work with other people Dave." He replied with a chuckle.

"I know they always secretly make fun of me." David informed him.

He continued to stare straight ahead.

"But you never make fun of me." He added.

Richard frowned.

"They do?" He asked.

David nodded as he continued to stare at the screen and Richard knew that he was avoiding making eye contact.

He didn't know how to respond to what David was telling him now.

"Did you know that you never make fun of me Richard?" David asked.

Now Willows grinned.

"Yes I had a rough idea that I don't make fun of you Dave." He replied.

He now realised that David was in fact making fun of him.

David slowly turned to face him.

"Are you making fun of me now?" He asked.

He now grinned too.

Richard struggled to keep a straight face as those huge over-magnified eyes stared into his and appeared to blink in slow motion.

"No!" He laughed.

David returned to the screen.

"You're a bastard Willows it's no wonder nobody likes you." He replied with a broader grin.

Almost immediately after he gained access onto the auction site buried inside Jane Chapman's fake dating website David found today's item again.

It was the image of Jade Harris.

Printed beneath the jpeg image were the digits 0060000.

Richard stared at the picture of the completely unconscious Jade.

"What's so special about her?" He asked.

David logged into the police criminal data base and showed an image of Carmen Richardson.

"She's what's so special about her." He replied.

Richard scanned his eyes over Carmen's arrest sheet from nine years ago.

"Soliciting almost a decade ago?" He asked.

David nodded and at the same time he showed Richard a saved copy of Carmen's current bank account.

Richard scanned over the bank account details before he raised his eyebrows.

"Bloody hell she's loaded!" He exclaimed.

He checked the details again and David nodded.

"I know I already love her!"

When David worked his magic on the third monitor Richard read an email sent from Detective Inspector Nicola Garwood to Walworth police station regarding Jade Harris.

The email indicated to both David and Richard that Garwood was more than keen to question the unconscious girl from the first monitor in conjunction with the case of the missing homeless.

"She's a suspect?" Richard asked.

Of course Garwood had no idea that her suspect was in fact the latest victim.

Richard thought it through for a few seconds before he stared at David.

"So let me get this straight." He began.

"She's been abducted." He stated the obvious.

He pointed to the image of Jade Harris.

"But she's a police suspect?" He asked.

David Stringer slowly nodded his head.

"Because they received an anonymous call naming her as the ring leader." David replied.

Richard nodded as he continued to stare at the screens.

"That was a very clever move." He uttered.

David returned his attention to his monitors where he pulled up a file of Arron Balcombe.

"This bloke is really, really rich!" He continued.

"So rich that he gave Ms Richardson four million pounds for her house and then he gave her three more houses too."

Richard was slowly losing track of where David was going but it would all become crystal clear very soon.

David again pointed to the image of the unconscious Jade Harris.

"She took over a shop at Walworth leased by her." He explained.

He then pointed at the image of Carmen.

"She got the shop free of charge from him." He added.

Now he pointed to the marketing image of Arron Balcombe.

"And now she's charging her just five pounds a month rent." He continued.

He again pointed to Carmen and then to Jade.

Richard shook his head.

"Hang on a minute." He began.

"Are you saying that Jade Harris pays Carmen Richardson just five pounds rent a month for a two bedroom flat and a shop?" He asked.

David nodded and then returned to Carmen's criminal record.

'Known associates: Jade Harris'

David took in a deep breath.

"This arrest is nine years old Richard so Carmen Richardson and Jade Harris have been best friends for like ever." He pointed out.

Now David returned to the bank statement of Carmen Richardson for Richard to view again.

"How much do you think she would pay to get her best friend back?" He asked.

Richard nodded because he could now see where David was taking him.

"She could easily afford to hire the mercenary team to get Sasha out of Mamuju." He replied.

He knew that David would be nodding his head which was exactly what he was now doing.

Richard stared at the monitors.

For a brief moment he could only wonder how Stringer accomplished what he had today.

Eventually reality returned and he chuckled.

"This is all well and good Dave." He said.

"But we don't know where this girl Jade is."

He pointed again to the image of Jade Harris on the monitor.

"We don't even know where to begin looking."

David grinned.

He had thought everything through in that short space of time.

"But, Richard." He began.

He searched through three empty pizza boxes as Richard stared at him and waited.

He somehow sensed that David had thought everything through.

Stringer returned his attention to his monitors.

"Bugger I ran out of food." He uttered.

Richard waited impatiently before he eventually returned Stringer to the topic at hand.

David again logged onto Jane Chapman's auction site.

"But..." He began again.

"If you can convince her..."

He pointed to the image of Carmen Richardson.

"That we can help her to get *her* back..."

He pointed to the image of Jade Harris.

"She might fund our mercenary team using her whopping great big bank account." He finished.

Richard thought the world of David.

He smiled that his friend was making suggestions to help but he realised that David was clutching at straws.

"The only problem is Dave that we don't know where this Jade girl is, remember?" He asked.

"We don't know where this place is."

He pointed to Jade's image on Chapman's auction website again.

David stared at Richard and then back at the auction website displayed on his monitor before he eventually responded.

"You're an idiot." He uttered.

"How did you ever get a job as an SAS planner?" He asked.

"I don't know how the army survived with you *in* it." He added.

Richard chuckled.

There was another pause.

"We don't have to find them."

Richard stared back at David.

"Why don't we have to find them?" He asked.

Richard realised that David had something up his sleeve, something that he had completely missed.

For a few moments David waited for him to catch up but he saw that it wasn't going to happen.

He stared back at the login to the website.

"Because Richard I can get you an invitation to the auction you idiot." He told Richard.

"And we can use her money." He added.

Again he pointed at the image of Carmen Richardson.

Richard stared at the screen and finally caught up with David.

"They'll tell us where they are!" He exclaimed.

David nodded.

"I wish I was as smart as you." He very quietly uttered.

Forty Two
Monday November 13th 2000

Jade Harris had now been missing for six days and her friend's Carmen Richardson and April Marsh knew that she had been taken.

In Carmen's new office sat the owner of Balcombe & Webb Property Developments forty six year old Arron Balcombe.

Against Carmen's better judgement he now knew everything that had happened with regard to Jade.

To Carmen's surprise he understood why she hadn't called the police and besides he recently included Carmen into his future business and personal plans.

He didn't want her face plastered all over the TV news or any unwanted attention toward the business.

Before Balcombe left for a meeting he told Carmen that he would obviously help in any way that he could and she thanked him.

"I just need to be able to figure out where to start looking." She told him.

A new addition to the joint business was twenty one year old receptionist Polly Aldington who sat outside Carmen's office on the ground floor of C.R. Property Management.

Polly was five feet six inches tall and she had long straight dyed jet black hair and in Carmen's personal opinion Polly had the most beautiful brown eyes that she had ever seen.

She was dressed in a white cotton blouse beneath a thin black cardigan and she also wore a short black cotton skirt with shiny black leather flat heeled shoes on her feet.

Polly and Carmen had been friends for some time.

It was Carmen that stopped Polly from becoming a prostitute herself with the help of Jade Harris at the time when this pretty young woman was just seventeen.

They had history and more importantly for Carmen she trusted Polly and right now Carmen chose to be surrounded only by those that she trusted.

That inner circle was a small one.

Seated opposite Carmen was April Marsh.

April hadn't said much at all since the disappearance of Jade.

She watched Carmen as she sat and stared out of her office window but eventually April spoke.

"You know every London gangster alive Carmen." She reminded her.

"Can't they do something?"

Without turning to look at April she slowly shook her head.

"I already phoned a few and none of them know what's going on." She replied in a quiet tone.

Now she turned to look at her plump friend.

"People are being taken from their manors and they don't have a clue." She added.

"So a fat lot of good they're going to be."

April sighed with frustration.

"Look, I know you don't want to go to the police but..." She began.

Carmen immediately stopped her.

"As soon as Jade's disappearance is made public they'll make her disappear properly April." She explained.

"She's still in London right now."

April stared across the desk.

"But you can't know that?"

Again Carmen stared across at her and eventually she replied.

"I can feel her I know she's still here, ok?"

April let out another sigh.

"That's lovely Car but your feelings won't help us find her will they?" She asked.

Carmen stared across at April.

"I'm trying to think of what to do next." She snapped.

"I need you to stop babbling in my ear." She added.

"Why don't you just go out for a smoke?"

She then returned her attention to the window.

After a few more moments of silence April smiled.

"So what do we know about the people that took her?" She asked.

"Did Jade ever remember the name of the security company that owned the van?"

Carmen slowly shook her head.

"It was a silver security van that's all we know." She replied.

April's smile broadened.

"Well that's a start."

Carmen stared across to April but said nothing at all.

It was over an hour later when the new receptionist Polly Aldington knocked on the door and entered before she closed it behind her.

"Carmen something really weird just happened." She said.

Carmen still stared out of her office window trying to think of how to find Jade or at least how to start looking.

She could deal with everything that life ever threw at her under normal circumstances but this was different because she was completely out of her depth and she knew it.

This time she didn't know somebody that could fix the problem and she was starting to consider April's suggestion of going to the police.

She turned her head to glance up at Polly.

"Sorry?" She asked.

"You know the house in Knightsbridge that Mr Balcombe told you about this morning?" Polly began.

Carmen nodded.

Polly sat down beside April.

"Well somebody just called and asked to view it." She said.

Carmen returned her attention to the office window and nodded.

"Ok." She replied.

"There's more Carmen." Polly added.

Carmen turned to focus on Polly again.

"Hang on how can somebody call here regarding a house that we don't even have yet?" She asked.

"You heard Arron Balcombe yourself we only discussed it this morning." She added.

Polly nodded.

"But that's not the weird part." She replied.

Carmen sighed.

"Have you called Arron Balcombe to ask his if he arranged a viewing already?" She asked.

Polly shook her head.

"No I haven't." She replied.

Polly glanced up at Carmen.

"I thought it best to speak to you." She replied.

Carmen nodded and again turned to stare out of her office window.

"Like I said Carmen something weird happened." Polly reminded her.

Again Carmen sighed and returned her attention to Polly.

"I understand that but as you know I'm a little pre-occupied with something at the moment." She snapped.

"Just call Arron Balcombe and ask him if he wouldn't mind dealing with it." She added.

"We don't even have that house on our files yet." She reminded Polly.

"He only left the keys here for the place this morning!"

Again Polly nodded.

"I'm aware of that Carmen but will you shut up and let me finish?"

There was a long pause of silence.

The last thing on Carmen's mind was a new house that she didn't even manage yet.

It was in fact why she employed Polly.

She was hired to deal with things like this.

She eventually snapped a little and reminded her new twenty one year old employee.

Polly sighed.

"I had no idea that working for you would be so difficult." She retorted.

April sat beside her with raised eyebrows.

Carmen bit her tongue and returned her attention hopefully for the last time toward the window and stared out onto Mount Street.

"The viewer Mr Handley asked for *you* to show him the house in person tomorrow." Polly eventually continued.

Carmen nodded and tried desperately not to snap at Polly again.

"Well he's probably a friend of Arron's so he can show him around the place." She replied with a sigh.

Polly shook her head.

"I doubt that very much." She replied.

"I've been trying to tell you Carmen that Arron Balcombe didn't send Mr Handley."

Carmen glanced across at Polly as April watched the conversation in complete silence because she had learned over the years when it was safe to speak and when it was not.

"Well if Arron Balcombe didn't send him who did?" Carmen asked.

There was a silent pause of around twenty seconds before Polly answered.

She took in a deep breath and then exhaled.

"He asked me to tell you that Jade Harris told him about it this morning." She quietly replied.

Suddenly Carmen stared at Polly.

"What?"

Forty Three
Tuesday November 14th 2000

It was just after nine the next morning when Carmen Richardson's pale green Aston Martin pulled up outside an exclusive vacant property at Queensgate terrace Knightsbridge London.

This was the property that technically still belonged to Arron Balcombe but the paperwork to transfer it to Carmen's C.R. Property Management would be finalised later today.

Carmen still had no idea how this Mr Handley or whatever his name really was, the man that called Polly yesterday could even know of the existence of this property.

But he claimed that Jade sent him.

At the very least Carmen needed to know whatever he knew or what he wanted for Jade's safe return.

She sat in the driver seat of her car outside the huge house and her heart pounded heavily.

She was dressed in a black knitted pullover with black cotton slacks and wore a full length black leather coat and over her shoulder was slung a black patent leather bag.

Eventually she climbed out from the car and headed toward the house and climbed the seven stone steps up toward the dark blue front door but then she stopped.

She held the front door keys in her left hand but now she slowly turned to scan the line of parked cars on the road where she had just parked her own.

She searched for a man or men that could be watching and waiting for her to enter the house.

She saw nobody.

"Just calm yourself down." She quietly uttered.

Carmen took in a deep breath and exhaled.

She hadn't realised just how terrified she was until she stepped closer to the blue Georgian door.

She pushed the key inside the lock and saw that her hand trembled.

Now she could feel her heart heavily pounding.

However, as far as Carmen was concerned her own welfare was irrelevant.

This Mr Handley had answers that could bring Jade back and that was more important than her own safety and Carmen continuously reminded herself this.

Before she turned the key inside the lock Carmen took one last look behind her at the road and still saw nobody.

She had arrived almost twenty minutes early and he probably hadn't arrived yet.

However Carmen felt eyes watching her from somewhere and as ridiculous as it seemed they felt to her like eyes in the distance.

She had an eerie sense that she was being watched right now as she pushed open the blue door.

Carmen *was* indeed being watched but not from behind.

She was being watched from sixty miles high in the sky.

As soon as she opened the front door her eyes slowly scanned the hall and she immediately noticed a stale smell due to this empty property standing vacant for a few months.

As the door slowly closed Carmen's brown eyes scanned outside from left to right but she could still see nobody out there.

She looked up to her right at the white security panel on the wall that flashed text on the screen because she had activated the silent alarm as soon as she opened the door.

Her trembling forefinger pressed the five digit code onto the keypad before she pressed 'enter' and the flashing text changed.

'Alarm system deactivated'.

She slowly headed toward a white door directly ahead that she knew led into the kitchen.

She planned to base herself there for the purpose of an exit into the back garden for a quick escape via the back door that she would unlock now in preparation.

She reached the kitchen door and realised that her heart still pounded.

"Get a hold of yourself." She whispered.

"He's not even here yet."

Carmen reminded herself again that this was all about finding Jade and that her own safety mattered very little.

Her fears would have to wait.

She knew that she needed to get through this and that she had to meet this man if only to find out what he knew or pay him whatever he wanted.

The kitchen door creaked as she pushed it open.

Carmen now stared inside and she immediately froze to the spot.

"W...Who the hell are you?" She asked.

"How did you get in here?"

Her heart pounded very heavily and she was close to passing out.

Carmen was gripped with sheer terror.

Seated at a kitchen table on her right was a man with short blonde swept back hair and blue eyes.

He wore a dark brown leather jacket with a white open necked shirt beneath it and blue denim jeans with shiny black shoes.

He actually sat drinking coffee.

Richard Willows smiled back at her.

"Good morning Carmen would you like a coffee?" He asked.

From the shock of seeing him sitting in the kitchen Carmen felt very light headed.

Her heart continued to pound much faster and heavier than before.

She knew that she was about to pass out.

She tightly held onto the door handle with her right hand and felt her legs weakening.

Richard smiled again.

"Thank you for meeting me at such short notice." He began.

"I do understand that you're an incredibly busy woman."

Carmen was still frozen to the spot.

Eventually she somehow managed to turn and glance at the inside of the closed front door in the hall.

She knew that she would never make it.

She slowly turned to face him when he quietly spoke again.

"I promise that you have nothing to fear from me Carmen." He assured her.

"I believe that we have something in common and can help each other."

Every single terrifying scenario flashed through Carmen's mind.

She was however aware that there was something about him and it prevented her from at least trying to make a run for it.

Still frozen to the spot she stared into his seemingly cold blue eyes and he spoke again.

"They took my sister too." He told her.

He had a tremble in his own tone and Carmen heard it.

She however remained rooted to the spot.

She was still too terrified to move forward or back toward the front door.

She managed to remind herself that she needed to know whatever this man knew about Jade.

"S...So who are you?" She asked him.

"How did you know to find me?"

Richard very slowly climbed to his feet and walked just as slowly to the kitchen work surface.

"Want a coffee?" He asked again.

He raised the mug that he'd been drinking from.

Carmen now slowly managed to edge toward him.

"There are people who know I'm here." She assured him.

He nodded with a smile.

"Good I'm going to need you to be that smart." He replied.

There was something about this man that told Carmen that she was in no immediate danger.

She didn't know what it was but nobody had come bursting through the front door and obviously she knew what Jade had told her prior to her abduction.

If he was representing them surely it would have happened by now.

Eventually she spoke again.

"I'm going to ask you again, who are you?"

He glanced across at her and flashed one of his smiles as he held out his hand for her to shake.

"My name is Richard Willows and I think that I can get your friend Jade back."." He replied.

Carmen stared down at his hand and then looked back up into his eyes.

"If this is a ransom let's get it over with." She told him.

Richard started to shake his head but Carmen interjected.

"But if anything already has or does happen to her..." She continued.

"I promise to spend every penny that I own at every waking moment to have you personally hunted down and executed." She assured him in a quiet tone.

Richard was more than aware that she meant every single word.

He made two cups of coffee and then glanced at Carmen.

"You're a dreadful hostess I had to go back out and buy milk." He boasted.

"Do you take sugar?"

Finally Carmen glanced down at the cups.

"Two." She said.

Willows smiled.

"Take a seat." He told her.

"Let's start by talking about getting Jade back before we discuss my sister."

Carmen slowly made her way to the table where she nervously sat down on the chair opposite where she earlier discovered him seated.

"I'm going to tell you again Mr Willows or whatever your name actually is." She began.

"If this is bullshit there are no limits to what I will do to make you pay." She assured him.

Richard sat down opposite her.

"I understand that you're an excellent business woman so let's talk business and tomorrow I have a friend that I think you should meet." He said.

Richard suddenly heard another voice.

"Is she as hot in person Richard?" David asked in his earpiece.

Forty Four
Wednesday November 15ᵗʰ 2000

It was around ten the next morning when a black Saab convertible pulled up outside the house where thirty three year old David Stringer lived and worked at Tranton Road Bermondsey.

Richard Willows looked across to the passenger seat at Carmen Richardson.

"I'd like to describe him as eccentric but that's not going to work." He told her with a chuckle.

"Or maybe completely insane bordering on genius." He added.

"I'm not sure which describes him better."

There was a pause.

"Either way he's going to be without a doubt the smartest person that you've ever met." He assured her.

David Stringer ventured outside yesterday and purchased coffee sugar milk and an electric kettle along with cups to pour it into.

He nervously invited Carmen and Richard inside.

"You cleaned String?" Richard asked in a whisper.

In the office upstairs Stringer began his show and tell by playing back satellite footage from earlier today.

The giant Russian Vladimir Kolov drove to the home of Jane Chapman at Watford.

He spent around half an hour there before he left and headed south and arrived at the home of Lisa Moore at Pinner.

He stepped inside there too and spent around the same length of time before he drove north-west to Amersham to meet with Debbie Davies.

David then froze the play back recording.

"At first I was quite surprised that he was meeting them all in person." He told Richard and Carmen.

"This is the first time that I know of that any of them have been in the same place at the same time."

He then looked up at Carmen as she stood behind his chair.

"I think they make a point of never being together." He told her with a smile.

Carmen stared into his over magnified eyes and he seemed to blink in slow motion.

Her mouth was already open to speak because of what she was viewing.

More to the point how she was viewing it.

"Where are we watching this from?" She asked with confusion.

David turned in his chair.

"From a French spy satellite." He informed her.

"They pass over here all the time." .

Carmen nodded.

"That's lovely but how are *we* watching it from a French spy satellite?" She asked.

Richard intervened.

"Don't ask." He advised with a chuckle.

Richard then explained the association between Vladimir Kolov Jane Chapman Lisa Moore and Debbie Davies to change the topic of conversation.

Stringer looked up at her again.

"There's still a lot more to show you Ms Richardson." He told her.

"Should we go halves on a pizza delivery?"

She stared wide eyed into his over magnified eyes.

"It's not even eleven o'clock in the morning." She informed him.

Carmen knew that this strange chubby man already knew far more than the police possibly could.

She glanced at her watch and then back down at him.

"If you're as smart as I'm beginning to think you are, you do the pizza ordering and I'll do the paying." She told him with a smile.

"And call me Carmen."

Standing beside her Richard shook his head at her offer of payment.

"That may have been your first mistake today." He said in a quiet tone.

He also scrutinised the monitors in front of him and David returned his attention to the same monitors.

"I'll hold back Carmen." He assured her with a grin.

Carmen now sat down beside him.

"Just make sure to order some ham and pineapple." She replied.

She then nudged David with her shoulder.

"Order the pizza and show me everything you know."

David started by showing her the dating website that was owned by Jane Chapman.

"I found this fake website by tracking payments from abroad in large quantities." He told her.

"And I mean large quantities." He over-emphasised.

He then tapped into the auction site but then turned to Carmen.

"This isn't going to be pleasant viewing." He informed her.

He then clicked on several jpeg images to show her a few of the women that had been abducted over the past months.

"This changes on a weekly basis."

After a few moments David clicked on a recent jpeg image that showed her unconscious best friend Jade Harris.

"We know from the floor behind her that she's at their warehouse facility." David said.

He turned to look at Carmen.

Tears now streamed down her face as she stared at the image of her unconscious friend.

"Sorry Carmen." David regretfully uttered.

There was a momentary pause before he spoke again.

"We can get Richard an invitation to the next auction to buy her back if you're willing to do that?" David asked.

Carmen could clearly hear his traits of naïve innocence clearly showing through.

Richard interjected again.

"Do you know anybody who would help us from abroad?" He asked.

Carmen immediately nodded as she stared up at him with tear filled eyes.

"Yes I do." She replied.

"I own a house on a Greek island." She told him.

"His name is Marinos Georgas."

Richard could see the anguish on Carmen's face.

"Can this Marinos be trusted?" He asked.

Carmen nodded without removing her tearful gaze from him.

"I choose my friends carefully." She replied.

Richard now turned his attention to David.

"When's the next auction?" He asked.

Stringer checked his computer for a few moments.

"In two days on Friday." He replied.

Richard turned to Carmen again.

"They want seventy thousand for Jade." He began.

Carmen shrugged.

"I don't care how much it costs."

"But the mercenary team to go into Mamuju to get my sister out is another hundred thousand." He explained.

Carmen nodded with a desperate smile of hope.

"A deal's a deal." She replied.

"Get my girl back and then we find your team of mercenaries." She promised him.

Richard turned to Stringer again.

Before he spoke Carmen had one more thing to add.

"I want your sister back from them as much as you do." She assured him.

"So let's work as a team from now and I promise to see this through to the very end including after Jade is back."

Richard turned to Stringer again.

"So mate, get me into that auction."

David beamed a grin.

"Thank you very much Carmen."

He worked on the auction site securing Richard an invitation on behalf of Carmen's long term friend Marinos Georgas from the Greek island of Kefalonia.

Carmen smiled at David.

"Get my girl back please." She told him.

He nodded.

"Working on it."

"Before I do anything I need to cook up and install a brand new image for your friend Marinos." He told her.

"They'll probably run a background check on him.

David then turned to Carmen and displayed that same cheeky grin.

"Shall we make him a shipping tycoon?" He asked.

Carmen couldn't help but chuckle.

"I think even he'd find that funny."

Carmen stood up and took her mobile telephone from her shoulder bag.

"I had better call him and tell him what's going on." She said.

Richard watched her for a few moments.

"You're sure he can be trusted?" He asked.

Carmen smiled still with tear filled eyes.

"Oh yes." She replied.

Forty Five
Friday November 17th 2000

It rained heavily for most of the night and although it was still raining at just after two in the morning it slowly eased to a drizzle.

Twenty eight year old PC Henry Noonan a special operations armed response officer sat in the driver seat of an unmarked car at Belmont road Ilford Essex.

Seated next to him was his friend and colleague PC Mark Crenshaw.

All of the side windows of the car were blackened.

When a small blue Fiat pulled up at the opposite side of Belmont Road the occupants had no idea that the two armed undercover policemen were inside it staring straight at them.

Twenty six year old Crenshaw was five feet eight inches tall with blonde cropped hair.

He confirmed that inside the blue Fiat were two occupants.

"This could be game time." He said.

Henry Noonan nodded with agreement.

"Charlie Sierra this is Zero-One, are you receiving, over?" Noonan asked into his radio mic.

The team's mobile Operations room was a dark blue long wheel based Mercedes van parked half a mile away around the corner at Winchester road.

In the back of the van sat thirty four year old Sergeant Alan Michaels along with PC Peter Stark.

Stark's role was to record every incident and radio transmission during this operation.

Sergeant Michaels was in charge of the entire team.

After hearing Noonan's transmission Michaels responded using his own microphone.

"Go ahead Zero-one." He replied.

Henry Noonan was five feet eleven inches tall and he had slightly greying red hair.

He relayed the new information regarding the situation at the far end of Belmont Road.

He glanced back through the blackened windows at the still occupied blue Fiat.

"I think you might be right this might be it." He said in a calm tone.

Crenshaw nodded as he also continued to stare at them.

"I hope so because I can't stand being in a car with you for much longer." He chuckled.

Noonan laughed too.

The two occupants inside the blue Fiat were still doing nothing.

While they sat waiting they had absolutely no idea that they were being watched by two armed police officers from the car beside theirs.

"Well they aren't moving." Crenshaw said.

Just then the radio silence was broken again.

They heard the next message directed toward their Sergeant.

"Hello Charlie Sierra this is Two-Three." A female voice said.

Noonan and Crenshaw stared at each other.

"That's Martine." Noonan said.

Crenshaw nodded again.

He slowly tilted his head to look down to the opposite end of Belmont road where he saw headlights from a second car.

It was now parked near their colleagues inside a second special ops car.

"Another car just came in at the other end of the street." He told Henry.

Noonan nodded.

At the opposite end of the quiet residential Belmont road a red Vauxhall pulled up on the opposite side and around two car lengths down from the second unmarked police car.

"This shit's finally getting interesting." Noonan uttered.

Twenty six year old WPC Martine Stone sat in the passenger seat at the other end of the street.

She glanced at her colleague thirty one year old Chris Carter who was second in command of this special ops team.

Martine called into Sergeant Michaels and informed him that a red Ford had just pulled up.

The occupants remained inside the vehicle just like the blue Fiat at the opposite end of the street.

"Keep your cool." Carter told Martine.

"We don't do a thing yet."

She nodded.

Chief Inspector Keith Curtis was sleeping in his bed when he received the telephone call from Michaels.

He switched on his radio on the bedside cabinet.

Curtis then lit a cigarette as he sat in his bed to listen in to the radio communications.

"If this kicks off Roberts I'll nail your arse to the wall." He uttered.

He continued to listen to the static noise from the otherwise now silent isolated radio channel.

Inside the dark blue van Sergeant Michaels instructed the driver to take a right turn out of Winchester road and park at the junction of Sunnyside road and Albert road.

They would then be positioned one street up from Belmont road itself just around the corner from where PCs Chris Carter and Martine Stone were positioned.

They would wait out of sight.

As the blue van turned right out of Winchester road the driver reported that a third vehicle was now turning into Belmont road.

"It's a silver security van."

The same silver security van eventually pulled up directly outside a house at Belmont road and the Romanian Captain looked out from the passenger window.

"Aceasta." He told his driver Lucian Banica.

'This.'

Abel Barbu turned to the two men in the back of the van and showed one finger to Emil Hagi and then the two fingered signal to Dorin Christescu.

'You are number one and you are number two.'

Both former soldiers nodded.

Barbu and his driver Banica watched as Hagi picked the lock of the blue door and one last time the Captain glanced upstairs to the darkened bedrooms of the house.

Chief Inspector Keith Curtis now sat on the side of his bed and pulled on one of his black socks with his phone tucked beneath his chin.

"Sam, get your arse out of bed." He told Henning.

"Belmont Road is about to kick off." He added.

"Yes get her up too but make sure she speaks to nobody." Curtis continued.

"This thing is about to kick off right now so both of you meet me at your HQ."

A second blue special ops van moved into Richmond road just thirty feet around the corner from Noonan and Crenshaw.

The second van waited to seal off Belmont road from one end to entrap everybody concerned when the identical mobile ops van with Sergeant Michaels inside covered the opposite end.

Nobody else would be permitted in and nobody now out of Belmont road.

From both Henry Noonan at one end and Martine Stone at the other reports were made that firearms were visible being carried by the three men currently entering the house from the security van.

The weapon types were unknown from both reports but both clearly stated that the three males dressed in black tactical combat clothing similar to their own were carrying firearms.

This would affect the approach for Sergeant Michaels positioned at the cross junction just around the corner because he didn't have the luxury of viewing this first hand.

This was an undercover operation and he also lacked the luxury of calling in local reinforcements unless it became a no-win situation.

Every member of his team knew and understood this.

After a brief telephone conversation with his boss Chief Inspector Keith Curtis who was now heading toward Whitechapel Sergeant Michaels made the radio announcement.

"Hello all stations this is Charlie Sierra."

Michaels then explained the situation to his team.

It was unknown whether the occupants inside the two spotter cars positioned at both ends of Belmont road were armed but the three individuals now inside the building were confirmed to be carrying firearms.

"When it hits the fan very shortly the two cars are going to run." Michaels informed his team.

"Let them go." He added.

"We don't want or need a shootout in a residential street."

In the unmarked police car at the far end of Belmont road PC Steve Crenshaw looked across to Henry Noonan.

"Are we seriously going to let these little shits go?" He asked.

Noonan stared back at him.

"You heard the man the house is the target."

The former Romanian Army Captain Abel Barbu entered the completely darkened house with Emil Hagi and Dorin Christescu.

He pointed to the staircase on the left and both of his men nodded.

They all very quietly reached the darkened landing at the top of the stairs where they saw three closed doors in front of them and one to the left that was slightly ajar.

Barbu pointed to the slightly opened door.

Both Hagi and Christescu stood on either side of it and armed their pistols that made a quiet high pitched squeal as they activated.

As usual the Captain's very nervous senses became heightened and he took a little time to compose himself for the task ahead.

Inside the red Vauxhall spotter car at the end of Belmont road twenty five year old Romanian Augustin Vasile sat in the passenger seat.

He waited with the driver for the clean-up operation that would begin after the Captain and his team removed the four women from inside the house.

Dragos Ungur also twenty five stared ahead watching the house.

"Păstraţi uitam." He told his seemingly bored passenger Augustin.

'Keep watching.'

Augustin Vasile sighed as he turned his head to the left and glanced out of the window toward the parked cars on the opposite side of Belmont road.

As he casually scanned the line of parked cars across the street Vasile again blew a mouthful of air from utter boredom.

But suddenly his eyes met with those of PC Chris Carter and then WPC Martine Stone through the front windscreen of their car.

They stared back at him.

His eyes widened with terror because he saw that they were dressed in black tactical police uniforms.

Captain Abel Barbu stood on the landing in front of the bedroom door that Emil Hagi and Dorin Christescu had just entered.

He alone heard the transmission in his earpiece from Dragos Ungur in the red Vauxhall Corsa at the end of the street.

His senses were already fully heightened but now he was suddenly gripped with sheer terror as his eyes scanned the darkened bedroom where his two soldiers had already entered.

'Este o capcană!' He told only himself.

'It's a trap!'

Hagi and Christescu by now positioned themselves at either side of a bed where two human shapes were bulging from beneath the covers but no heads were visible.

Their Captain's eyes stared wide through his black balaclava as he quietly backed himself away from the room without uttering a single word.

His actions were purely for the purpose of self-preservation.

His heart continued to pound but more rapidly now.

He could feel his face covered with sweat beneath the black mask and his hands trembled as he reached beside him for the bannister rail.

The Captain slowly backed himself down the stairs.

When he eventually reached the bottom he turned and sprinted out to the silver van and jumped into the passenger seat.

"Du-te, du-te!" He ordered.

'Go, go!'

Without a second thought Lucian Banica started the engine and skidded away toward Richmond road at high speed past Henry Noonan and Steve Crenshaw and turned right toward the A118 Winston road.

They then turned left and headed toward the city of London.

"Ceea ce sa întâmplat?" Banica asked his trembling Captain.

'What happened?"

Barbu pulled off his balaclava and Lucian could see the absolute fear in his eyes.

"Masini de politie de la ambele capete ale drumului!" Barbu replied.

'Police cars at both ends of the road!'

Banica stared across at his Captain as the van headed west.

"Emil și Dorin?" He asked.

'Emil and Dorin?'

Barbu shook his head.

Lucian Banica slowed down the van.

"sunt ei conştienţi?" He asked.

'Are they aware?'

Officers Henry Noonan and Steve Crenshaw already watched the silver security van speed past and now it was the turn of the blue Fiat beside them.

They watched as it sped down Belmont road past the red Vauxhall on its left and the second unmarked police car on its right and then it turned left and out of sight.

"I can't believe we're letting them run." Crenshaw uttered.

Noonan glanced across at him.

"That could be two guns that can't shoot you today."

The red Corsa that was reported by Martine flashed past Noonan and Crenshaw in the same direction that the van took.

It then also took a right and headed toward London as reported by the second blue van that was positioned around the corner.

The two blue vans now moved into position across both entry points of Belmont road and sealed it off.

Nothing would enter into Belmont road and no more out.

They had two men trapped inside the house.

Henry Noonan started the engine after receiving the radio instruction from Sergeant Michaels.

Michaels remained inside the blue van that now completely blocked the entrance at the other end of Belmont road.

Noonan pulled up nose to nose with PC Chris Carter and Martine Stone with the house in question on his left.

In the darkened bedroom at the front of the house the two Romanian soldiers stared at each other after they heard cars pull up to a stop right outside.

They already heard vehicles speed away and knew that their Captain had suddenly vanished.

They both knew that something was very wrong and fear now began to creep in.

Hagi stared down at the two still forms beneath the covers that he already knew weren't just motionless.

They were too still and when he pulled back the covers they both stared down at two headless dummies.

The atmosphere suddenly turned electric.

Panic set in and both men frantically scanned the room.

Hagi suddenly spotted two silhouettes out in the darkened landing and they were dressed in what looked like black tactical uniforms.

"Stand still!" PC Colin Simms shouted very loudly at him.

Hagi watched both men adopt a kneeling stance and they both had weapons pointed in his direction.

The man that knelt beside Simms now yelled.

"Drop the firearm!"

Both Special Ops officers had firearms pointed at Emil Hagi, the only Romanian within their line of sight.

"Drop your weapon!" PC Mark Fuller shouted.

Hagi then dropped his stun gun onto the floor and held his empty hands high in the air for them to see.

They weren't carrying stun guns.

Theirs fired real bullets that would kill him.

Out of the line of sight of Simms and Fuller, Dorin Christescu still frantically scanned around the room pointing his gun in in every direction that his eyes travelled.

"Drop the weapon!" A female voice suddenly yelled at him.

The voice came from somewhere inside the completely darkened room.

Christescu continued to frantically search until he finally found her.

He stared down wide eyed at twenty six year old WPC Vanessa Fisk.

She stared straight back up at him from where she was lying on the floor beside a tall brown chest of drawers.

She instinctively knew that he wasn't going to let go of what still looked in the darkened room to be an ordinary 9mm pistol.

"I said drop the weapon!" She yelled.

His stun gun automatically followed his eyes and now pointed directly down at her and the red beam settled at the centre of her forehead.

The blonde police woman concluded that he was going to fire if she didn't shoot him first.

"Suit yourself!" She silently mouthed.

They stared straight at each other as Christescu moved his left hand over to steady the right that held his pistol.

Vanessa Fisk immediately fired two shots in rapid succession into the chest of Dorin Christescu that echoed loudly throughout the entire house.

The force sent him sprawling backward and he landed slumped over the two headless dummies that were partially concealed on the bed.

Simms and Fuller quickly entered the room as she slowly climbed to her feet and now pointed her hand gun at Emil Hagi.

His hands were still raised in the air and he now trembled with uncontrollable fear.

Outside the house Henry Noonan and Steve Crenshaw saw multiple lights being switched on by the residents of Belmont road as they heard the radio message from their Sergeant.

"Shots fired, I repeat shots fired!"

They hurriedly climbed from the car as did Chris Carter and Martine Stone in front of them.

Colin Simms reported by radio that the house was now secured.

Sergeant Michaels now stood outside the front door with Noonan Carter Stone and Crenshaw and called for local police back up to deal with the now wakened residents of the street and to cordon off the entire area.

Emil Hagi was taken into police custody by the special ops team.

Dorin Christescu was killed from two gunshot wounds to his chest.

The second round passed straight through his heart both courtesy of twenty six year old WPC Vanessa Fisk.

Forty Six
Friday November 17th 2000

In the very early hours of the morning Nicola Garwood was woken by Sam Henning.

He insisted that she meet him at task force headquarters at Whitechapel immediately and with no explanation until she arrived.

Still half asleep she dressed and drove into the city centre with a sense of urgency from Dulwich village but still with no knowledge of why.

"This had better be good Henning!" She uttered to herself.

She drove through central London more than six hours earlier than she usually needed to.

A short while later she sat in the cubicle office with Sam Henning and Chief Inspector Keith Curtis from New Scotland Yard where they all listened to the events as they unfolded at Belmont road Ilford, Essex.

When it was all over and a single arrest was made with another of the abductors declared dead at the scene, Nicola turned to Sam.

"And I'm guessing that I wasn't to be trusted with any of this?" She asked.

Chief Inspector Curtis answered her question.

"That was my fault Garwood."

Curtis went on to explain that because after it was discovered that her boss Chief Inspector Roberts removed information from the building it was essential to be absolutely sure that he was the only person other than Henning that knew about the bogus safe house at Ilford.

"If you knew it would've meant that there were two of you instead of one." He insisted.

Eventually Nicola although reluctant knew that what they did was the right thing and she nodded with acknowledgement.

"Ok I get that." She conceded.

But now she stared across to Curtis again.

"So do we know for sure that these people got the information from Roberts?" She asked.

"I'm only asking in case anybody else here seems to have forgotten that we're talking about the Chief Inspector of the entire bloody task force." She reminded them.

Sam nodded but Nicola still didn't know if he was nodding in agreement with her or nodding that they knew for certain that Roberts had passed on the details of the bogus safe house.

Sam said nothing but Curtis seemed to know what he was talking about.

"Sam and Roberts are the only two people in this building that knew about that house." He began again.

"What differs between them is that Sam was fully aware that it was full of armed coppers." He added.

Curtis now glanced across Sam's desk at both Henning and Garwood with a much more serious, as opposed to the earlier smug look on his face.

"So who wants the bad news?" He asked them both.

Before either could speak up he continued.

"It's still not enough to nail Roberts."

Both Garwood and Henning stared back at him.

"You're kidding right?" Nicola asked.

Curtis shook his head.

"We know that it could only have been him but there's no tangible evidence to prove it."

He took in a long deep breath.

"Let's say that we try to nick him in the morning." He began.

"We have a new safe house that they just happened to hit with no link to Roberts at all." He added.

"But I'm guessing that he has to react in some way."

He now stared directly at Nicola.

"I'm also banking on the guy in custody singing like a bird."

Nicola shook her head with disbelief.

"And what if your bird can't or won't sing his name?" She asked.

Curtis broke into a grin.

"If we can't take Mohammed to the mountain we have ways of convincing the mountain to come to Mohammed." He assured her.

His grin broadened.

"On the bright side we now know for a fact where our mole is, don't we?" He asked.

"If we can set him up once more we'll have him."

Again Sam nodded.

"He's right Nik." He told her.

"I have no doubt now that the info came from Roberts and remember he doesn't know that he's the only other person who knew about it." He told her.

"I told him that half a dozen people knew of the existence of that house."

Curtis now looked at Sam.

"He's going to want to know why you told him it was a safe house." He began.

"So you've got to play dumb and tell him that you were only informed that you had a new building and that's it."

Henning nodded with a mock smile.

"Thanks guv."

Nicola suddenly chuckled.

"It just dawned on me that if this all goes wrong, for once I'm the only one that he can't scream and shout at."

Curtis chuckled too.

"Actually we just implicated you." He replied.

Just under seven hours later Sam and Nicola stood at the back of Chief Inspector Martin Robert's full office as the TV cameras rolled.

Roberts informed the world's press that one of the abductors involved in the case of the missing homeless was arrested while another was unfortunately shot dead at the scene.

Nicola stood beside Henning with her arms folded while he stood with his hands inside his grey trouser pockets.

They both watched as the chief grimaced his way through the press conference and when it slowly wound down Garwood leaned to her left.

"You'd think he'd show us his happy face as he informed the world that an abductor had been caught." She commented.

She still watched as the chief answered questions via several hand held microphones.

"I was just thinking how overjoyed he looked." Henning whispered.

It was still only the two of them that knew the truth at task force headquarters.

Even Jacob Saunders was excluded because right now the fewer people who knew the better.

Keith Curtis explained this and both Garwood and Henning of course agreed that it was the safest option.

When the press release ended the two Detective Inspectors made their way to the door along with the first few members of the press.

"Detective Inspector Henning, do you have a moment please?" The chief called out.

Sam stopped in his tracks.

"Good luck!" Nicola whispered with a giggle.

"I'm going to try to find out if Roberts was on the client lists of Jade Harris." She added.

When Sam joined him Roberts glared for a moment.

"I'd like a word when everybody's gone." He whispered.

Sam nodded.

He then watched as the chief shook hands with several members of the press and thanked them for attending until he closed the door after the last one.

Henning stood in front of the desk and waited for the tirade that was bound to be headed his way as Chief Inspector Roberts slowly walked around to the opposite side.

To Sam's surprise Roberts remained calm.

"Did you know that the house at Ilford was a set up?" He asked.

There was a short pause before Henning replied.

"I found out this morning Sir." He lied.

"When the house was allocated we were only told that we had a new one to take on board that already had four young women in it." He lied again.

The chief now motioned for him to take a seat.

"Well it seems that somebody may have fed the traffickers information." He told Sam.

"It could just be pure coincidence Sir but we're going through lists of who had access to the address and who could possibly gain access to them." He replied.

Roberts agreed that was a good plan of action.

There was another pause before the chief spoke again.

"Do we have any immediate suspects?" He asked.

Sam shook his head.

"I personally don't want to spend too much time thinking about it Sir." He said.

"For me the house at Ilford was more than likely watched and then hit." He lied again.

The chief's next enquiry was regarding the location that the prisoner was being held.

"That seems to be a huge secret." He told Sam.

Sam nodded again.

"It is Sir." He replied.

"New Scotland Yard figure that if this outfit are bold enough to hit our safe houses they're bold enough to attempt a rescue."

There was another pause as Roberts waited for an answer.

"So?" He eventually had to ask.

Sam realised that Roberts was waiting to be informed of the whereabouts of the prisoner although at this time nobody even knew Emil Hagi's name or nationality.

Eventually he replied.

"He's being held at Woolwich nick Sir."

Just then Sam had an idea, another bite for Roberts because it was possible that he might just take another one.

"There's a discussion about who's going to interview him." He added.

"It needs to be a very senior officer of course." He added.

He soon departed from the room leaving the very senior officer Chief Inspector Martin Roberts alone with his thoughts.

Forty Seven
Friday November 17th 2000

It was just after seven on a dark cold evening when Richard Willows stood in the living room at his two bedroom apartment near Wapping Wharf.

He tied his silk burgundy tie.

His swept back blonde hair was combed and he was dressed in a black pinstriped suit with a white shirt and polished black shoes and he stared into the full length mirror.

He then pressed a small dark brown mole onto the front left side of his neck that was designed and built by David Stringer.

The tiny mole acted as a transmitter using the vibrations of his throat while a much smaller version was carefully inserted into his ear that acted as a receiver.

"How's that Dave?" He asked on the isolated frequency.

Inside his office room at Tranton road David Stringer took a swig from a bottle of red fizzy pop.

"Loud and clear and your signal's good Richard." He eventually replied.

David had just locked onto a passing French spy satellite.

"They'll be picking you up next to Potters Field Park just around the corner from your place." He reminded Richard.

"I'm guessing that from there they take you to wherever it is that they hold the auctions."

"The fake ID I created for Marinos passed their examinations." He added.

Richard again stared at himself in the mirror.

"And you'll watch where they take me from above?" He asked.

David confirmed that he was correct.

"By the end of tonight we'll know where their warehouse is." He told Richard.

There was a pause.

"As long as they don't kill you before you get there of course." He added with a chuckle.

At Mount Street Mayfair Carmen Richardson was included with two identical moles of her own courtesy of the somewhat smitten David Stringer.

Carmen was also issued with a slender magnet to retrieve the tiny mole from inside her ear later.

It was a home-made device that he issued only to her.

She was amazed at the clarity of the conversation that she was now a part of and learned that Stringer could even talk in isolation with either of them by somehow switching frequencies.

Richard was ready and at ten minutes past eight he stepped out from his apartment and headed toward Potters Fields Park to be picked up by Jade Harris's abductors.

He would then be taken to the site of the auction while watched from the night sky by his friend David Stringer.

When Richard arrived at the pick-up point at Weaver's lane a light blue Ford van with no windows at the back waited with two men seated in the front.

He could see that they were eastern European.

He immediately recognised their accent and as he climbed into the back of the van he very quietly spoke to himself.

"The two men in the front of the van are Turkish." He very quietly uttered.

The small mole positioned on the front left side of his neck worked on the vibrations of his throat and it meant that Richard could speak as quietly as he wished.

At the other end of the conversation David would hear him loud and clear.

Richard could feel the van starting to move.

David Stringer saw that it was heading east and he relayed the information to Richard.

"Remember that they could have hidden microphones inside the back of the van so say nothing from now on."

"And they might have hidden cams so no silent responses either." He added.

He consequently received no response from his friend.

At Mount Street Mayfair seated across the desk from Carmen was April Marsh.

She rapidly scribbled something onto a note pad on Carmen's desk.

'What's going on?'

She slid the pad across to Carmen.

Carmen read the question and promptly scribbled a response.

'He's sitting in a van!'

It was around forty minutes later that David announced for the benefit of both Richard and Carmen.

"Ok I can see that you stopped at the end of the Stanley industrial estate next to north Woolwich pier and this looks like it Richard."

"In the event of a quick escape whatever you do, don't run south or you're going swimming." He chuckled.

Richard understood that the river Thames was directly to the south of the van.

As he waited on the wooden bench in the back of the windowless blue van the back doors opened and he was motioned out.

He was escorted through a narrow alleyway between units 4A and 4B that were joined at the back by a small door at the centre that led into both buildings.

Inside he saw six sliver vans that had been recently stripped of their signage although one imprint remained.

'London's finest!'

At Bermondsey David stared at his monitor.

"Ok I've seen you walk inside." He told Richard.

"If you can just touch your throat mic so that I know that you can still hear me as you're now inside a steel structure I'd appreciate it."

He then heard a light 'thud' as Richard gently touched the transmitter on his neck.

"Thanks." David responded.

Richard was escorted across the warehouse floor to another brown door by Barak Yazici and his driver Atif Rahman from the Turkish abduction team.

Yazici now sported a solid white cast over his right forearm.

He led Richard through into the hospitality lounge also known as 'the bar.'

Richard stood and scanned the room for a few moments.

"You have a bar?" He asked.

Barak Yazici smiled.

"It is hospitality suite." He replied.

He was obviously unaware that Richard's question was for the benefit of David Stringer.

"Do they do fizzy pop?" David asked with a chuckle in Richard's ear.

There were already many people in the bar area that casually chatted while they stood with a drinks in hand or sat on the plush cream leather furniture just as they would at any other bar.

Richard was quite taken aback.

These people as wealthy as they may be could actually sit or stand and discuss the weather, economics or whatever they talked about while they waited to place bids on living walking and breathing people.

'How self-righteous are you lot?'

Richard knew that tonight he needed to keep his emotions in check.

Barak Yazici turned to him.

"Mr Handley can I offer you a drink?" He asked.

Richard smiled.

"Do you have scotch?"

Yazici nodded with a smile.

"Please wait with Atif." He replied.

"I will get your drink and then take you to the woman that you seek."

Richard nodded with a smile of his own.

His eyes scanned the room to see if there was anybody famous that he recognised.

He noticed that many were not from the UK and had probably travelled in to make their purchases or to explore for their first visit.

In truth he also knew that he was guessing and didn't really know anything for certain.

When Barak Yazici returned he handed Richard a glass of neat scotch.

"Please Mr Handley after me." He said.

Richard then followed him with Atif Rahman behind.

As they walked through the bar area Richard glanced down at a small silver dog cage that was situated between two cream leather sofas.

Inside it was a pretty young woman that he guessed was in her early twenties.

She smiled back up at him.

A well-dressed man sat on the sofa to the left of the girl in the cage and an older woman was seated on the sofa on the right of it.

The man and woman obviously knew each other prior to today.

They talked over the cage and because the pretty young girl inside it glanced up and half-smiled at Richard he guessed that she was a part of some marketing ploy and actually worked within the organisation.

He was led by the Turkish men to another enclosed area inside the adjoining warehouse.

He passed through a small aisle and on his left he saw rows upon rows of black steel cages most of which were occupied.

Richard now had his first very brief glimpse of the warehouse itself.

In the enclosed area he saw a makeshift wooden construction that resembled a stage with a long scaffold pole that ran across the top.

There were old burgundy curtains that hung on either side and served as an entrance and exit where the exhibits could be ushered to and from with their hands chained to the scaffold pole above.

'You lot thought of everything.'

Richard now stood with Yazici beside him amongst ten or more empty blue plastic chairs.

Barak Yazici then introduced Richard to another Briton.

"Mr Handley this is Mr Downing he is in charge here."

Richard shook hands with Mark Downing who was also dressed in a smart black suit.

"So you like the crazy girl?" Downing asked.

Richard raised his eyebrows.

Downing pointed to the Romanian Captain Abel Barbu who now sported a large plaster across his nose and he chuckled.

"Crazy girl head butted him earlier tonight when he woke her up."

He then pointed to the broken forearm of Barak Yazici that was now set in a cast.

"She did that too."

Richard grinned before he replied.

"It's my client that wants to buy her Mr Downing."

"As you know I represent a Greek businessman." He added.

He discretely grinned at the Romanian Captain with his very recently broken nose.

'Good girl!' He thought to himself.

On the stage in front of them a woman was suddenly shoved onto the platform from the right side.

She wore just filthy turquoise briefs and her hands were tightly chained together and to the scaffold pole above her head.

Richard immediately noticed heavy bruising all over her body.

When he first saw her on David's screen she was unconscious.

Now her eyes were opened and a large rag had been shoved into her mouth and covered with a wide strip of shiny black duct tape.

Downing pointed to the tape that covered her mouth.

"That's not to keep her quiet it's to stop her from biting one of us." He explained with another chuckle.

The man that brought her into view now started to chain her ankles together.

Richard stepped forward but he was stopped by Mark Downing.

"Let him sort out her feet first mate." He insisted.

"She's a nut job."

When the Romanian driver Lucian Banica secured Jade's ankles together Richard climbed up onto the stage directly front of her.

Jade stared him straight in the eye and showed him nothing but contempt.

Richard stared back before he broke into a warm smile.

"My client Mr Marinos will be very pleased with his purchase." He said.

He continued to maintain eye contact with Jade.

"And he probably thinks that she should stop fighting." He very quietly added.

"This is the girl that Mr Marinos from Kefalonia wishes to purchase." He told Downing.

He turned to face Downing.

Mark Downing smiled back at Richard.

"We'll be happy to ship her out so let's talk business." He replied.

Richard nodded before he turned to stare back into Jade's green eyes.

"I think you'll be quite happy to meet Marinos." He quietly told Jade.

She still stared into his eyes but her own were now filled with tears.

Jade knew that Carmen had found her.

"No more fighting them." Richard quietly told her.

"Mr Marinos would like to see you in one piece."

Richard turned and headed back down toward Mark Downing but turned again to Lucian Banica as he led Jade away.

"Can you put some clothes on her?" He asked.

"She won't be any good to my client with Pneumonia."

Banica nodded.

Richard saw that Jade had stopped struggling for now.

Downing led Richard back out to the bar area.

"So the price is seventy thousand?" Richard asked.

Downing nodded.

"But you can guarantee it for eighty, Mr Handley." He replied.

"Don't forget this is an auction." He reminded Richard.

Richard nodded with a shrug of his shoulders.

"Ok so how much do you want to make absolutely sure?" He asked.

Downing sipped his whiskey and stared into Richard's eyes.

"Forty thousand in cash now and fifty on delivery and crazy girl won't make an appearance at the auction."

Richard nodded again.

"So we're talking seventy thousand to buy her and another twenty in your pocket to make sure." He said.

He looked to be considering Mark Downing's offer for a few moments.

Richard then stared back up at him.

"If it secures her for my client it's an acceptable raise Mr Downing."

Mark Downing grinned.

"So we have a deal Mr Handley?"

Richard grinned too and reached out his hand to shake.

"We have a deal Mr Downing." He replied.

He sipped his scotch as they shook hands.

Mark Downing and Richard Willows continued to grin at each other.

'I'm going to kill you last.' Richard thought to himself.

Jade wasn't on Richard's mind.

His twenty two year old sister Sasha was.

At Mount Street Mayfair April stared across the desk.

"What's happening?" She asked.

She saw tears streaming down Carmen's cheeks.

Carmen waved her hand.

"Just go and have a smoke." She sobbed.

"I'll tell you in a minute."

Inside the small locked silver dog cage between the two now vacated cream coloured leather sofas, Nikki Fright who was abducted from Stanley Morton's home at Love lane Micham on August 4th knelt and peered through the bars.

Her long wavy brown hair was down and make up had been applied by Debbie Davies.

She was dressed in just a skimpy pink two-piece bikini.

Her instinct was to scream out because she was here completely against her will but she didn't.

She knew that everybody inside the warehouse was here to purchase people like her.

As instructed by Debbie Davies she stared through the wire bars and smiled up at passers-by.

After all she was just eye candy.

She would be released and would wake up somewhere in a field in Scotland with Veronica Willard.

The blonde woman that she knew was called Debbie promised them.

Veronica Willard was taken during the abduction of Claire Grover from St Andrew's road Enfield almost three months ago on August 11th.

Through the bars of the small cage Nikki glanced across the room at Veronica who knelt inside an identical cage and wore an identical small bikini.

People walked past both cages in all directions.

They forced a secret smile to each other.

It was a shared smile of hope.

In return for their freedom they would both play the part of eye candy to passing bidders and buyers although they were not in fact for sale.

Debbie Davies made the deal that if they did this they would be freed just like agreeable others had been before them.

Nikki and Veronica were the two women that were purposely roused and were seen by Tania Downing on the night that she visited the warehouse two weeks ago on November 3rd.

The promise of hope however can blind natural rational instinct.

To the right of Nikki Fright beside the cream leather sofa stood Debbie Davies the woman that proposed the agreement that would lead to them both waking up in a field somewhere in Scotland.

At least they would be free.

Davies spoke in a foreign language to an older woman.

The older woman continued to glance down at Nikki through the thin metal bars of the cage and Nikki would of course force a smile up at her as she was instructed to do.

Occasionally the woman would look to her right at Veronica inside the other small cage.

Davies and the underground brothel Madame from the small town of Walsrode North West Germany continued to talk in German.

'You can buy them each for twenty thousand.' Davies informed her.

The German Madame again glanced through the shiny silver bars at Nikki and then at Veronica.

'Or you can buy them together for ten thousand more' Davies added.

The German Madame viewed them both once more before she turned back to Davies and smiled as they shook hands.

The deal was that they were to kneel inside the locked cages in the bar area to act as eye candy for visiting prospective buyers.

As payment both would receive their freedom.

The reality was that they had been placed on display in the bar area because Davies had not yet found a buyer for them.

Now that one of the Romanians had been caught time was running out.

Unbeknown to Nikki Fright and Veronica Willard they had just been sold to an underground brothel in Germany.

Their future lives would begin tomorrow.

Davies would start to inject them with Heroin in preparation for lives of enforced addiction and prostitution.

Forty Eight
Tuesday November 21st 2000

It was just after eight in the evening when the huge Russian Vladimir Kolov sat in his living room and flicked through the TV channels unable to decide what to watch.

He was dressed in a pair of old blue denim jeans and a white shirt with just black socks on his feet.

"There are only repeat programmes." He sighed.

His beautiful younger wife Inna walked past in front of the TV and into the kitchen.

Inna wore a chunky white woollen pullover and very tight fitting white denim shorts that showed off her long slender tanned legs.

Her long straight dark brown hair was down past her shoulders but as soon as she stepped into the kitchen she pulled it back into a ponytail and tied it with a pink elasticated band.

She casually walked to a drawer beneath the kitchen window where she removed six large clear plastic bags before she closed the drawer.

She then opened a cupboard door beneath the sink where she took out a large roll of silver grey sticky duct tape.

Inna continued to hum a tune that she heard twice that day on the radio and she just couldn't get it out of her head.

She walked to the small wooden door that led down into the basement.

She then stepped through and closed the door behind her and made her way down the stone steps into the dimly lit basement beneath the house.

Lying on the cold hard dusty basement floor were four semi-conscious women.

All of them continued to slip in and out of consciousness as the effects of chloroform slowly wore off.

The industrial white paper masks were removed a few hours ago and were burned along with all of their personal belongings including outer clothing.

All four were bound with handcuffs to keep their arms chained behind their backs.

Their legs were kept together by the same silver grey duct tape tightly wrapped around their ankles.

Occasionally one would move or whimper but none were in any condition to mount any kind of resistance.

Inna continued to quietly hum the same tune as she walked to the first girl on her right.

She had long matted brunette hair and brown eyes that occasionally flickered into life.

Inna sat down beside the bound semi-conscious brunette where she gently lifted the young woman's head and rested it onto her own lap.

Her eyes briefly flickered and she saw Inna who continued to hum that same song staring back down at her.

Inna warmly smiled.

She then separated one of the six clear plastic bags before she placed it onto the cold dusty floor and then she pulled a long length of shiny silver duct tape from the roll and used her teeth to bite it away.

With the long length of duct tape between her perfectly straight white teeth Inna picked up the single clear plastic bag and slowly slipped it over the brunette's head.

She then tightened it around her neck before she wrapped the strong sticky tape around and around and sealed off her oxygen.

She continued to hum that tune.

Suddenly the brunette opened her eyes wide and stared up through misty plastic into the beautiful brown eyes of Inna Kolov.

Inna continued to hum that song as she smiled back down at her.

"We must all leave here." She whispered.

The brunette was completely helpless with her hands tightly chained behind her back.

Because Inna had tightly wrapped several layers of duct tape around her ankles she could only attempt to kick out with sheer panic but with no force.

It took around four minutes as she quietly sung to herself until the bound fatigued woman kicked out for the last time.

Her head finally rested down onto Inna's lap with her eyes wide open but they were still.

Inna held her for a few moments.

"Now you sleep." She quietly told the dead woman.

She carefully placed her head down onto the concrete floor still encased and sealed inside the clear plastic bag just to be sure.

Inna moved onto her next victim who was a woman of just twenty one years of age.

She was barely a woman.

She had long matted blonde hair and Inna meticulously carried out her murder as she continued to hum that song that she just couldn't get out of her head.

Her third victim had auburn hair and if she could stand she would be around five feet five inches tall and she was also just twenty one years of age.

Inna Kolov murdered three women within the space of twenty five minutes while she casually hummed along to a song in her head.

She now sat down beside eighteen year old Amy Hadlow who was taken from New Inn Yard on October 20th and brought here by Inna's husband.

The so called doctor that was in fact no more than a two year medical student examined all four of these women just yesterday.

All four were given the all clear to be transferred to the warehouse at Woolwich.

Time had however run out since the death of Dorin Christescu and the capture and incarceration of Emil Hagi.

Hagi might talk at any given moment.

The Kolov's were fleeing to somewhere in Europe and could leave no trace that these four young women had ever been inside the house at Oakland's avenue.

Inna gently stroked Amy's short blonde hair as she bit off another length of silver duct tape that again she held between her teeth.

She then slowly slipped the smooth clear plastic bag over the helpless and barely conscious Amy's head.

Inna continued to hum as she lifted Amy's head to wrap the tape tightly around the bottom of the plastic bag around her neck.

She then rested Amy's encased head onto her own lap just as she had the three young women before her.

Amy suddenly opened her eyes and Inna could see that they were full of fear and panic as the clear plastic bag inflated stretched to its seams and then deflated and stuck to her face.

She squealed and her legs kicked out but they were bound together by her ankles.

Inna Kolov watched down with a warm caring smile.

"Sleep my angel you will feel no pain." She whispered.

She continued to hum that tune.

The clear plastic bag inflated like a mist-filled balloon and Amy's eyes flickered as she slipped in and out of consciousness for the next two minutes or so.

Eventually her entire body suddenly stiffened for the final time with one last kick of desperation as she urinated in her filthy pale peach underwear.

She then slumped into a limp torso with her head now rested on Inna's lap.

Inna smiled down into the now vacant eyes of Amy Hadlow.

"Rest now you suffer no more."

She gently lifted Amy's head and carefully rested it onto the hard concrete floor and again still encased inside the clear plastic bag.

Inna climbed to her feet and walked toward the staircase and checked the back of her tight white denim shorts.

"Damn!" She uttered.

She saw that they were covered with grey dust from the floor.

She patted it off before she climbed back up the steps and into the kitchen where she closed the basement door behind her.

She then walked back into the living room and again in front of her husband as she headed into the hall where she picked up her telephone and dialled a number.

When the call was answered she checked herself in the mirror.

"Barak it is Inna."

"I am well thank you." She told the Turkish leader.

"It is done and you must come to take them away."

When the call was finished Inna strolled back into the living room and sat down next to Vladimir where she curled up with his arm around her.

"It is done Vladimir." She told him.

He nodded and still flicked through the TV channels.

"What are you watching?" She asked.

Vladimir shrugged his huge shoulders.

"I watch everything and yet nothing." He replied with a sigh.

Inna giggled as she settled down to watched TV with Vladimir's arm around her.

Forty Nine
Tuesday November 21st 2000

In the cubicle office at task force headquarters Nicola Garwood sat at her desk.

Sam Henning sat at his and Detective Sergeant Jacob Saunders stood in the space between them.

Henning informed them both that the suspect being held at Woolwich police station wasn't speaking.

"He isn't even giving us his name." He informed them.

"But Keith Curtis seems to think that this fella is or was a professional soldier." He added.

Jacob Saunders frowned before he delivered his own news.

"The three vehicles that were allowed to leave Belmont Road were all stolen."

Nicola Garwood still studied the file of Jade Harris on her computer monitor and she glanced up at Saunders.

Saunders then grimaced again.

"The vehicle registrations were all clones." He informed her.

She glanced across at Sam before returning her attention to Jacob.

"What about the security van?" She asked.

Jacob shrugged.

"The registration number matches a silver van but the vehicle is registered to an active builder." He replied.

"It was also cloned." He added.

Nicola shook her head and sighed.

"And I'm guessing they've suddenly disappeared from current CCTV coverage?" She asked.

Jacob nodded.

"I'm afraid so guv."

But Nicola wasn't finished.

"Ok so what about the security company themselves?" She asked.

Saunders displayed another grimace.

"Indigo Security Services don't exist." He informed her.

Garwood stared up at him with disbelief.

"What?"

Jacob looked decidedly uncomfortable and he waited for Nicola to erupt as soon as she learned what he was about to tell her next.

"It's actually worse than that." He continued.

Garwood almost laughed.

"Jacob, so far today you've told me that we have three stolen vehicles that we have no way of tracing and that have probably been crushed by now." She began.

Jacob braced himself in preparation for her rage but Nicola remained calm yet sarcastic.

"Let's see, we also have one dead abductor and another who probably doesn't speak a word of English."

Now she stared back up at Jacob.

"And now you've thrown in a security company that has been seen multiple times on our seven hundred CCTV cameras that never actually existed."

"And not a single member of your team ever considered checking them out?" She asked.

Saunders nervously ran his fingers through his black curly hair.

"Yes guv." He began.

"Like I said it gets worse yet."

Saunders went on to explain that not only was the security company bogus but when playbacks were viewed on the camera systems it was discovered that there wasn't just one van seen on the major roads.

Vans not van had often been seen at the exact same time.

"So wait you're telling me that they have a bloody fleet?" She asked.

Saunders nervously nodded.

"We found five different vans on camera with Indigo security services advertised on them." He informed her.

Garwood shook her head.

"So this bogus security firm have been operating freely right under our noses for the entire time?" She asked.

There was another pause.

"And now they've obviously gone underground." She uttered.

Saunders nodded again.

"It would appear that they're more organised than we originally thought guv."

Garwood nodded her head as she continued to stare up at Jacob.

"No shit Sherlock." She quietly uttered.

The subject turned to New Kent road Walworth.

Jacob explained that forensics had uncovered vital evidence.

"The stain on the carpet in the living room is human blood group O negative and they've also confirmed that it doesn't belong to Jade Harris." He began.

"It turns out that she's a regular blood donor and her blood group is AB negative."

"There were also fragments of human skull discovered at the scene and whoever it belonged to probably died when the struggle took place."

Garwood nodded.

"Call it instinct but I knew there was something about that girl." She replied.

"So now we have blood and fragments of skull in her flat that aren't hers and she's nowhere to be found."

Sam glanced up from his desk.

"You also have no dead body from the flat." He reminded her.

Garwood shook her head.

"I know but we do know that there was a struggle, a pool of blood, fragments of somebody's skull and all of her clothes still in the flat."

"She ran Sam." She insisted.

Sam shrugged his shoulders.

"We have fragments of skull we have blood and we have evidence that there was some kind of struggle." He replied.

"They're your only facts right now Nik."

Sam glanced back over at her.

"I'm still not convinced about Jade Harris." He added.

"Something just doesn't add up like how conveniently we were handed her name by an anonymous call." He continued.

"And the bottom line is that if she walked in here now, without a confession that she killed whoever bled out in that flat and produced the body you have nothing to charge her with."

"You have suspicion that's all."

Garwood nodded again as she stared into her computer monitor.

"That's if I ever bloody find her." She quietly sighed.

When Jacob Saunders eventually left the office Nicola looked up at Sam.

"Anything new on you know who?" She asked.

Sam sat back in his chair and displayed a thoughtful look.

"When he called me back after the press conference he wanted to know where the suspect was being held and I told him that it was classified information for obvious reasons." He told her.

"But I did eventually tell him that he was being held at Woolwich nick." He added.

"Keith Curtis told me to let it slip to him."

It was Nicola's turn to look confused.

"Why would he want you to do that?" She asked.

Sam grinned.

"Our prisoner isn't at Woolwich nick." He chuckled.

"He's in Lambeth nick."

Nicola looked even more confused.

"So why tell him that this guy's at Woolwich?" She asked.

Sam grinned again.

"Because I also told him that we were waiting for a senior officer to interview him but we hadn't decided who yet." He added.

Nicola's eyes widened.

"Do you really think he'll put himself up for that job?" She asked.

Sam shrugged.

"We're clutching at straws but you never know." He replied.

"After all he did put himself up for the job here in the first place." He reminded her.

"And all the time the prisoner isn't where he thinks, we hold all of the cards."

Fifty
Friday December 1st 2000

Thirty four year old Carmen Richardson wore her short light brown leather jacket and a thin white knitted pullover beneath it with blue denim jeans.

She and Richard Willows arrived at the departure lounge at Gatwick International Airport two hours early for their pre-booked 7pm flight to the Greek island of Kefalonia.

She owned a beautiful house on the island with eight bedrooms facing the Ionian Sea in a small southern village called Lourdatta.

Richard wore a short black leather jacket with a white open necked shirt beneath and he also wore faded blue denim jeans.

"So is this Greek island going to be sunny?" He asked.

Carmen smirked before she turned to face him.

"It would be if we were going in March." She replied.

"But from about October to the end of February it rains quite a lot." She chuckled.

"It's actually known as the raining season."

Richard raised his eyebrows.

"That explains a lot." He said.

He watched Carmen's smile broaden.

She glanced across at him again.

"But don't panic because Marinos will fetch us from the airport in his canoe."

Carmen's light hearted responses were her way of trying to block out the reason that they were flying out to the Island.

Richard eventually chuckled.

"We couldn't have done this in the Bahamas could we?" He asked.

Again Carmen smiled.

"I don't own a house in the Bahamas."

She glanced down at her passport.

Richard could see that she was now deep in thought.

"Are you sure that these little moles won't get picked up by some kind of airport security gadget?" She asked.

Richard smiled back at her.

"That's why we're wearing them." He informed her.

"Dave completely deactivated them and they show absolutely no signal to pick up." He assured her.

"I travel with them all the time, they just look like moles."

She studied him for a few moments.

"How many people have you killed?" She unexpectedly asked.

Her question caught Richard off-guard but eventually he glanced down at the floor.

"Too many if I'm honest." He replied.

She continued to watch him but then she decided that it was a question that she had no right to ask.

She was really searching for confidence and reassurance of some kind from him.

Eventually Carmen started to search through her beige leather shoulder bag.

"I just want to put Jade's passport into my pocket." She said.

Again she turned to Richard to see that he was grinning.

"What?" She asked.

"Stop fussing." He replied.

Suddenly Carmen removed her phone from her bag.

"I have to call Polly to make sure that she knows what to do over the next few weeks." She said.

Richard then watched her speak on the phone to Polly Aldington.

Carmen explained to Polly that Arron Balcombe would over the next few days deliver some paperwork regarding particular properties to view.

"Can you give them straight to April and make sure that she sorts at least one of them out as we discussed?" She asked.

The moment that Carmen returned her phone to her bag it rang and she sighed as she took it out again.

Richard watched with amusement because this time it was April.

"If you were sitting right next to Polly just now why didn't you say something?" She asked.

Richard chuckled to himself.

"Arron thinks that the maisonette in Tooting would be ideal." Carmen said into her phone.

Suddenly on the airport loudspeaker their flight was announced.

"Listen we're boarding our flight now so just make sure that everything ticks over for me, ok?" She asked.

"I'll call you when we're at the house in Kefalonia."

Fifty One
Monday December 4th 2000

Nicola Garwood just walked through the security door and into the ops room when Sam Henning grabbed her arm and pulled her toward the cubicle office.

"Quickly in here!"

As Sam pulled her into the office he looked back to see Jacob Saunders approaching and he stopped him.

"Give us ten minutes mate." He told Saunders.

He then closed the door behind him.

Nicola turned to face Sam.

"What the hell is going on?" She asked.

She could see that Sam was not his usual calm and casual self.

"He took the bait." He told her.

Nicola was still confused.

"Is this another fishing tale Sam?" She asked.

Sam stared at her and waited for the proverbial penny to drop but he could see only a look of confusion.

"Roberts is on his way to Woolwich nick to interview the prisoner." He finally told her.

Nicola walked quite nonchalantly around her desk and sat down.

"But isn't he going to get there to discover that the prisoner isn't actually at Woolwich?" She asked.

Sam grinned.

"Of course he's not." He replied.

He sat behind his own desk.

Sam went on to explain that Chief Inspector Keith Curtis earlier called and informed him that this morning Martin Roberts called Woolwich police station.

Roberts informed them that he was on his way to interview the suspect in custody and he stated that he was to be left alone with the prisoner to gain his confidence.

Nicola sighed and nodded her head.

"But what part of the prisoner isn't actually at Woolwich nick has your senile old person's mind forgotten?" She asked with a giggle.

Sam pointed a finger at her.

"Watch it you!"

He then leaned back in his chair.

"Roberts is going to conduct an interview with somebody that he believes is the suspect." He told her.

"Curtis is already there with one of his Detectives that'll play the part." He added.

Nicola stared across at Sam.

"And what if we're wrong and Roberts had nothing to do with any of this and the house at Ilford was purely coincidental?" She asked.

"And then when he discovers that he was actually interviewing a bloody copper from New Scotland Yard?" She asked.

She stared across at Sam again.

"Your mate Curtis can explain it all to him." She finally added.

Sam laughed.

"Well actually he and I only have a few weeks before we retire." He reminded her.

Then he gave her a playful wink.

Nicola stared at him with her eyes widened.

"Thanks you twat!" She replied.

It had been more than five hours since Sam told Nicola that Roberts was driving to Woolwich police station and they had heard nothing since.

Saunders was now inside the cubicle office and had no idea what was happening at Woolwich but he did know that both Detective Inspectors Garwood and Henning were very quiet.

Suddenly the office door opened behind Jacob and Chief Inspector Keith Curtis from New Scotland Yard stepped inside and closed it behind him.

Both Sam and Nicola stared up at him.

Curtis grinned at Sam.

"We're not retiring yet." He said.

Sam raised his eyebrows.

"You need to be talking to Mrs Henning." He laughed.

His wry grin suddenly disappeared.

"What are you doing here anyway?"

Curtis turned to Saunders beside him.

"Who are you?"

Jacob reached out his hand to shake.

"I'm DS Saunders Sir." He told Curtis.

He realised that the round balding man was of rank.

Curtis nodded without shaking Jacob's hand.

"Where do you get coffee from around here?" He asked.

Jacob immediately started to explain the route to the canteen but he suddenly stopped mind-sentence.

The Chief Inspector continued to stare into his eyes.

"You mean where do I personally get your coffee from don't you?" Jacob realised.

Curtis smiled.

"You should be a Detective."

When Saunders left the room, both Garwood and Henning continued to stare at Curtis.

"Has something happened?" Sam finally asked.

Curtis removed his notepad from his inside jacket pocket.

"At eleven thirty four Chief Inspector Martin Roberts entered the interview room with who he believed to be an unknown suspect from the human trafficking ring currently operating within the city of London." He recited.

There was a pause as Nicola gasped.

"Oh my god you got him!"

Curtis went on to explain in great detail from his note pad how the very senior officer Roberts was as he requested left alone with the suspect.

At Eleven fifty six he purposely passed the under-cover officer who he believed to be the suspect a white capsule that is believed to be a form of suicide pill possibly and probably containing Cyanide.

Garwood sat with her mouth wide open as did Sam as Curtis continued with his explanation.

"At eleven fifty nine myself, CI Curtis and two officers entered the interview room where Chief Inspector Roberts was arrested under the Human Trafficking Act."

"He was also charged with perverting the course of justice and he has been detained at Woolwich police station pending further investigation." He added.

Curtis displayed a broad grin.

Garwood and Henning stared at each other before they both looked back up at Curtis but he wasn't quite finished.

"And now here comes the bad news." He continued.

"As they have bugger all for me to do at the Yard as usual and as I'm also a Chief Inspector, guess who your new boss is for the immediate future?" He asked.

Sam started to laugh.

"Oh no it just got worse than it was before!"

But Nicola was still stunned at the news and she stared up at Curtis.

"So what happens with Roberts now?" She asked.

Curtis shrugged.

"It's not about what happens but how much happens to him." He replied.

"The capsule is being examined right now but we know what it is."

Garwood glanced over to Sam and then back up at Curtis.

"But haven't you illegally entrapped him?" She asked.

Curtis shook his head.

"Before I travelled to Woolwich I had it authorised." He informed her.

"Sir Christopher Dwyer was more than keen to see how this played out and he was willing to take a thick ear for it." He added.

There was another pause.

"This is pure insanity." Nicola quietly uttered.

Again she and Sam stared at each other before Curtis turned to leave the cubicle office.

"I want a full briefing from the pair of you downstairs in my office in an hour." He told them.

He then stopped at the door.

"Oh and if that young fella turns up with my coffee send him down with it will you?"

He then left the cubicle leaving Sam chuckling.

Nicola stared at the closed door like the proverbial rabbit that was caught in the headlights of an oncoming truck.

Fifty Two
Saturday December 9th 2000

In the summer months the Greek Island of Kefalonia was incredibly beautiful and warm.

A long and narrow twisting turning dirt track road led down from the southern face of Mount Ainos to several small holiday hotels and a few private residences that faced the clear blue transparent Ionian Sea.

In the distance to the south the nearby smaller sister island of Zakynthos was clearly visible.

But this wasn't the summer months.

It was now early December and it had rained here almost constantly for just over a month and not a single tourist could be seen.

It was actually the perfect time for Carmen and Richard to arrive.

At the bottom of that winding dirt track road were three commercial hotels on the left and three beautiful palatial homes on the right.

At the far right end of this private and secluded area facing the Ionian Sea was the huge eight bedroom house that was owned by Carmen Richardson.

From her lounge window Carmen pointed south to the vague island of Zakynthos.

"Jade and I took a holiday there and we kept wondering what it would be like here on this Island." She told Richard with a fond smile.

She then turned to him.

"We took a chartered boat to this very beach a few days later and by chance we found this place for sale."

Richard smiled as he looked down at the grey tiled floor.

"I can see now how important she is to you."

Seated behind Carmen and Richard was Carmen's friend Marinos who she and Jade actually met on that day that they visited the island for the very first time.

Thirty year old Marinos Georgas was five feet eleven inches tall with short dark brown hair and dark brown eyes.

Carmen's opinion was that he always seemed to have a cheeky grin that was full of mischief.

Marinos was native to the island.

It often seemed that he knew just about everybody that lived on it and everybody seemed to know him as a loveable rogue.

He also had a sense of humour to match David Stringer.

Between them Richard and Carmen explained the entire story to Marinos and the reason that they had arrived late last night.

After he heard everything Marinos sat upright.

"So you saw my friend Jade?" He asked.

Richard nodded.

"She's ok."

Of course there was no question that Marinos would help and immediately agreed to act as the wealthy business man Mr Marinos.

He would meet with a small boat at the port of Sami the day after tomorrow to pay for and collect Jade.

"There is no question that I would do this of course." He told them both.

Richard now turned to Marinos again.

"I know that this is going to sound like a stupid question." He began.

"But do you know of anywhere that I could get my hands on a rifle?" He asked.

Marinos broke into a smile.

"A high powered rifle is good?" He asked.

Richard's eyes lit up.

"Of course, my cousin Denis has one." Marinos said.

"I will collect it tonight."

Richard now turned to Carmen.

"The Indigo cargo ship is anchored not far from here." He told her.

"Miguel Sanchez has flown to Turkey for three weeks on holiday believe it or not." He added.

Carmen shrugged.

"It doesn't surprise me." She replied.

"I would imagine they're all going into hiding for a while."

Marinos looked confused.

"How do you know these things?" He asked.

It was Carmen that smiled with a response.

"Now that would take some explaining." She chuckled.

She immediately thought of David Stringer sitting at a computer.

There was silence for a few moments while Marinos digested what he had been told.

Richard glanced back at Carmen.

"I was thinking of a slight change of plans regarding my sister." He told her.

Carmen stared back at him.

"What changes?" She quite angrily asked.

Richard reminded her that the day after tomorrow Jade would be back.

"This is only about Sasha after." He added.

Carmen continued to stare.

"What changes?" She asked again.

"As you can imagine getting my sister back is always on my mind Carmen." He began.

"But I think that we could spend that money in another way to be absolutely sure that we get Sasha back too." He told her.

Carmen still stared into his eyes.

"Richard, don't you dare play games with her life!" She snapped.

Richard rigorously shook his head.

"No hear me out."

He went on to remind Carmen that his original plan had been to use a team of mercenaries to break into the military base at Mamuju and remove Sasha by force.

One of his concerns with that idea was the lack of loyalty from the team of mercenaries if they could in fact even find a team willing to take on such an assignment.

"I know of another way and I think it'll cost less than a hundred thousand." He told her.

Carmen continued to stare at him.

"And I genuinely think that this way would be not only less risky but pretty much fail safe." He added.

Carmen still stared into Richard's eyes.

"Are you talking about buying her back from them like we are Jade? She asked.

Richard smiled as he thought it through.

"Actually I think it'll save you about fifty thousand." He told her.

"And Miguel Sanchez isn't that far from here."

"Richard, a deal is a deal." She eventually replied.

"We get my girl back here the day after tomorrow and then let's talk about your new idea with regard to Sasha." Carmen suggested.

Richard smiled.

"They're traders Carmen and you're the best business woman that I know of so let's trade with them."

Fifty Three
Monday December 11th 2000

Chief Inspector Keith Curtis was temporarily placed in command at task force headquarters Whitechapel and things were about to dramatically change.

The abductions immediately ceased after the capture of Romanian Emil Hagi and the death of Dorin Christescu at Belmont road Ilford Essex.

The former Chief Inspector of the task force Martin Roberts was also detained in custody with any hope of bail categorically denied.

Roberts was going nowhere.

The supposed Russian diplomat Vladimir Kolov and his family had flown to his native Russia and vanished without a trace.

This left Jane Chapman Debbie Davies Lisa Moore and Mark Downing to clear up the operation hence Downing making twenty thousand on the quick sale of Jade Harris.

Debbie Davies made the deal with the German Madame with the discounted sale of Nikki Fright and Veronica Willard along with a few more that evening at the auction.

Nikki Fright and Veronica Willard were sold at a much cheaper rate than they would have been under usual circumstances.

There was a new sense of urgency.

Before he fled the country Vladimir Kolov visited the three women at their respective homes again and was watched by David via an overhead satellite.

Kolov instructed them to completely close down the operation and leave absolutely no trail so that it could be resumed at a later date when the current situation settled.

At task force headquarters they still knew very little.

Not anything like the facts that David Stringer knew.

Chief Inspector Keith Curtis sat at his new desk with Sam Henning and Nicola Garwood opposite him.

"So we know that Kolov has definitely left the country." Curtis informed them.

"This probably means that their operation has been closed down." He added.

Sam nodded with agreement.

Nicola Garwood however wasn't fully convinced.

"But we still haven't located Jade Harris Sir and the evidence is quite overwhelming." She told Curtis.

"There was an unidentified blood sample and fragments of skull found at her flat and it looks as though she fled the scene in a hurry." She told him.

"I still think she has something to answer for Sir." She told her new boss.

Curtis sighed.

"Here's the problem with the Jade Harris situation." He began to explain.

"Roberts named her during his initial interview." .

"And Roberts knows that if we can't break this case he'll meet lesser charges and get out within five years at worst." He told her.

"So if he claims that she's involved it's more likely that she isn't."

He leaned onto his desk.

"And also take into account what she did for a living for years prior to opening up that shop." He continued.

"I bet that on her client list I could name five very high profile ministers and judges that would have no choice other than to provide her with an alibi just to keep her quiet." He added.

He sat back in his chair.

"And besides without a body to match the DNA from the blood found at her flat we have no victim and if we have no victim we have no murder." He informed her.

"You can't realistically charge her with murder without a murder victim Nik."

Curtis then stared at her.

"I think that whatever happened, Jade Harris is out of the country." He told her.

"We know she's got a current and valid passport and I don't know how but I do think she's out of the country." He repeated.

He leaned forward again.

"Get Interpol to put a flag up at all of the European airports and sea terminals just in case she has." He continued.

Nicola nodded.

"Yes Sir."

The new chief sighed.

"If she does suddenly pop up you can question her but if she pleads ignorant to whatever happened at her flat we have bugger all to charge her with." He added.

"Remember Nik her DNA isn't at the scene, the place was clinically cleaned."

Sam now nodded in agreement.

"He's right regarding the Roberts situation Nik." He told her.

"We can't trust anything that Roberts tells us as a statement of fact without evidence to back it up and with regard to Jade Harris there is no evidence."

Curtis nodded.

"And he also knows that if we crash this case he could actually walk away."

Curtis again glanced at Nicola.

"If she turns up somewhere you can hold her for twenty four hours for questioning." He said.

"But if you have nothing after that you've got to let her go."

Nicola looked down at the file of Jade Harris in her hand.

"Yes Sir." She replied.

Curtis glanced across at her once again.

"Drop the Sir crap in private Nik we're in this together." He told her.

"I'm not Roberts."

Curtis now turned his attention directly to Sam.

"I've been authorised to give you a stay of execution." He chuckled.

Sam raised his eyebrows.

"You were planning on executing me?"

Curtis chuckled.

"I have authorisation from the powers that be to ask you to stay on for an extra three months." He explained.

"That's when they'll start to wrap this thing up if we haven't closed it." He added.

"And I would really appreciate your help Sam."

Sam looked down at the floor with a grin.

"It's impossible to say no when you throw down that guilt trip with those puppy dog eyes." He replied.

Both Curtis and Nicola grinned.

Sam then looked up at his former and new boss.

"But if you don't want to have to deal with Mrs Henning it stops after that." He insisted.

Curtis mocked a look of utter horror.

"Bloody heck nobody wants that to happen."

"Right, let's get back to work because we're on a time limit to crack this before they start to wind us down." He informed them both.

Fifty Four
Monday December 11th 2000

It was a little before one in the morning when a black Mitsubishi pick-up truck turned right onto a narrow dirt track road that lead after ten minutes to the old road that would take it right to the peak of Mount Ainos.

The truck would then travel down the northern face and into the quiet Kefalonian sea port town of Sami.

Marinos Georgas drove the borrowed black truck and beside him in the front passenger seat was Carmen.

Richard sat in the back as they headed for their rendezvous point to pay for and collect Carmen's friend twenty nine year old Jade Harris.

It was hardly surprising that the only person inside the black pick-up truck that spoke was Richard.

He was the only one that had ever faced or been involved in anything even remotely similar to whatever they headed toward now.

He prepared the high powered rifle and looked to the back of Marinos.

"This is a nice truck Marinos." He said.

Marinos turned his head.

"It belongs to my cousin." He replied with a smile.

Richard nodded and held out the rifle.

"Thank him for the use of this." He said.

A beaming grin appeared on the Greek islander's face.

"Not that cousin." He replied with a chuckle.

Carmen now interjected.

"Marinos has about ninety thousand cousins on the island." She chuckled.

"If you need anything here he has a cousin that has at least one of them." She added.

Marinos laughed.

"This is true!" He assured her.

Richard achieved what he set out to do which was to break the silence and prevent them from over thinking about what lay ahead of them at Sami.

Carmen turned to Marinos.

"At least it stopped raining for a while." She said.

He nodded.

"But I think rain would have been good tonight." He replied.

Carmen glanced out of the window and up at the clear, pitch black star filled sky.

"David, are you listening in?" She asked.

There was a pause before David Stringer spoke from his office bedroom fifteen hundred miles away at Bermondsey south east London.

"I'm here Carmen." He replied.

She smiled.

"Good, for some reason I feel a hell of a lot safer knowing that you're up there watching." She told him.

"There's a small fishing boat tied up next to The Indigo at the strait between the islands of Kefalonia and Ithaki." David said.

"Is it one of theirs?" Richard asked.

David confirmed.

"Yes Richard the small boat is actually Greek but it's tied to The Indigo."

Carmen stared back at Richard.

"They're definitely here for the delivery." He informed her.

Stringer interjected.

"I'll let you know as soon as there's any movement."

At the peak of Mount Ainos Carmen looked to her right and back down toward the southern coast of the island at thousands of lights that looked like bright white and yellow pin pricks resting on a black carpet.

Marinos glanced to see what she was staring at and then he smiled.

"You are still in love with my beautiful island?"." He asked.

The pick-up truck rolled down the northern face of the mountain and Marinos pointed to the bright lights in the distance ahead.

"That is Sami." He told them.

He turned to Richard.

"It is a beautiful and historic town so please avoid destroying it."

Their eyes met in the rear view mirror and Richard smiled.

"I'll try." He replied.

It was around twenty five minutes later when Marinos slowly drove into the deserted town of Sami while Richard's eyes scanned the area.

"I can't believe how quiet it is around here." He said.

Marinos nodded.

"It is only this quiet here now." He replied.

"There are only two hotels in the area and both are being rebuilt soon so no tourists stay here and of course it is also the season of rain." He explained.

He then pointed to the bay on their left.

"This is where the delivery will be." He said.

He then pointed to the right.

"There is a house where you both can wait."

Richard looked over to the right.

"Is it your house?" He asked.

Marinos grinned.

"It is owned by my cousin." He replied with a chuckle.

Richard grinned.

"Your family reunions must be fun."

Marinos parked the pick-up truck facing away from the port and ushered Carmen and Richard across a square toward the house.

Richard concealed the rifle beneath his jacket so that only the barrel was visible beside his leg although Sami was seemingly deserted and there was nobody to see it anyway.

Inside the house Marinos guided them up the stairs to a bedroom that had a single window directly facing the port.

"You sit here." Richard told Carmen.

She nervously nodded and sat down on a small wooden chair in the completely darkened room.

Suddenly the realisation of what was about to happen kicked in and Carmen realised that she was shaking uncontrollably.

Richard turned to Marinos.

"Is this another bedroom?" He asked.

He pointed to the wall beside him.

Marinos nodded.

"I need to be in there and completely alone." Richard said.

He then looked at Carmen.

"No distractions." He told her.

Again Carmen very nervously nodded in silence.

She sensed that the time was rapidly approaching as the preparations were made.

She sat in front of the window while Richard positioned himself in the adjoining bedroom with the high powered rifle pointed through the slightly opened window.

The silent wait began.

Around ten minutes later they both finally heard the voice that would bring an icy chill to Carmen.

"Ok the small fishing boat has left The Indigo at Steno Ithaki." David Stringer announced.

When Richard relayed the information to Marinos, the Greek left the building and walked across the dimly lit and dead quiet empty street to the black pick-up truck.

Around fifteen minutes later Marinos saw the red and green port and starboard lights of a small fishing boat that headed in his direction and he pressed the button of his black torch twice to guide it toward him.

A small blue and white boat that had a darker blue rubberized canopy covering the rear approached the quayside where the engine slowed to a stop.

A tall thin man on board tossed a rope to Marinos and he secured it to a mooring post beside him.

The night was suddenly dead still.

A second man appeared after the engine was switched off and both stared at Marinos.

Marinos the Greek shipping tycoon wore a black suit with a white open necked shirt beneath it.

He spotted the short 9mm machine gun that was pointed at him.

"You speak English?" He asked.

The tall thin balding man nodded.

"You have something for us?" He asked.

Marinos nodded back at him.

"Show her to me." He told the Spaniard.

The tall thin Spaniard laughed.

"You must show the money first my friend." He said.

He stepped off the boat and was now almost nose to nose with Marinos.

Marinos however would not back down.

He never would.

"Behind me inside the house with the yellow door are two high powered rifles." He lied.

"One is pointed at you and the other now at your friend." He added in a very calm and quiet tone.

The man looked past the shoulder of Marinos and saw the yellow door and then he saw the opened window above it.

"You do not come to *my* island to make demands." Marinos told him.

"Now show me the girl and get your money."

They stood nose to nose and stared into each other's eyes for a few moments more before the Spaniard looked behind to his colleague.

"Muestrale." He told his friend.

'Show him.'

Richard was poised in the completely dark room with a steady hand and his rifle pointed toward the boat.

"If you shoot Richard, take out the man on the boat first so that he doesn't leave with Jade." David reminded him.

Stringer's voice now came with cold and very ruthless efficiency.

"Roger that." Richard replied.

His rear sight and foresight were in perfect alignment with the chest of the man on the boat and with a completely steady hand.

"Whatever happens, that boat doesn't leave with her still on it." Richard calmly assured him.

Carmen stared out at Marinos as she listened to the clinical and surreal conversation between David and Richard.

She suddenly realised that she was in way, way over her head as she heard them casually discussing killing the two men down at the boat while she was gripped with sheer terror.

Her heart hammered against her chest.

The man on the boat lifted the blue rubberized cover to reveal the unconscious Jade still dressed in just her filthy underwear.

Her hands were tied behind her back and her ankles were tied with the same dirty red rope and she wore a white paper mask that covered her nose and mouth that was lightly doused with chloroform.

The thin Spaniard now turned back to Marinos.

"Now give me the money!" He insisted.

Marinos slowly stepped backward and leaned inside the opened window of his truck and pulled out a large padded envelope that he handed to the man.

"Now put her in my truck." He told the Spaniard.

The tall thin man grinned.

Again he glanced back at his friend on the boat and nodded toward the truck before he returned his stare toward Marinos Georgas.

The tall and thin man didn't take his eyes off Marinos until he eventually glanced down at the envelope and opened it to see the cash.

His companion lifted Jade's limp torso onto his shoulder and carried her to the back of the truck.

He dropped her into the open back where she lay completely motionless.

Even from afar Carmen could see that Jade hadn't moved.

Tears started to roll down her cheeks.

Marinos glanced to his right to study the motionless Jade and then returned his gaze to the Spaniard.

"Now leave my island and never return here." He told him.

The Spaniard arrogantly chuckled.

Marinos now stared deep into his eyes and could only think of his friend Jade.

"If you ever return you will never leave this place alive."

There was another pause as they stared.

"I make you that promise." He assured him.

Marinos with his heightened emotions at seeing his friend this way wanted to do so much more but he somehow managed to refrain.

The man's grin slowly disappeared as he stared back at Marinos.

"We will meet one day again." He promised.

Marinos stared back at him.

"I hope." He replied.

Marinos watched the small fishing boat head back out toward the Strait of Ithaki and behind him inside the house Richard began to unload the rifle.

"This Marinos is worth knowing Dave." He told his friend.

He returned the ammunition to his black jacket pocket.

"He's ballsy I'll give him that." David chuckled.

David then turned his attention to Carmen through his microphone.

"We have her back Carmen and I just watched her move." He said.

"She's alive but unconscious."

He received no reply.

Marinos picked up Jade from the open back of the truck and laid her down onto the softer back seat inside the warmer cab where he untied her hands and feet and removed the white paper mask.

Inside the darkened room at the window Carmen sat with her head in her hands where she quietly uncontrollably sobbed.

"Carmen?" David said into her earpiece.

Again he received no response.

Richard glanced down at the floor and smiled again.

"Leave her for a few minutes mate." He told David.

Richard listened the quiet sobbing from the other side of the wall.

There was a pause before Stringer replied.

"Is she having a girl moment?" He asked.

Willows smiled again.

"No mate she's having a best friend moment."

Carmen, with tears rolling down her face nodded in silent response to David.

Of course he couldn't hear or see her.

She silently mouthed to both of them as tears streamed down her face.

"Thank you."

Fifty Five
Monday December 25th 2000

It was just after eleven on Christmas morning when David Stringer sat on the right side of his office bedroom and hacked into the files of Jane Chapman's computer.

Buried deep inside he found what he was looking for.

It was an encrypted file and in the very unlikely event that her computer was ever confiscated by the authorities Chapman ensured that they would never be able to decode it.

David Stringer however could.

Attached to this particular file should it ever be opened without the aid of another twelve digit password was a completely destructive computer virus.

It would destroy not only the file but would cause her entire computer to completely crash and wipe itself so that it could never be used as evidence against her.

Jane Chapman wrote and embedded the virus herself.

David now sat and read detailed files that thirty six year old Chapman kept in order to keep a track of their organisation's affairs.

He read that from August 1997 to July 2000 Chapman, photographer Lisa Moore, Debbie Davies and Mark Downing had successfully removed from the streets of London 1407 homeless and destitute men.

Chapman kept detailed files after issuing these men like cattle, numbers in order to replenish the ever increasing demand for enforced labour.

They were mostly transported to Siberia, Serbia, Bulgaria, Romania and the more recent addition on the island of Madagascar where a huge mine became operational.

The four were responsible for the abduction sale and transportation of these numerically filed homeless men.

There was another numerical figure that David didn't read because no such figure existed on her computer.

It was the fact that after these unfortunate men were sold Jane Chapman had nothing more to do with them.

From the 1407 men taken from the streets of London from August 1997 to July 2000 more than half, 717 to be exact had since perished from malnutrition, disease or severely violent beatings from their handlers.

This brought the need for Chapman Moore Davies and Downing to continue supplying the forced labour.

David didn't know who he was reading about next but the file was dated 18/07/2000 and her only description was 1012 (F). 00042000.

Nothing that was entered onto Chapman's computer could be used as evidence against her.

The recorded file of twenty three year old Hannah Anderson was from Chapman's point of view quite self-explanatory.

She was simply victim number 1012 she was female and was sold for £42,000 sterling.

Hannah Anderson was 1012 (F) 00042000.

The beautiful young Hannah was now somewhere in northern Albania.

Inside an attached file was victim 1013 (F).

1013 (F) was Hannah Anderson's best friend twenty two year old Amanda Golding.

Amanda of course died in the back of Firat Alican's black London taxi.

It occurred in the early hours of Sunday July 16th from a fatal combination of alcohol and Rohypnol.

It caused her blood pressure to lower to the point that her heart simply stopped beating.

Her body was weighted and dropped into the river Thames behind unit 4B of the Stanley estate at north Woolwich on Monday July 16th 2000.

Turkish Firat Alican performed her watery burial for fifty pounds.

David unknowingly now read the fate of the six squatters that were taken from the house formerly owned by Stanley Morton at Love lane Micham in the nearby county of Surrey.

He read that 1117 (M) twenty seven year old Mark Prichard, 1119 (M) twenty four year old Michael Stott and 1121 (M) nineteen year old James Creasley were transported to the recently operational salt mine on the island of Madagascar.

They were sold for £18,000 sterling each.

1122(M) otherwise known as twenty eight year old Robert Croft was transported to a different mine at southern Turkey for the same price.

Robert Croft and Mark Pritchard were since deceased.

The girl with the bright red hair at Love lane, twenty two year old Jackie Miles 1120 (F) the girlfriend of Michael Stott was transported to Mamuju on the Indonesian island of Sulawesi.

She was the first person that the Indonesian men had ever seen with bright red hair and she was immediately very popular.

David continued to read and about twenty two year old Nikki Fright 1125 (F) also from the squat at Love lane.

She was still held at unit 4B on the Stanley estate north Woolwich.

She was awaiting shipment to the sea port of Bremen Germany.

She would not wake in a field somewhere in Scotland as promised by Debbie Davies.

The next file that David opened was dated Monday August 14th

It contained information regarding twenty two year old Claire Grover 1127 (F) twenty four year old Sara Crossley 1128 (F) and twenty six year old Veronica Willard 1129 (F)

They were taken from their shared house at St Andrew's road Enfield north of London.

Claire Grover was transported to Saudi Arabia and her unconscious voyage started on Monday August 21st

David read that she was sold for £83,000.

Lot number 1128 twenty four year old Sara Crossley suffered complications after extended use of Chloroform.

She died on Sunday August 13th although of course no official cause of death was entered into Chapman's files.

The twenty four year old died from a massive heart attack.

Twenty six year old Veronica Willard who David could only read as 1131(F) was still held at unit 4B at the Stanley industrial estate north Woolwich also awaiting transport to the sea port of Bremen Germany.

David sat back in his chair and took a long deep breath as his eyes for the first time welled with tears.

"This is mental." He quietly uttered.

He had witnessed many things that he often wished that he had never seen since he began in this line of work but nothing could have prepared him for this.

Eventually he returned to reading.

He discovered that the beautiful Bridget Oakes 1149 (F) who was taken from her own bedroom at Norton road Wembley was now somewhere in the Philippines.

Olivia Fletcher 1148 (F) was still at unit 4B at the Stanley industrial estate awaiting both sale and transportation.

He went on to read about the four women that were abducted from the safe house at Caterham Surrey.

Denise Ruane 1143(F) was somewhere in Syria, Linda Edmunds 1137 (F) somewhere in South Africa, Jane Carey 1138 (F) and Deborah Franklin 1141 (F) were both somewhere in Libya North Africa.

He read about the death of Dawn Sheppard 1106 (F) at Folkestone Kent.

She was entered as a 'no sale' item and her body like Sara Crossley's was burned behind unit 4B at the Stanley estate.

After David read similar 'no sale' entries regarding eighteen year old Amy Hadlow and three more girls from Oakland's Avenue near Ponders End shortly prior to the departure from the country of Vladimir and Inna Kolov he copied and saved the file.

He now realised that they too had been murdered.

David read 1736 separate entries.

There was something else that he didn't read and therefore couldn't know.

It was that from that total of 1736 entries made on Jane Chapman's computer 589 had since in one way or another met with their deaths.

Many of the 589 victims probably welcomed their deaths as a blessing.

Only one from 1736 escaped and regained her freedom.

Just one person from 1736.

Twenty nine year old Jade Harris was recovering at the house owned by Carmen Richardson on the Greek island of Kefalonia.

She didn't however escape completely unscathed.

It occurred on the night of Friday November 17th immediately after her sale was agreed by Richard Willows with Mark Downing.

Barak Yazici Firat Alican and Atif Rahman repaid her for the death of their friend and colleague Doruk Gezmen.

They used her own baseball bat before she was rendered unconscious in preparation for her trip to the Greek island.

Jade suffered a dislocated jaw, a broken collar bone, six broken ribs and every one of her back teeth on the left side were completely smashed with the bat.

Jade was however at least alive.

She was slowly recovering.

The former high class prostitute had since made a vow to Richard Willows.

Richard and Carmen would soon return to London.

Jade Harris would follow them in the not too distant future.

The former elite SAS Captain now wanted his sister back.

Jade Harris wanted payback.

This was by no means over...

Not the End